Shapes in the Fire

Shapes in the Fire
M.P. Shiel

Ægypan Press

Shapes in the Fire
A publication of
Ægypan Press
www.aegypan.com

To Mistress Beatrice Laws

Dear Beatrice, —

The pieces of this inkling of a Book, which, with much longing, I dedicate to you, were not all written in the same night, but separated in their execution by intervals for eating and sleeping; and as you know me to be of at least not less nervous vigor than your sweet self (for in Thee is not vigor gobbled up in sweetness?), so you, too, red ruddes, should read them (in spite of the sub-title), with like intervals, one by one, not gulp them like porridge or a novel, — which, you know, are homogeneous, these being designedly heterogeneous — or you will hardly, I think, get at what one meant to imply (Easily, you know, in the crash of the orchestra, do the light flute-notes lose themselves on the tired ear: a fact which seems to indicate that works of art, especially such as pretend to be more or less *musical* should be not only pretty short, but separately imbibed; so that *the Concert,* for one thing, is wrong; and with it, the book, such as this, of short detached pieces, which is a literary Concert; only that *here,* you have it in your option to extend your concert into as many nights as there are pieces; and your concert-giver, too, hath it more in his dominion what piece shall company with what, and what shall be the precise complexity and information of the whole.) Well, but to maintain the dear fiction of the Winter's Night, I will say this (epistolary — and not as they write big in the volume of the Books, lest you pout): that the curtain having risen, I will present you first a diary-extract of a poor friend now dead; then a little more drama which I have encountered in the chronicle of one Aventin von Totten-weis; and next a rather dark experience of my own in the dim Northern seas, which, in dream, yet revisits me. Then will be a short interlude for cigarettes, ices, and whispy-lispy, during which will be rendered a piece just splashed down anyway, for a male reader or two, and in some places dull (to *you* I mean) and in others pretty cheap, — this, however, being a day of cheap things, sweetmeat; you yourself, perhaps, not so overdear, and only overdear to the beglamoured eyes of male-made me. This, then, you should *skip* (recalcitrant roe that thou art on the Mountains of Endeavor!) Go out on the verandah, pig's-eye, and there heave, the open secret of that torse my soul remembers to the chaste down-look of Dian's astonished eye-glass, and the *schwärmerei* of the winking Stars. But soon, at about midnight, return; for now, to the tinkle of a silver bell, will unfold itself the life-history, very well translated by me from the original, of a poor man of Hindustan, not, I verily believe, unloved of the gods, but loved, you perceive, in *their* peculiar fashion: *those people* (as the late Mr. Froude uncommonly said to the dying Carlyle) probably having reasons for their carryings-on, of which *we* cannot even dream. And truly, dear, this is marvelous in our eyes, or at least in mine. Well, but now, just as that dark Daphne with the gems entangled in her hair turns paling in flight from the red rape of day, I shall (spiritualest wine coming last, you know, as at that Marriage) once more introduce myself in character this time of lover, and tell how I wooed one of the ladies of my heart at world-illustrious Phorfor. Immediately whereupon, Beloved, shall the Day break, and the Shadows flee away. — Yours, pour toujours et une Nuit d'Hiver!

The Author

Table of Contents

PART I
Shape I
Xélucha.. 11

Shape II
Maria in the Rosebush 19

Shape III
Vaila... 45

INTERLUDE
Premier and Maker 73

PART II
Shape I
Tulsah... 113

Shape II
The Serpent-Ship 125

Shape III
Phorfor.. 141

Xélucha

"He goeth after her . . . and knoweth not . . ."

(From a diary)

Three days ago! by heaven, it seems an age. But I am shaken — my reason is debauched. A while since, I fell into a momentary coma precisely resembling an attack of *petit mal.* "Tombs, and worms, and epitaphs" — that is my dream. At my age, with my physique, to walk staggery, like a man stricken! But all that will pass: I must collect myself — my reason is debauched. Three days ago! it seems an age! I sat on the floor before an old cista full of letters. I lighted upon a packet of Cosmo's. Why, I had forgotten them! they are turning sere! Truly, I can no more call myself a young man. I sat reading, listlessly, rapt back by memory. To muse is to be lost! *of that* evil habit I must wring the neck, or look to perish. Once more I threaded the mazy sphere-harmony of the minuet, reeled in the waltz, long pomps of candelabra, the noonday of the bacchanal, about me. Cosmo was the very tsar and maharajah of the Sybarites! the Priap of the *détraqués!* In every unexpected alcove of the Roman Villa was a couch, raised high, with necessary foot-stool, flanked and canopied with *mirrors* of clarified gold. Consumption fastened upon him; reclining at last at table, he could, till warmed, scarce lift the wine! his eyes were like two fat glow-worms, coiled together! they seemed haloed with vaporous emanations of phosphorus! Desperate, one could see, was the secret struggle with the Devourer. But to the end the princely smile persisted calm; to the end — to the last day — he continued among that comic crew unchallenged choragus of all the rites, I will not say of Paphos, but of Chemos! and Baal-Peor! Warmed, he did not refuse the revel, the dance, the darkened chamber. It was utterly black, rayless; approached by a secret passage; in shape circular; the air hot, haunted always by odors of balms, bdellium, hints of dulcimer and flute; and radiated round with a hundred thick-strewn ottomans of

Morocco. Here Lucy Hill stabbed to the heart Caccofogo, mistaking the scar of his back for the scar of Soriac. In a bath of malachite the Princess Egla, waking late one morning, found Cosmo lying stiffly dead, the water covering him wholly.

"But in God's name, Mérimée!" (so he wrote), "to think of Xélucha dead! Xélucha! Can a moon-beam, then, perish of suppurations? Can the rainbow be eaten by worms? Ha! ha! ha! laugh with me, my friend: *'elle dérangera l'Enfer'!* She will introduce the *pas de tarantule* into Tophet! Xélucha, the feminine Xélucha recalling the splendid harlots of history! Weep with me — manat rara meas lacrima per genas! expert as Thargelia; cultured as Aspatia; purple as Semiramis. She comprehended the human tabernacle, my friend, its secret springs and tempers, more intimately than any *savant* of Salamanca who breathes. *Tarare* — but Xélucha is not dead! Vitality is not mortal; you cannot wrap flame in a shroud. Xélucha! where then is she? Translated, perhaps — rapt to a constellation like the daughter of Leda. She journeyed to Hindustan, accompanied by the train and appurtenance of a Begum, threatening descent upon the Emperor of Tartary. I spoke of the desolation of the West; she kissed me, and promised return. Mentioned you, too, Mérimée — 'her Conqueror' — 'Mérimée, Destroyer of Woman.' A breath from the conservatory rioted among the ambery whiffs of her forelocks, sending it singly a-wave over that thulite tint you know. Costumed cap-à-pie, she had, my friend, the dainty little completeness of a daisy mirrored bright in the eye of the browsing ox. A simile of Milton had for years, she said, inflamed the lust of her Eye: 'The barren plains of Sericana, where Chineses drive with sails and wind their cany wagons light.' I, and the Sabæans, she assured me, wrongly considered Flame the whole of being; the other half of things being Aristotle's quintessential light. In the Ourania Hierarchia and the Faust-book you meet a completeness: burning Seraph, Cherûb full of eyes. Xélucha combined them. She would reconquer the Orient for Dionysius, and return. I heard of her blazing at Delhi; drawn in a chariot by lions. Then this rumor — probably false. Indeed, it comes from a source somewhat turgid. Like Odin, Arthur, and the rest, Xélucha — will reappear."

Soon subsequently, Cosmo lay down in his balneum of malachite, and slept, having drawn over him the water as a coverlet. I, in England, heard little of Xélucha: first that she was alive, then dead, then alighted at old Tadmor in the Wilderness, Palmyra now. Nor did I greatly care, Xélucha having long since turned to apples of Sodom in my mouth. Till I sat by the cista of letters and re-read Cosmo, she had for some years passed from my active memories.

The habit is now confirmed in me of spending the greater part of the day in sleep, while by night I wander far and wide through the city under the sedative influence of a tincture which has become necessary to my life. Such an existence of shadow is not without charm; nor, I think, could many minds be steadily subjected to its conditions without elevation, deepened awe. To travel alone with the Primordial cannot but be solemn. The moon is of the hue of the glow-worm; and Night of the sepulcher. Nux bore not less Thanatos than Hupuos, and the bitter tears of Isis redundulate to a flood. At three, if a cab rolls by, the sound has the augustness of thunder. Once, at two, near a corner, I came upon a priest, seated, dead, leering, his legs bent. One arm, supported on a knee, pointed with rigid accusing forefinger obliquely upward. By exact observation, I found that he indicated Betelgeux, the star "a" which shoulders the wet sword of Orion. He was hideously swollen, having perished of dropsy. Thus in all Supremes is a *grotesquerie;* and one of the sons of Night is — Buffo.

In a London square deserted, I should imagine, even in the day, I was aware of the metallic, silvery-clinking approach of little shoes. It was three in a heavy morning of winter, a day after my rediscovery of Cosmo. I had stood by the railing, regarding the clouds sail as under the sea-legged pilotage of a moon wrapped in cloaks of inclemency. Turning, I saw a little lady, very gloriously dressed. She had walked straight to me. Her head was bare, and crisped with the amber stream which rolled lax to a globe, kneaded thick with jewels, at her nape. In the redundance of her décolleté development, she resembled Parvati, mound-hipped love-goddess of the luscious fancy of the Brahmin.

She addressed to me the question:

"What are you doing there, darling?"

Her loveliness stirred me, and Night is *bon camarade.* I replied:

"Sunning myself by means of the moon."

"All that is borrowed luster," she returned, "you have got it from old Drummond's *Flowers of Sion."*

Looking back, I cannot remember that this reply astonished me, though it should — of course — have done so. I said:

"On my soul, no; but you?"

"You might guess whence *I* come!"

"You are dazzling. You come from Paz."

"Oh, farther than that, my son! Say a subscription ball in Soho."

"Yes. . . ? and alone? in the cold? on foot. . . ?"

"Why, I am old, and a philosopher. I can pick you out riding Andromeda yonder from the ridden Ram. They are in error, M'sieur, who suppose an atmosphere on the broad side of the moon. I have reason to believe that on Mars dwells a race whose lids are transparent like glass; so that the eyes are visible during sleep; and every varying dream moves imaged forth to the beholder in tiny panorama on the limpid iris. You cannot imagine me a mere *fille!* To be escorted is to admit yourself a woman, and that is improper in Nowhere. Young Eos drives an *équipage à quatre,* but Artemis 'walks' alone. Get out of my borrowed light in the name of Diogenes! I am going home."

"Near Piccadilly."

"But a cab?"

"No cabs for *me,* thank you. The distance is a mere nothing. Come."

We walked forward. My companion at once put an interval between us, quoting from the *Spanish Curate* that the open is an enemy to love. The Talmudists, she twice insisted, rightly held the hand the sacredest part of the person, and at that point also contact was for the moment interdict. Her walk was extremely rapid. I followed. Not a cat was anywhere visible. We reached at length the door of a mansion in St. James's. There was no light. It seemed tenantless, the windows all uncurtained, pasted across, some of them, with the words, To Let. My companion, however, flitted up the steps, and, beckoning, passed inward. I, following, slammed the door, and was in darkness. I heard her ascend, and presently a region of glimmer above revealed a stairway of marble, curving broadly up. On the floor where I stood was no carpet, nor furniture: the dust was very thick. I had begun to mount when, to my surprise, she stood by my side, returned; and whispered:

"To the very top, darling."

She soared nimbly up, anticipating me. Higher, I could no longer doubt that the house was empty but for us. All was a vacuum full of dust and echoes. But at the top, light streamed from a door, and I entered a good-sized oval saloon, at about the center of the house. I was completely dazzled by the sudden resplendence of the apartment. In the midst was a spread table, square, opulent with gold plate, fruit dishes; three ponderous chandeliers of electric light above; and I noticed also (what was very *bizarre)* one little candlestick of common tin containing an old soiled curve of tallow, on the table. The impression of the whole chamber was one of gorgeousness not less than Assyrian. An ivory couch at the far end was made sunlike by a head-piece of chalcedony forming a sea for the sport of emerald ichthyotauri. Copper hangings, parnlled with mirrors in iasperated crystal, corresponded with a dome of flame and copper; yet this latter, I now remember, produced upon my glance an impression of actual grime. My companion reclined on a small Sigma couch, raised high to the table-level in the Semitic manner, visible to her saffron slippers of satin. She pointed me a seat opposite. The incongruity of its presence in the middle of this arrogance of pomp so tickled me, that no power could have kept me from a smile: it was a grimy chair, mean, all wood, nor was I long in discovering one leg somewhat shorter than its fellows.

She indicated wine in a black glass bottle, and a tumbler, but herself made no pretence of drinking or eating. She lay on hip and elbow, *petite,* resplendent, and looked gravely upward. I, however, drank.

"You are tired," I said, "one sees that."

"It is precious little than *you* see!" she returned, dreamy, hardly glancing.

"How! your mood is changed, then? You are morose."

"You never, I think, saw a Norse passage-grave?"

"And abrupt."

"Never?"

"A passage-grave? No."

"It is worth a journey! They are circular or oblong chambers of stone, covered by great earth mounds, with a 'passage' of slabs connecting them with the outer air. All round the chamber the dead sit with head resting upon the bent knees, and consult together in silence."

"Drink wine with me, and be less Tartarean."

"You certainly seem to be a fool," she replied with perfect sardonic iciness. "Is it not, then, highly romantic? They belong, you know, to the Neolithic age. As the teeth fall, one by one, from the lipless mouths — they are caught by the lap. When the lap thins — they roll to the floor of stone. Thereafter, every tooth that drops all round the chamber sharply breaks the silence."

"Ha! ha! ha!"

"Yes. It is like a century-slow, circularly-successive dripping of slime in some cavern of the far subterrene."

"Ha! ha! This wine seems heady! They express themselves in a dialect largely dental."

"The Ape, on the other hand, in a language wholly guttural."

A town-clock tolled four. Our talk was holed with silences, and heavy-paced. The wine's yeasty exhalation reached my brain. I saw her through mist, dilating large, uncertain, shrinking again to dainty compactness. But amorousness had died within me.

"Do you know," she asked, "what has been discovered in one of the Danish *Kjökkenmöddings* by a little boy? It was ghastly. The skeleton of a huge fish with human —"

"You are most unhappy."

"Be silent."

"You are full of care."

"I think you a great fool."

"You are racked with misery."

"You are a child. You have not even an instinct of the meaning of the word."

"How! Am I not a man? I, too, miserable, careful?"

"You are not, really, *anything* — until you can create."

"Create what?"

"Matter."

"That is foppish. Matter cannot he created, nor destroyed."

"Truly, then, you must be a creature of unusually weak intellect. I see that now. Matter does not exist, then, there is no such thing, really — it is an appearance, a spectrum — every writer not imbecile from Plato to Fichte has, voluntary or involuntary, proved that for good. To create it is to produce an impression of its reality upon the senses of others; to destroy it is to wipe a wet rag across a scribbled slate."

"Perhaps. I do not care. Since no one can do it."

"No one? You are mere embryo —"

"Who then?"

"*Anyone,* whose power of Will is equivalent to the gravitating force of a star of the First Magnitude."

"Ha! ha! ha! By heaven, you choose to be facetious. Are there then wills of such equivalence?"

"There have been three, the founders of religions. There was a fourth: a cobbler of Herculaneum, whose mere volition induced the cataclysm of Vesuvius in '79 in direct opposition to the gravity of Sirius. There arc more fames than *you* have ever sung, you know. The greater number of disembodied spirits, too, I feel certain —"

"By heaven, I cannot but think you full of sorrow! Poor wight! come, drink with me. The wine is thick and boon. Is it not Setian? It makes you sway and swell before me, I swear, like a purple cloud of evening —"

"But you are mere clayey ponderance! — I did not know that! — you are no companion! your little interest revolves round the lowest centers."

"Come — forget your agonies —"

"What, think you, is the portion of the buried body first sought by the worm?"

"The eyes! the eyes!"

"You are *hideously* wrong — you are so *utterly* at sea —"

"My God!"

She had bent forward with such rage of contradiction as to approach me closely. A loose gown of amber silk, wide-sleeved, had replaced her ball attire, though at what opportunity I could not guess; wondering, I noticed it as she now placed her palms far forth upon the table. A sudden wafture as of spice and orange-flowers, mingled with the abhorrent faint odor of mortality overready for the tomb, greeted my sense. A chill crept upon my flesh.

"You are so *hopelessly* at fault —"

"For God's sake —"

"You are so *miserably* deluded! Not the eyes *at all!*"

"Then, in heaven's name, what?"

Five tolled from a clock.

"*The Uvula!* the soft drop of mucous flesh, you know, suspended from the palate above the glottis. They eat through the face-cloth and cheek, or crawl by the lips through a broken tooth, filling the mouth. They make straight for it. It is the *deliciæ* of the vault."

At her horror of interest I grew sick, at her odor, and her words. Some unspeakable sense of insignificance, of debility, held me dumb.

"You say I am full of sorrows. You say I am racked with woe; that I gnash with anguish. Well, you are a mere child in intellect. You use words without realization of meaning like those minds in what Leibnitz calls 'symbolical consciousness.' But suppose it were so —"

"It is so."

"You know nothing."

"I see you twist and grind. Your eyes are very pale. I thought they were hazel. They are of the faint bluishness of phosphorus shimmerings seen in darkness."

"That proves nothing."

"But the 'white' of the sclerotic is dyed to yellow. And you look inward. Why do you look so palely inward, so woe-worn, upon your soul? Why can you speak of nothing but the sepulcher, and its rottenness? Your eyes seem to me wan with centuries of vigil, with mysteries and millenniums of pain."

"Pain! but you know so *little* of it! you are wind and words! of its philosophy and *rationale* nothing!"

"Who knows?"

"I will give you a hint. It is the sub-consciousness in conscious creatures of Eternity, and of eternal loss. The least prick of a pin not Pæan and Æsculapius and the powers of heaven and hell can utterly heal. Of an everlasting loss of pristine wholeness the conscious body is subconscious, and 'pain' is its sigh at the tragedy. So with all pain — greater, the greater the loss. The hugest of losses is, of course, the loss of Time. If you lose that, any of it, you plunge at once into the transcendentalisms, the infinitudes, of Loss; if you lose *all of it* —"

"But you so wildly exaggerate! Ha! ha! You rant, I tell you, of commonplaces with the woe —"

"Hell is where a clear, untrammeled Spirit is sub-conscious of lost

Time; where it boils and writhes with envy of the living world; *hating* it forever, and all the sons of Life!"

"But curb yourself! Drink — I implore — I *implore* — for God's sake — but *once* —"

"To *hasten* to the snare — that is woe! to drive your ship upon the *light/mouse* rock — that is Marah! To wake, and feel it irrevocably true that you went after her — *and the dead were there* — and her guests were in the depths of hell — *and you did not know it!* — though you *might* have. Look out upon the houses of the city this dawning day: not one, I tell you, but in it haunts some soul — walking up and down the old theater of its little Day — goading imagination by a thousand childish tricks, vraisemblances — elaborately duping itself into the momentary fantasy *that it still lives,* that the chance of life is not forever and forever lost — yet riving all the time with undermemories of the wasted Summer, the lapsed brief light between the two eternal glooms — riving I say and shriek to you! — riving, *Mérimée, you destroying fiend* — She had sprung — tall now, she seemed to me — between couch and table.

"Mérimée!" I screamed, "— *my* name, harlot, in your maniac mouth! By God, woman, you terrify me to death!"

I too sprang, the hairs of my head catching stiff horror from my fancies.

"Your name? Can you imagine me ignorant of your name, or anything concerning you? Mérimée! Why, did you not sit yesterday and read of me in a letter of Cosmo's?"

"Ah-h . . . ," hysteria bursting high in sob and laughter from my arid lips — "Ah! ha! ha! Xélucha! My memory grows palsied and grey, Xélucha! pity me — my walk is in the very valley of shadow! — senile and sere! — observe my hair, Xélucha, its grizzled growth — trepidant, Xélucha, clouded — I am not the man you knew, Xélucha, in the palaces — of Cosmo! You are Xélucha!"

"You rave, poor worm!" she cried, her face contorted by a species of malicious contempt. "Xélucha died of cholera ten years ago at Antioch. I wiped the froth from her lips. Her nose underwent a green decay before burial. So far sunken into the brain was the left eye —"

"You are — *you are Xélucha!*" I shrieked; "voices now of thunder howl it within my consciousness — and by the holy God, Xélucha, though you blight me with the breath of the hell you are, I shall clasp you, living or damned —"

I rushed toward her. The word "Madman!" hissed as by the tongues of ten thousand serpents through the chamber, I heard; a belch of pestilent corruption puffed poisonous upon the putrid air; for a moment to my wildered eyes there seemed to rear itself, swelling high to the roof, a formless tower of ragged cloud, and before my projected arms had closed upon the very emptiness of insanity, I was tossed by the operation of some Behemoth potency far-circling backward to the utmost circumference of the oval, where, my head colliding, I fell, shocked, into insensibility.

*W*hen the sun was low toward night, I lay awake, and listlessly observed the grimy roof, and the sordid chair, and the candlestick of tin, and the bottle of which I had drunk. The table was small, filthy, of common deal, uncovered. All bore the appearance of having stood there for years. But for them, the room was void, the vision of luxury thinned to air. Sudden memory flashed upon me. I scrambled to my feet, and plunged and tottered, bawling, through the twilight into the street.

Maria in the Rosebush

Dreadfully like an immortal goddess i' the face!

— Homer

*A*lbrecht Dürer — artium lumen, sol artificum — pictor — calcographus — sculptor — sine exemplo — one day sent, as we know, a black-and-white wash of his face, untouched by pencil, to his friend, a certain Raphaelo Santi at Rome: a piece of work said to have been much admired of the Master. Two years later, Dürer dispatched just such another to the morganatic Gräfin von Hohenschwangau — a great lover of Art, herself an artist — and it was the burning of this portrait that was the undoing of the Lord of Schwangau himself and so of all that branch of the race of the Herzogs of Swabia, till now.

The history is in part archived in the Bertha room of the little yellow-stone Schloss which now occupies the heights of the Schwanstein — a spot strange "picturesqueness," wondered at within the last decade by some of those British pilgrims who have taken the Constance route to see at Oberammergau. One stops at drowsy Füssen on the torrent Lech, and mounting an Einspanner, penetrates five miles into the richly-forested mountains. The new castle, like the one which preceded it, occupies the loneliness of a sharply-defined ridge-summit, and looks down upon the grey old lazy race of swans which haunts the Schwansee below, and upon the vague blue dream of yet three lakes visible from the height; but the oldest castle of all was lower down, near the plain, on the borders almost of the See. The top of Schwanstein could not, in fact, have contained its massive spread. For gaunt background, the bare breasts of the cleft Säuling.

The incident is, moreover, sketched in a rare old folio of one Aventin von Tottenweis, called: Beiträge zur Kentniss der Mittelalterlischen Malerschulen, mit verschiedenen damaligen Familien-Geschichten.

Matthias Corvinus of Hungary, having the lust to harry Turks south of Danube, had drawn in his wake many a thirsty sword of Southern

Wehrfähige from Franconia to utmost Rheinpfalz; and even when only the fame of the Ungarn king still lived, Caspar of Schwangau, observing with disquiet a fleck of rust on his two-handed sword, and a white wire in his long beard, enticed after him a small body, *Freiherren,* barons, holding, some of them, in feof of his house, and set out on the well-worn route: by no means with injurious intent to any person, but merely in order that that might happen which our Lady of Zugspitze, in her gracious pleasure, might will to happen.

And now, scarce any rough work presenting, the band meeting only with cullions and caitiff curs, and so dispersing by mere centrifugal perversity and dissent, — what more simple than that Caspar, headlong man, should find himself alone with sword and jazeran at Stamboul; cross over into the Troad; thence by the Ægean to the legs of Piræus; and in the neighborhood of Colonus, near the very grove, sacrosanct, solemn, where the *Semnai* gave everlasting rest to way-weary Œdipus, there finally be meshed?

In precipitate fashion, he wooed, and partly won. She was of ancient priestly family, a genuine *Hellene* of antique descent, unmixed, chaste, and overtall in the half-revealing draperies of the old daughters of the gods.

Over the Knie-pass, west of Wetterstein, a train of sumpter-mules, following behind them, labored out of the Tyrol toward the flat tableland of Ober-Bayern, under a burden of precious things, a Hera by Praxiteles, immortal amphoræ, MSS., paintings older than the Lyceum. This was the Countess's *dot.*

The grandeur of the alp must have been novel after sylvan Colonus, and even Caspar's eye was not callous: but Deianira saw here nothing but rudeness. Only, let once a lonely *Sennhaus* appear, the overhanging roof of thatch weighted with boulders, the variegated *Sennerinn* herself in thick-waisted shin-frock at the door, and instantly the Greek interest would flutter up at the hint of fitness, the making hand of man, and the artist reined to look with sidling head.

And so they came to the Schloss by the Schwansee; drawbridge and portcullis felt a throe, and through a double hedge of pikes and harquebuses they passed by the base-court to the great black round Keep, tower-flanked; and here in the gloom of the old Ritter-saal, before castle-chaplain, and God, and every saint, Caspar tendered the left hand of a true knight, and his whole passionate and subservient heart.

Said old Wilhelm of the Horneck, garrulous as a rattle, inveterate tri-ped, having shot out an oaken limb ever since the reign of Caspar's father: "But, Gräfin, you must e'en know that these are not the days that have been. Hey for the fair, gallant times when Wilhelm was tall as the rest; and land and laws were supple to the will of the grand reckless old Adels; and a free imperial knight might e'en marry a scullion, and forthwith have her 'nobled without ado. But Wilhelm is old now, Gräfin, and things do flow to change. There was Lippe-Detwold wedded a wench from the marketplace at Strassburg; and there was Heinrich von Anhalt-Dessau married a hind's pullet in Schwarzwald, as indeed nearly every Anhalt-Dessau has stooped to the *unebenbürtig* since the time of Conrad *le Salique*. Ennobled! the whole company of them, and nothing said. But now! by the Three Kings, the Empire melts, with your upstart free cities, and the rest. Why, can you credit it, dear lady, that the Elector Frederick himself, a Reichs-unmittelbarer-Furst, who married a ballad-singer from the Court at Munich when I was a lad, can't yet obtain a dispensation, and the children remain what you guess? And here now is our own Herr Graf gone to the diet at Ratisbon to talk with Maximilian, if something cannot be done for *you;* and there's Maximilian, stubborn as a Lombard mule, or a bürger of Augsburg —"

A luminous narrow lake of grape-purple, clear hyaline, showed gaudily beneath her half-opened lids.

"Is that, then, the reason of the Count's absence?"

"What! did he not tell you? I thought I heard him —"

"Possibly. It can be of no moment."

"Of no moment! hear her! by the gebenedeite Jungfrau Maria of Eichstadt! and the children then are nothing —"

"What children?"

"The children that are coming, though late — that are e'en now coming, I think —"

Her face was as when a drop of blackest dragon's blood falls and melts into a silver bowl of cream.

"Twittering sparrow that thou art, Wilhelm!"

"Aye, aye, Gräfin, Wilhelm's no eyas — an old fowl. I was burg-vogt of this castle half a score of years before our good lord was born: and right proud of it: and you think me an eyas, a stripling! people have me for an unfledged eyas! I who remember when, near seventy years ago, the grandfather of the wild Wolf of Rolandspitze broke loose over the land, stormed the old palace of the Emperor Arnulf at Regensburg, and carried off gold plate, pictures —"

"Yes? tell me. . . ."

"Ah, you like to hear about pictures: too much, I think: and the Graf grows jealous — deadly jealous — of all your fine Kram and Putz, and the love you pay them! Say little, see much: that's my motto: I follow a point with my eye, as the needle said to the tailor. And let old Wilhelm, who has heard more marriage-bells mayhap, aye, and funeral-knells, than you, give you this hint —"

"But the Wolf! you mean the robber-baron of this region?"

"The same; he of the Felsenburg on the yon side of Lech; his grandfather sacked Regensburg Palace, seizing much treasure, all which his vile Lanzknechte trundled home —"

"Do you remember anything in particular?"

"Remember, aye; old Wilhelm's memory is as clear today. . . . The varlets took everything: the Blessed Sacrament chalices from the altar of the Doppel-kapelle, and, if you *must* know, there was *one* famous picture, spoken of at the time, called the Madonna in der Rosenlaube —"

A luted note escaped her.

"And has he it now, the Wolf?"

"They do say it was hung up in the shrine of his chapel of St. Gereon."

"Wilhelm! it was a work of your own Meister Stephan, a disciple of Wilhelm von Cöln! Dürer has written me concerning him. But to recover it?"

"Recover — what? you judge ill of the fangs of Roland of Roland spitze, if you think —"

"Leave me now. Return later in your Nestor dress — the picture, you see, grows. And prepare me instantly a messenger for Ratisbon to call back the Count."

The apartment, circular in shape, terminated a long series of darksome corridors from the central Ritter-saal. High up, two Gothic slits in the Cyclopean walls let in a parti-colored gloom. Within, *lychnoi* and cressets perpetuated a dim Feast of Lanterns; making vague the majesty of a Zeus Herkeios in the center; painted French watches; an Isis of Egypt; an open letter, and a drawing in red chalk, from Raphael, on a table of ebony arabesqued with walrus tusk; chryselephantine panels of Byzantium; a deep-blue macaw from the South Seas, and two small golden serpents, deadly, black-freckled, of Hindustan, in a glazed Doric temple, love-offerings of Venice, the great merchantman, sent in adoration of the exotic beauty-queen of the Schwangau; enameled pyxes of Limoges, pietas in wax, enoptra (mirrors), tapestries — a whole incrustation, dubious, sheeny, of all that fine Kram and Putz of which old Wilhelm had spoken.

That very night, while the messenger was still on the road to Ratisbon, Caspar broke through the hangings of the doorway, rosy with ardor.

"Ah, *Herzchen, Herzchen* — *to* see you again!"

By the deep low couch where she lay in a *peplos* of Genoa velvet he fell upon a knee, full of the consciousness of her sex, all-gone anew at the vaguely-lit contrast between the china whiteness of skin, and the thick convolving lips, fierce scarlet, of Rossetti's apocalypses. He bent to kiss her with a reverent, chivalric slowness, she motionless.

"And I have lorded it over the best Ortenburg, and Agalolfinger, and Hapsburg of them all — and you are to be Countess of Halsenheim!"

"Did you not meet my messenger?"

"Not I: is aught amiss?"

"Nothing; only I sent to you —"

"Tell me, tell me, *Schätzchen* — ah, the boy — when he comes" — laying close siege to her ear — "shall be Graf von Halsenheim, with a nine-pearled coronet to his head!"

"The wolf of Roland-spitze, is he *strong?*"

"Strong, aye, with a pack of three hundred *faitour* jackals of Schwartz-reiters in his black hold. But why?"

"Does he not fear you?"

"Not he! not yet! though, by the bones of the Eleven Virgins, the wolf may yet know the meeting of the hound's teeth on his quarters —"

"But he loves gold?"

"Loves it, and takes it on the Duke's high-road. But why, *Liebling*, why —"

"Did you know that he has Stephan's Madonna in his chapel?"

He let slip from him like cold snow the naked thick arm which he had been kneading with caresses. He stood erect.

"Pictures again — and *already!*"

"Hence I sent for you," she answered, with eyes opening slowly wide, "it is, or should be, a great work: Albrecht Dürer writes me —"

"Tell me not of this Dürer — a low-born Bürger *Schelm*, drubbed, they say, by his own *wife* —"

"Base woman. No law of man could make such union good."

"Pah! do you not know that the dauber is son to a goldsmith of Ungarn!"

"He is a son of the gods."

"There is but one God, Deianira, and" — crossing with low head — "Jesu Christ whom He hath sent."

Her eyes smiled and closed.

"This hunting after beauty, beauty," he continued, calming, "is not good, *Liebling*. Best make sure that God and his blessed saints look not upon it as sinful with holy eye askance. What then is this divine 'beauty' that you speak so of? By'r Lady, I see it in none of these gimcracks of yours! Give it up, *Zuckerkorn!* God's creatures for beauty, say I; look, if you want to see it, all lustrous, grand, in yonder mirror —"

"But I was not made by man for man's eyes."

"You were made, I swear it, by God for *my* eyes."

"And if you find me perfect, it is, — perhaps, — your eyes that are imperfect. The chance toppling of stones *may* form a hut, you know; but chance never built a temple to the Endless. The Greek women placed a statue of Hyacinthus in their sleeping-rooms, that their offspring might catch something of its wonder. Nature, you see, is nearly everywhere rude, crude, and waits for the rearranging touch of *our* hand. Glance only at that" — she pointed to the Zeus — "no man of flesh ever looked so; you certainly never saw one such. Not by the imitation of nature was *that* shape born to life; but by four-winged imagination, yoked to the divine instinct of loveliness, and riding in pæan triumph, scornful almost of nature. The Assyrians copied nature, and you know —"

"Nay, nay, I am no schoolman in these matters. You want, it seems, this Wolf of the Spitze hunted, and the smudge torn from his claws; well, by St. Hubert, hunted he shall be, and torn it shall be — by power of gold — or secret nightfall — or open storm —"

He had succumbed again to her side. She, inclining to him, bore a dead kiss to red pyre in his beard.

A page entered with a packet. An adventurer Italian, Count della Torre de Tasso (now great Thurn und Taxis) had lately set up a riding-post throughout the Empire. His courier had reached thus far from Nürnberg.

The packet flew open. First there was Brunehild, princess of the Visigoths, mortal bane of ten princes of the Merovingians, carved in hone-stone, and initialed "A.D."; the furrows of eighty years of crime; the blood-dabbled grey hairs tied to a horse's tail; the indignant hoofs spurning to broken death their guilty incubus; the triumph-smile of young Clothair near. Next, a letter in Latin, flourished at the end with a couplet from Ovid; and next, a curling folio of canvas, washed with a head. She held it open with her two extended arms.

"This then is he!"

Caspar had leant over to look.

"The burger-son of Nürnberg?"

"Dürer."

"Well, he has a goodly, pleasant face enough. But methinks the fellow presumes, *Herzchen*. A bonfire of these child's toys, if you wish to pleasure me! And a letter interdicting —"

"Nay, the *next* letter," she said, smiling an arch *câlinerie*, "will be a boast that I have the Stephan Madonna of the Rose-bower — safe!"

The Dürer-head, stretched on a framing, took rank by the couch. The light of a fierce, fond criticism beat upon it, and Caspar, entering unawares, was witness how, sitting on the edge, she searched the pale azure eyes with intent forgetfulness, so that he touched her before she knew.

And he frowned to see the swell of sudden pink which leapt to her throat.

And the next day when, fulminant with rage, he broke into the room, Dürer had vanished, and he noticed it: but his mind was of such sort as to bear the stress of only one disquiet at a time, and he said nothing of the daub. In his hand he flourished a document; a torrent of invective came from him.

"The blasphemous *Frevler!* His weasand for it, as I am true knight and Christian gentleman! See, *Herzchen,* see, this he has sent me – he – *he* – the meanest *Mittel-frei,* self-styled Graf and Wolf! His great-grandfather" – stamping to and fro – "digged the trench round his five-acre farm with his own hands. And this to *me!* His life for it – I will worry, worry, worry the poisonous rat from his stench-hole, by the Holy Mother of God! Self-styled Count! Slitting throats at noontide! claiming right to coin money in his own vile lair, like an *Adeliger!* taking of tolls! tribute from the villages! Walpurgis-tax – Michælmas-tax – hearth-shilling – Frohn-arbeit – levied all upon other men's bauers – and his own grandfather a lubber-lipped *Land-sasse!* Deems himself *rechts-fähig,* by ——! Ha, Sir Count!" – with robust emphasis of foot – "thy weasand for it, then! I did but write, *Herzchen,* making stipulation for the stolen Madonna you wot of in return for honest Schwangau money rendered. He replies by a threat to harry me – harry *me* –"

Her eyes were wide.

"But you *will* obtain the Madonna?"

"Ah, that will I, and within the sennight!"

"By strategy and surprise, then – not by open assault."

"How so?"

"For the sake of your own safety; and partly lest the man, having warning, destroy the work."

She made her arms a lulling charm, and slowly cooled his judgment to the temper of hers. Long after a windy night-fall, a picked body of cavaliers crept through the dripping woods of the heights above Füssen, taking their secret way to the Felsenburg.

The enterprise was as hardy as could be. Caspar only realized the steepness of the danger he had dared when he stood once more within his own good castle-gate. It was then breaking day. Helmeted still, visor down, glistening in wetted armor-plates, he winged his feet with the good news towards the bedchamber of Deianira. As often, she had passed a sleepless night; her bed was unruffled. Thence with eager outlook he hurried to the apartment where the *lychnoi,* in a sleepy twilight inviolate as yet of the crude day, laved the empty couch of the

Greek. An angry "wetter!" broke from him. In a corridor he came upon Wilhelm of the Horneck, always a shaker before the cock, a heap of age, built upon his staff.

"How, now, Wilhelm? The Gräfin!"

"Not in her chamber, and not in her Kunst-kammer?"

"In neither, man, by my faith."

The old fellow, sudden and quick in jealousy for his overlord's dignity, looked bilious, suspecting truth.

"Follow me," he said, "old Wilhelm's eyes — old Wilhelm's wits — 'twas always so — the dagger to cut every knot — from the time when your grandfather, Otto, took to too fluent rouses of Hochheimer grape —"

"Come, come, old man, less of lip and more of limb!"

Wilhelm led the way up the steep, unequal steps of a turret, along a dark passage, and pointed. Caspar stood before the open door of an extremely small room cut from the wall. Within, on a low table — almost an altar — of pierced bone, burned a right flank of three long vestas, stuck on pricket-candlesticks; a left flank of three; and, somewhat retired from them, a center of three; and beyond them, hanging to the wall, a washed head; and before them, priestess of this shrine, the breast-banded back-view of Deianira, the gorgeous grace of her samite *peplos,* she erect, with perked head, searching, searching the pale azure eyes. She had not heard the clinking approach of Caspar's armor.

A harsh "Ha!" broke from him.

She started into pink confusion, and then, instantly calm again, "Ah, you have brought it then, the Madonna!"

The rattle of his metal broke an awful silence as he turned and marched to her apartment, she clinging expectant to his side. A not very large parcel, placed by a halberdier, lay in wrappings on the floor.

"Help, help me!" she cried, eagerness trembling in her fingers as she undid it; and then, "but, oh! see there! fie! you have defaced it," and now, after a moment's breathless inquisition, "but — it is not — beautiful — not supremely; it lacks — not scrupulousness — certainly not that — but the — *This* is not Art, thought, — it is Nature, impulse! I am sorry I gave you the pains."

Caspar stood tapping the frown of his resentment to ultimate smoothness beneath the tip of his steel boot, till she, remembering that he needed reconquest, set herself leisurely to the work. His *bonderie* lasted till mid-day, and then he was hers again.

Falconry, and the dear delights of woodcraft in the forest near, filled his mornings; and once, when the Madonna had been relegated to forgotten obscurity, she rose to meet him as he entered the door of the art-room, plumed, horn by horn, holding still the spear and straight short sticker, faintly streaked with dry blood of the boar.

"Tell me, have you had good venery this morning?"

She lavished on him the whole Æaean incantation of her loveliness, languishment of kisses, listening with quite disproportionate interest to details of the chase, the halloo, conduct of pack and prickers, the bringing to bay, the dimensions of the quarry. Then suddenly:

"Tell me, where is — Arras?"

"Arras? In Frankland, surely. But what now?"

"They make tapestry there?"

"Aye."

"And you have heard of Raphael? You *must*, I think, — in Welschland?"

"Well, well, *Herzchen.*"

"Raphael, you know, highest of all — he has lately executed, so Pietro Perugino writes me, ten great works, altogether immortal, on *cartone*, at the invitation of your Pope, and these have been sent to Arras and the factory there to be woven into fabric. You see now the full connection? You see? And I hear that now their purpose is served, little account is made of them, and they lie dust-grown, neglected; to be purchased, therefore — think of it! — perhaps for little, by a wily bargainer, crafty to hide his eagerness of acquisition. Ah, and you will go! You will go!"

"Now, by St. —"

The name of the saint fainted on his lips, as a wind at the caress of a pearl-shelled grotto of roses, and down a steep incline, topped by angry impatience, and based by growling complaisance, slid Caspar; so that after not many days, accompanied by a very few pikes, he rode his moody way over the plain of the Schwangau. The sentinels on the turrets saw the little band swallowed by a glade of the forest, as they wound slowly forward on their long journey to Frankreich.

It was shortly after this that Albrecht Dürer — most dreamy-wandering of bürger-sons — his whole life a pious Wanderjahr — arrived.

Passing near on foot, he hoped for the minute-measured privilege of some talk with the exalted lady who had been pleased to approve him. Old Wilhelm of the Horneck himself, with no overflow of courtesy — eyeing yellowly, with rheumy eye, the dusty hose, and belted *wamms*, and short cloak, all of rather worn brown stuff — led him from the base-court, up to the Saal, and so along the corridors. A satchel, hanging diagonally, contained *butter-brod*, and two pieces of chalk. Deianira, just emerging from the hangings of her sanctuary, saw, and knew; and uttered a bated cry.

Dürer, too, knew, and his heart, failing, sank; regretting his rashness. More blushes than a girl's covered him. A sudden noon-day sun could not have dazzled and winded him more.

Some little time before this, while on his Italian trip he had written to a friend: "In Italy I am a gentleman; in Germany a parasite." Add to this that the genius was, by nature, shyer than a kid.

She greeted and led him to the chamber with a heart-simple old majesty, beyond anything he saw in the high dames who sailed athwart his eyesight in his humble Hofmaler attendance at the court of Maximilian and (afterwards) of Charles. Climaxes of crimson rushed every moment across his face. She sitting over against him. Andromache in his eyes, Helen, Artemis' self; and she said unexpectedly this:

"Well! you have come in lucky time: within — shall I say three weeks? — Raphael's Sistine cartoons *will be here!* Ten of them — a banquet of wine. And I know you will not think of going without seeing them!"

He could evoke nothing but a murmur of thanks.

Airy German magi, Novalises, idealists, will not hear of Time; for if the *condamné* actually finds a night eternity, and the Monk Felix one hundred years a second — whose shot brings down the volatile truth? Both, or rather neither, they say; for the thing computed is in each case reflexive of the computer merely, externally inane. Albrecht and Deianira, with their quick brains, might well have realized some such thought, had they compared the pace of these weeks of waiting with others past and to come. But crowded speculations of a different sort were insistent upon their attention.

At first, it was all decked words, picked turns of phrase, some of the open bashfulness remaining on the one side, the secret diffidence on the other; a continuous torrent of mere opinions; the world-old dogmatism of the artist, self-sure, but with claws now tucked-in; Deianira's theories quite different from his, yet seeming almost to coincide, by means of trimmed, only half-expressed convictions, on this hand and that.

Everything was gazed into; Stephan produced. "What curious work! so minute; but —" and she stopped.

"He is my favorite of the Cöln school," said Durer; "his limpid piety seems so to illumine all he did. Wynrich I place on a much lower grade: you never saw his Sancta Veronica in the Munich Pinacothek? No? Rather an inanity. And yet the old Cöln *tempera* was so excellent that he ought —"

"You place a *very* high value on medium, do you not?"

"Well, as a workman, a fairly high value, perhaps. You, I daresay, do not —"

"Not *so* high, maybe."

"But this of Stephen is fine — ah, delicate, virgin. He painted the

Dombild, too, in the Cathedral, but that, you would see, is much immaturer; here he is at his perfectest — the chastity of detail — of the crown, of the cherubs in the medallion — but you, doubtless, do not —"

"The Greek writers, painters, sculptors" — evading direct reply — "placed, I think, little value in details by themselves, except in so far as they conduced to the intended effect of the whole as a whole."

This was a point of view new to Dürer. He blushed. And timidly:

"You think they were right?"

"They *may* have been wrong," she said, and smiled.

Thus to begin. But the rapid days brought rapid realization of the equality of all infinite things, and so a full resumption of self-reverence, and so greater freedom of thought and speech; the words falling out now less knit, foreknown — and more, ever more, of them, torrents laughing with light and feeling. No more careful retraction of claws, but roughish play, the free fraternity of two natural, high-strung people, conscious of themselves and of each other. Dürer had been everywhere, looking at things through the crystal simplicity of a devout, open intellect; lowliest pilgrim to Venice, to the Flemish cities: a lynx in the castle of Barbarossa at Gelnhausen, and among the ruins of the great old Charlemagne palaces at Aachen and Engelheim. The *quattrocentisti* had hewn their work, and ended; and out of that strength was coming, had come, sweetness as of ambrosia; Botticelli, the Holbeins, Buonarroti, all breathed the same new air; the Van Eycks had been painting in their wonderful new oil-varnish medium at Binges. All this movement, art-life, the delicate young monk-mind had felt, cutting clean the rein of aspiration, dreaming dreams, high but pure. Raphael had sent him two life-studies in chalk. He poured into the ear of Deianira fairy tales of art-history, gleams, hints, half cabalistic in their effect; secret treasures stored in monasteries grey as the dawn of German things; suspected gems in the vaults of the church of the Augustines at Nürnberg, and in the cloisters of St. Catherine at Augsburg; old Abbots — Alfred and Arinam of Bayern; Gosbert and Absolom of Triers — mixing in their *tempera* occult substances, dying with their selfish arcana; the splendid art of the Hohenstaufens; the rich gold-ground honey-medium work of the thirteenth century; the perfect *impasto* of John van Eyck; *protégés* of the old Emperors at Prague; the Maastricht school; subtle distinctions between Rhine-men and Westphalia-men, Dutch and Flemish; Israel von Meckenen; and the beauties of Wurmsur and Veit Stoss, and the only three-quarter beauties of Martin Schoen; a whole snowflake cataclysm of wanton words.

"Do you know," he asked, "what di Cosimo mixed in his colors for the Death of Procris? Only guess!"

"And what does it matter *what* he mixed?" she answered, freely pouting now, a long-legged Aphrodite playing angry at baby-tricks of little Eros.

They parted lingeringly late in the night, and lay dreamlessly dreaming of the next day's bacchanal of reason, the word-orgy, and dancing rivulet of fancies.

For him she threw off something of the anchorite quiescence, and there were days when they took long walks together over the plain, and so into the shade of the forest; Albrecht's temper, naked to all influences of nature, softening at the great old trees, and deep glens, and dank, religious gloom; she maintaining the Greek coldness, feeling nothing. And long-drawn floats on the lake filled the halt twilight. A steep flight of stone steps at the back of the castle, mossy underfoot, overarched every-way with a wide wilderness of bindweeds, led at this point down the hillside, and so plumped into the See. By this way they reached the high-prowed little shallop, itself a swan, moored to the platform.

Albrecht sometimes flung from a zither an old psalm-air or daintytripping Minne-lied to the drugged breezes and wavelets of the See. Not yet had Jacob Stainer gone through the forest with little tapping steel-hammer, and found that ever the oldest tree had in it the mellowest Memnonmusic: Mittenwald and the violins were therefore future; but every peasant of Bavaria, even then, was a maker and twanger of the zithers whose universal twitter filled the land with sounds.

"Look!" cried Deianira, "see — see how the presence of a man's hand reforms the callous landscape!"

It was the 23rd of June. Here and there, on the heights round Schwangau, cones of flame, smoke-plumed, burned upward to the deepening sky.

"*Sonnenwandfeuer,*" said Albrecht, "lit by the bauers. It is the Eve of St. John."

"St. John! — why, it is the celebration of a solar myth — this, you know, is the summer solstice — the myth which underlies the story of Œdipus."

"Hardly, I think. We light the fires because St. John —"

"And yet — they lack — arrangement. A supreme artist might so place them in reference to each other as actually to lift the scene into ideality. Chance does nothing."

This *banne camaraderie* fructified into intimacy. Albrecht put a modest hand into the wallet of his brown cloak, and drew out the MS. of his little book, not yet completed, *De Symmetriâ Partium;* she envisaging him, sitting on the couch-edge, elbows meeting draped knees, chin joisted on fisted hands. And he read — Monk-Latin, with acolyte intonation — and she, with sure scalpel of inward criticism, listened, searching, searching his face. Now, the figures of Dürer in the "Trinity with Heavenly Host" and the "Christian Martyrs," painted by himself, as well as his still surviving two heads, are beautiful indeed, but probably not true of his face, for his gift was never the presentation of a superlative degree of human "prettiness." The painter had, in fact, the spiritual face of a stripling seraph; such a face, that, had he been Italian, had his life passed in Florence and not Nürnberg, he must have been Raphael and not Dürer. A crinkled head of long, gossamer, auburn hair was the pensive playmate of every breath; and blushing maidenhood, and the innocent eyes of old recluses, and the kiss-compelling lips of Byron, transfigured him to the meek beauty of Leonardo da Vinci's John at the Last Supper.

And in fond repayment of the *Symmetriâ Partium,* Deianira produced from an alcove her own work of the last three years: a triptych with the rape of Persephone; old Wilhelm as Nestor; and, large on chestnut panel, a return of a *sennerinn* on Rosenkranz Sunday from Almen-leben on the heights; the bell-cow decked with edelweiss and rhododendron; the crowned *sennerinn* on its back; the train of meek kine, calved; the gratulatory length of village-street full of the laughter poured from every gossiping doorway; the bashful lover, broad-faced, in felt steeple-hat, presenting to Gretel the necessary nosegay — reward of all her lonesome ward of love. And she had only seen it once, crossing the Alp to Schwangau, years before. Albrecht, without a word, self-abased, looked at it, she smiling at his blank face. What spurred his wonderment was the lifefulness — he well knew the scene — and then, far above all, the unlikeness to any life anywhere. Never Bavarian peasant, or peasant or man in the world, owned such meaning traits, look so strange and high. Here, then was contact with a new school, perpetuated by one disciple, grandest of all, the school of Apelles, and old Rhodian masters of the Doric Hexapolis. It was shortly after this revelation that Dürer wrote to his friend Melanchthon that sentence so full of pathetic meekness: "admirator sum minime meorum, ut olim; et saepe gemo meas tabulas intuens, et de infirmitate meâ cogitans."

And now change was manifest in the spirit of their intercourse; a third distinct phase, like the evolved presentments of a planet's face — so natural, self-unconscious. The penumbra of a profound melancholy fell upon these souls — penumbra, because though poignant, it was not painful, but, on the contrary, full of luxury. Without shadow of apparent cause, they walked continually on the borders of the misty-dripping lake of tears, by the twilight banks of a spectral river of sighs. The art-talk dropped utterly; and, in its place, talk of life; and especially of death;

and all mournful things. Albrecht had secretly wondered whither had vanished the present of his washed head: but exploring alone one day, he saw the square of deeper darkness on the wall of the little cell; entered, knew, looked at the nine extinguished tapers on the low altar-table; and frowned down a tingling tumult of ecstasy and pang which rushed through all his frame. Soon subsequent to this the doleful mood grew on.

"Pirene," said Deianira, "wept and wept, so *bitterly* wept, that she melted into a fountain."

"And Kriemhild," said Albrecht, "when she heard of the death of Siegfried, so *bitterly* laughed, that the ringing rafters made the house to tremble."

Here was intensity for intensity; deep calling to deep. Deianira had been no dyspeptic worm in painted Hoch-deutsche MSS., new-printed books. They droned of old German women; Thusnelda, the magnificent; Rumetrude, misty-weird; Carolus and his paladins in the romaunts; tragic bignesses of Niebelungenlied; the true heart of Bertha; lily-chastity of Theodelinda; all the ah and pain of woe-worn Tannhäuser of the Hörselloch. They fell into comparisons between Ajax and Amadis; asked which was the pitifulest, Hercules Furens or Orlando, not yet "Furioso."

"Read to me," he said.

"What?"

"Something *sad.*"

She filled the night with a reading-from-the-scroll of the long lamentation and wringing of hands of Euripides' *Trojan Women*.

At home with Plato and Aristotle, less familiar with the Tragedies, he caught perhaps not half; but the half filmed his eyes with a constant moisture. As the slow, variegated words, each a perfect round messenger from her, wafted clean and light like bubbles from a pipe, floated about him — rhythmic chorus, and pomp of sententious rhesis* — he then first realized the Greek language, and all the fresh joy and wonder it is. And as all modes of beauty are akin — beauty of form to beauty of sound to beauty of odor — these need but approximation under right conditions to blend into harmonies, and so produce the ultimate delight. Albrecht, listening, drank an exhalation from her of mingled frangipane and ambergris, and roamed from the Paphian face of sea-foam white, to the braided bosom, to the fine linen *zonè*, to the broken billow of draperies at her feet, to the dainty arrangement of sandal-straps; and again back to the dead-white face. A rare exaltation — verging on tears — like the rarest flame of interstellar ethers — ached through his physic man.

---

* The very number of lines determined for wise reasons.

The invitation had been that he should stay to see the Raphael cartoons. Looking now, each saw in the other's eyes that this must not be.

He slung his satchel, containing the chalk-sticks and the *butter-brod* crusted now to stone, upon his back.

The setting sun was the very genius of gold on the waters of the Schwansee. Languid undulations curved into purple and saffron and crimson before the breasts of the swans, and the beaked prore of the shallop. From the terraced garden which sloped to the edge of the See on the castle side, an oppression of violet-beds and roses pervaded the whole spirit of nature. Yet not a breath ran upon the water. All was a conflagration; the bordering tree-tops burned unconsumed; yellow streaks stretched quite up to the zenith; the sun and his immediate train stepped down incarnadine to *couchée* and purple bed, pomped and appanaged like dormiturient old queens of Assyria, drunk with blood and wine.

Their most commonplace words were uttered in a tone of profoundest sadness.

"Helen," said Dürer, splashing one of the birds, "had for father — a swan. Her mother Eurotian Leda. I seem to see a perfect fitness in the myth."

"The poets," she answered, looking never at him, "would have pawned their hope of Elysium for power to give a higher impression of her beauty; and as of her beauty, so of the pain, the tragedy of her."

"The pain, the tragedy! So it is, then, and must be, with beauty! Calvary is witness."

"Cursed be it, I say; and the hunger of it!"

She hid from him the sudden passion of her face.

The sun set; the mist and melancholy of a *morne* twilight grew deepening down upon the lake. A flight of crows, the sad fate of a nightingale in a grove near, the flap of a swan, were evidence of the silence. They heard distinctly a change of sentries at the turret-portal next the see.

"You return to Nürnberg?"

"Not yet. I am a wanderer, you know, a confirmed wanderer."

"Rest is best."

"For myself I look for one rest henceforth — the rest that remaineth to the people of God."

"I meant what you mean."

"A roam among the alp-heights, perhaps — some sketching —"

"You will be still near me then."

"Near you? Ah yes! still near you."

The mournful mood of Gethsemane was in them; the old torrent of words ran low.

Moving red lights gleamed through the barred window-slits of the donjon. It was night. A faint breeze arose, and wooed to truancy hairs of Deianira's filleted, uncovered head, and was heavy at a perfume it met around her, and died at the sweet tumult it won from the old gilt Æolian *phorminx,* seven-stringed, which lay since the previous night in the shallop. She took it, and the insistence of the plectrum won from her a softly-sung hymn of Andromache.

> Hector, the harmer
>   Moan'd at the night of thee;
> Myrmidon armor
>   Paled at the light of thee.
> (Your lutes of lotus wood
>   Libyan wail for him!
> Your lutes with wax conglued
>   Sweetness exhale for him!)
> Plowman of blessings!
>   Whelp-son his lingering,
> Tears his expressings,
>   Harps knew his fingering!
> Zeu! who through Ancient Night
>   Urgest thy traveling,
> Yet metest ever right
>   Doom of thy raveling;
> Red has the flame of noon,
>   Rushed to obscurity —
> Rash let the crapèd moon
>   Rend up her durity!

"Ah! that was a chillier wind."

The moon, which had uttered a scared face, drew quickly the grey curtains of the night and disappeared.

"It grows cold for you; you must go now within the Schloss."

"It is lonely there."

"Is it lonely?"

"And I am not cold. Touch my hand." At his touch she shivered. A single drizzle-spray fell upon each of them.

"Still I must go," he said.

A sob!

"We may meet again."

"You will never come again."

"Time and tide happeneth to us all, you know."

"But — you will never come again."

They had reached the platform of the bowered stair. He stepped from the shallop and stood with her. The mizzle had become clearly sensible. The moon had utterly vanished.

Her hand was in his. He stooped and kissed it — on back, in palm — ready to be mad as she. Luckily, her face was quite turned from him.

"God —" he said.

From her working lips came no sound. Her bosom rowed like two oarsmen struggling for life from the suck of the whirlpool.

He was gone. She stood and watched him to the other side of the lake, and the embankment there. He made fast the boat. A curtain of masonry ran here parallel to the See to defend the castle-back. Before he reached it the mist had swallowed him. As he finally disappeared from her, she buried her face in the voluming folds of her left arm, and the thin, low wail of a little child welled from her. Slowly she ascended the stairs.

The end would have been different, had Dürer, like Deianira, been all artist; but the Nürnberg painter was first of all saint, and artist after.

But there was evil news at the Schloss of Schwangau in those very days. The old nose of Wilhelm perked high, sniffing danger on the wind. Bauers and yeomen from round Füssen and Eschach, leaving their farms, came crying to the Burg-vogt for protection. Sathan himself was loose. At Hopfen a whole street had burned, the church of St. Magnus been pillaged. Two villages flamed together. Roland of Rolandspitze, biding his time, collecting his forces, had not forgotten his Madonna.

He was a species of Swabian Eppelein von Gailingen, a Sud-deutscher Wild Boar of Ardennes.

On the third day Caspar arrived — almost by stealth — with his little band of men-at-arms. He had heard tidings of trouble on the way. His blood was up.

Flushed with enthusiasms, high passions, he came to where the wool stood bundled before heron the distaff. "Ah . . . ah . . . ah!" was all he could say, as he did, and did again, perfervid violence to her lips; she enduring with pensive patience. "But you look not *so* well, *täubchen* — not so well — a look of care — to be expected now, perhaps — and I have brought the smudges — aha! that pleases it then? Ah . . . ah . . . sugary ecstasy that thou art! — three of them — yes, *only* three — the other seven lay buried in some hole — the factory is a monstrous place, you must know — and they showed me there scant courtesy, by'r Lady; but three, by much entreaty, and a threat or two thrown in, I did get — these being easily unearthed — for a few gulden. Ha! and here they come."

Two waiting-men bore-in a long narrow box, opened; the cartoons had been cut into strips. Deianira rose, and adjusted them on the floor: Stephen stoned; Paul in prison at Philippi; the light at noon-day "above the brightness of the sun." For a minute, over each, the impeccable energy of her scrutiny worked intensely; then, without fail, she knew the truth of form, composition, drapery, effect. Coming to him, she rewarded him with a cold kiss. And coldly she said:

"Thank you — they are very lovely."

Even he could see it, and went away wondering at her inertness, the death of her enthusiasm.

But action, action was the word — no dallying over daubs! "Come, man, news, news!" he cried to Wilhelm, towing the three-goer into a small room. Wilhelm, who was directness itself where the talk touched upon the old trade of war, was minute on the defenses of the castle, ammunition, provisions, his own share in everything, the ravages of the Wolf. Only a few hours before a Wappen-herald had arrived at the gate, demanding the return of the Maria, loud with threats of siege.

"His strength, man?"

"Over three hundred, they say."

"And ours?"

"A hundred and twenty, beside a flock of bauers."

"And gold in our coffers?"

"Scarcity of that till harvest."

"Ha! and where is now my cousin of Swabia?"

"At Augsburg they say."

"Good! a dispatch to him instantly, requisitioning succors, and the same to every friendly burggraf of the region. The ripped bowels of this *Verräther*, Wilhelm! And other news?"

"Nothing — only —" the old man halted, half loving his suzerain's quiet mind, and half the solace of the oily tongue.

"Well, Wilhelm, well —"

"Nothing — a visitor to the castle — the painter of Nürn —"

"Now, by —"

"For more than two weeks —"

"Ha!"

"Two weeks," the conciseness melting before a fervor of doddering communicativeness, "and never by my goodwill, either — 'tis not till now that Wilhelm of Horneck has waited to see the back of a noble house broken by some strolling troubadour or runaway bauer's pup with fair face. You may have heard of Trautmandorfs wife and the mummer nigh a century gone. And did ye ever know old Wilhelm to predict you false? With right jealous eye, I tell you, I looked upon the long intimacies of speech — and wantonness of glides on the lake — by night — with worrying of — harps and zithers —"

"Enough, Herr of Horneck, enough —" Caspar had drawn back a foot, and was frowning into the old man's soul.

"Worrying of harps — and confluence of bent heads over Kram and Putz — and now that he is gone, the rekindling of the tapers before the painter-head — put your trust in old Wilhelm's eyes for seeing! — nine of them — burning continually, like the fires which they used to say the prince-bishop of Bruchsal plenished near the tombs of the Emperors in the crypts of Spires Cathedral — and the door of the cell kept locked, and a daily double-visit paid to the head —"

"Enough, man, I say —"

"But, for that matter, 'tis a left-handed wedlock — you are not bound. Well I remember the case —"

"Traitor! Silence!" His roar was the lion's; the old man cowered, silent; Caspar walked away.

It was then late in the day. That very night a fresh troop of bauers fled into the castle, with tidings of added woes. At dawn the plain before Hohenschwangau was dotted grey, well beyond artillery range, with the leaguering tents of Roland.

And there was brisk work before long. The *Burgh-wache*, though insufficient to make even the proper show of strength, had no lack of fire, through hope of speedy help, and confidence in Caspar's generalship. He was in every place, a strong, ubiquitous spirit of disposition, inspiration. Two parallel bastioned curtains defended the front and sides of the donjon; before each of these a fosse and drawbridge; and before the outermost drawbridge an out-work barbican. Upon this last the chief besieging party, under Roland himself and his brother Fritz, concentered their efforts with scaling-ladders, petards and grenadoes, potent enginery; and upon this detachment Caspar in person, from a bastion of the first curtain, directed a saker and culverin hail-rain. But before nightfall the out-work had fallen to the reverberating *hochs!* of the brigands.

Early the next day the storm reopened. The enemy, with manifold advance and retreat, now attempted the bastions of the first escarpment. Still no sign of Swabian support. A sigh for sleep, only for sleep, arose among Caspar's men. During the night a strain in the relief of sentinels had made itself felt, so meager the garrison. Caspar himself had mounted guard.

In the afternoon, passing by Deianira's room, tired, he entered, pining for her. Hardly since his coming back had he seen her. Freely now, from his heart, he forgave her the entertainment of the bürger-son, knowing well her child's love for pictures and suchlike. Here in these recesses the volleying of howitzer and mortar, saker and falconet, whizz of arrows, smiting of pikes, was only buzzingly audible. She lay on the couch at full length, beautifully asleep, or only on the borderland of wakefulness. In this dim state, hearing the ghost of his footstep, she stretched out her arms, both of them, at full length before her, inviting to the luxury of her embrace; and he, smiling ineffably, trusting, gentle, came to her, bending himself down, happy at the sweet, voluntary friendship of her arms about his neck. She, in her half-sleep, murmured:

"Albrecht, Albrecht, thou art come . . ."

Caspar stumbled backward with that pale, distorted rigidity of face seen in the agonized brave fellows on the bastions when a sudden arrow entered their hearts. He reeled like a dying man from the chamber.

Deianira, vaguely conscious of disturbance, slowly opened her eyes, and was alone.

But in little time Wilhelm of Horneck came dashing into the room, youth in every third projected leg, and before her fell prone to his old knees, with outstretched clasped hands, a world of prayer in his eyes.

"O Gräfin — save the Count — you only can — for the love of God! Gräfin! There may be yet time — he thinks to make a sally — stark mad, raving! And the men, seeing certain death, refuse to follow him. Some devil, some furious devil, rides him. Save him! Only some fifty against three hundred! Gräfin! his eyes are two rolling suns of flame; and help must come tonight — tomorrow — for very certain, if he would only wait —"

She, surprised, rose. Outside they met men rushing hither and thither with wild looks. One said:

"They are gone — just passed the inner Fallbrücke. God help them!"

The desire to see overcame her, and, mounting the steps of a turret, she took a seat on a planchette within the boldly-projecting machicolation near the battlements, looking through an aperture. Here she was alone, the donjon being as yet safe from shot. The small band — multifariously armed, hellebardiers, brigandined archers, carabiniers, Caspar at their head — were then issuing from the outer bridge. Just now there had come a lull to the storm; the enemy were in lager. The sun was low, hidden behind a crag of Säuling. The castle party moved down a gentle slope.

A flourish of trumpets, a shout, arose — two — triumphant on one side, death-challenging on the other. Quickly before the lager-tents sprang a crop of dragon's teeth; midway they met.

Deianira's eyes rested only upon Caspar. A certain unusual tingling feeling, vaguely working, was struggling into form within her — akin to admiration. To the minute when the fight began her face was calm. Then she saw him in the thick of things, firm, Actè-bluff when thunder-bolts are abroad, and breakers break upon its rock. The first dawn of a smile rose orient upon her lips. A small body of men — the very pick of the castle — surrounded now every-way by the enemy — formed his immediate *entourage;* the rest, blocked, sustained the shock of the brigands. Every minute a life ended — two to one on the side of the besiegers, who did double-battle with the dogged despair of Caspar's men. He, it was clear, was bent upon some object away from him; his sword the very tooth of pestilence in his hand, his helmet-plume floating above all heads, certain token of coming death. The dawn spread to Deianira's eyes; an eager luster grew gradually radiant in them. And soon the end of Caspar's quest was evident — the Wolf himself, distinguished by his raucous shouts of cheer, huge battle-axe, suit of fluted armor. The brool of Caspar's roar rang challenging out; they were near now. Roland, a towering bulk, nothing loath, rabid with the taste of blood, struck spur to charger; casting axe, drawing sword. They dashed together. The warring *Lanzknechte* made way, and left large field: it was a recoil of the wave from the basalt, like the scampering of chaff from flails. The two men fought alone. Deianira drew a deeper breath.

It was at this precise moment that the sun, sinking hitherto behind a fork of the Säuling, burned forth a perfect red circle in the inter-space between the riven rock. Its beams, falling upon Caspar panoplied in plated steel mail, made him rich, splendid; a luminous molten glory of cuirass and gorget, arm-piece and helmet and greaves; it welded him to his bossed and prancing warhorse, and turned them, him and it, into a homogeneous Centaur of fluent and refulgent gold.

"O! — but it is beautiful!" The effect was so sudden. It took her breath away. Her hands clasped, rigidly. A swelling wave of feeling flowed in her. Beautiful! And why? This, as usual, was the first question of her analytical mind. As she faintly heard the ringing outcries raised from the clattered metal of the warriors, saw the swift avenging flash of Caspar's blade, she knew quickly why. It was in the nature of a revelation to her. The doer, then, was great as the maker? Conduct as art? Marathon lovely as the Parthenon? The Crusades as Aphrodite? Caspar as Raphael? Was it *so,* then? And if not, how came this sight so to lift her bosom with the beauty-sense — with love perhaps? It was more than a revelation — it was a regenesis, the birth of a little child, as natural, as definite, as the conversion of Lydia. Not since their meeting-day to this hour had Caspar appealed unconquerably to the predominant in her — her abandonment to beauty. Now he loomed in quite another light: he was immense — he was thrilling! With an æsthetic inquisitiveness, she peered at the illumined interchange of tierce and quart, shrewd thrust, ponderous hew: the two men were nicely parallel in skill, virulence; Caspar not quite so tall, his warhorse larger. Only to look at him, facing so great danger, at so great odds, with so great manfulness, was joy! And now the thought rose bitingly within her that this all was for *her* sake; of all the pillaged Madonna of Stephan was the inception; and his boylike sincerity of affection, his minute love for her, races on her errands over Europe, all seemed precious and different, now. She would design, in the fullness of her gratitude, a highly-finished pattern, and send it to Milan to be gold-embossed in arabesque on a suit of plated armor for him, great son of Peleus that he was! She would make her arms a constant ensorcelment about him! But now, sudden fears took hold upon her: — if he never returned? Of this she had not thought. She turned a bitter face from the sight of his cleft helm. But immediately afterwards Caspar, executing a *demi-volte* on his charger, hewed with his whole momentum, and Roland the Wolf toppled with centrifugal brains from his saddle.

Deianira stood up, most tall, laughing, with clapping hands.

Seeing the fall of his brother, Fritz with a body of cavaliers galloped towards the Count. But the *restes* of Caspar's band, some twenty men, closed round him. They effected, still fighting, a slow retreat, till the ordnance of the bastions covered them. They reached in safety the castle-gate.

Deianira with haughty, crimson face — proud of him — of herself, that she was his, he hers — had descended the steps of the turret. As she passed along the corridor, she came to the shrine of the Dürer-head; stopped, thinking; then took from her bosom a key, unlocked the door, and entered. For a long time she stood, searching the painter's face; his innocent, azure eyes. Then, slowly, she extinguished the tapers, — all except one; which she held uplifted in her hand

She waited presently for him on the couch of her own sanctum, devising garlands of gratulation with which to crown him. He came, striding rapidly, his face bloody, passing through to another part, almost forgetful of her in the flush and heat of the moment. And she held out wide arms to him. He started into fury: — just so — just so — she had looked *before!* The action goaded him to a memory *so* bitter, that he stamped, with the one roar:

"Woman!"

Caspar's stamp was like the tramp of a shod bull. The flooring shook. A box of tarsia-work slid with clatter from an inclined plane to the ground; an enameled *chasse;* a little hung marble temple fell to fragments; and among the fragments writhed the black-speckled gold of two small serpents, presents from Venice, the great merchantman. He saw and did not crush them with his foot. Raging, he dashed from the room.

But, already, in the corridor, he stopped. Such was the depth and power of his love for her. There was something fatherly in it — she so much younger than he! And this time, at least, she had wished to embrace *him* — *this* time she did not dream. The thought somewhat relaxed the tension of his wrath. What had maddened him above all was the shame of it — to his father's house — to his own son that was to be. A goldsmith of Ungarn's cub! But still, he would return to her — later on. Only first, the daubed head! The swift smoking-out — as of a pest — of that and every other memory of the bürger from the castle; and then he would see.

With masterful stalk he ascended to the alcove. A sensation of pleasure suffused him when he found it in darkness. He groped on the table; struck light to one of the tapers; raised it to apply the flame to the canvas; and — *started so,* that his armor rattled.

The picture was already consumed.

He could see the burned edges within the frame where the fire had died.

In a flash the whole truth illumined him — the whole brave story of her struggle — self-conquest — sacrifice. He threw down the light, and ran — rapidly ran — toward her room, remembering now, with sudden vividness, the Doric temple of marble. As he fell in, she lay stretched on the couch, with closed eyes, the purple gloom of the *lychnoi* on her face, an arm overhanging the edge. On the back of her hand, peering near, he discerned a minute *piqûre*. . . .

*H*igh in a tower of the donjon sat Caspar of Schwangau. The chamber was a small oval one, ponderously hung with old figured tapestry; and it was hot and bright with a multitude of burning wax tapers; and its air was heavy with the breath of flowers. Flowers were everywhere — rose, and narciss, and lily, and jasmine — sprays of yew, and bitter rosemary, and rue — piled on the floor, heaped high against the tapestry, covering the bed where the body lay. He was alone, and it was late in the night. The door was twice locked. He felt no pain — only a dull, nightmare speculation rode him. A slow, endless inquiry as to Beauty, and the nature of it, infinitely repeating itself in a numbed brain. What was it, what was it, at all? He propped the frown of his brow on his hand, thinking it out. It was an oppressive word to him merely. *She* knew, but slept. On her waking he would exact from her minute exegesis.

Only in some faraway, lotus-choked region of his consciousness did he know her verily dead. Her face was not stern to him – still soft, and white. Her hair underspread her wide to the knees. His anxiety now was that she should look her very loveliest on the bed – he knew that to be a care to her. Twice he had taken from her black head a garland of yellow roses, which he had discarded for another of white, and then for one of red; and then he had yielded to endless doubts, and replaced the yellow. And why roses at all? Why not violets? lilac? Choice of all lay round him; and one or other, to the ideal eye, was beautifulest, best – but which? She, in her heart, knew exactly. On her waking he would learn without fail. The unnoticed hours of the night passed over him. He sat in shirt and hose, bootless, thinking it out. Every now and again he would rise to readjust something on the quiet bed. Chance, she often said, "does nothing" – one must create Beauty by wise, directed energy of soul. He unstrapped her sandals, deeming her bare feet fittest; and in a few minutes was bent upon replacing them, but stopped, deciding again that it was best so. He rearranged fifty times the folds of her violet robe. Then the room grew so hot that mechanically he opened a narrow casement. A fulgor of watching constellations brooded steadily over the hushed morning hour. The window looked sheer upon the lake. A swan chased his flapping mate over the ruffled surface, with noises. Water and death – wherein lies their intimacy? This was a new question for him. There *is* a relation. The funeral-train which winds by the seashore is ever the saddest of funerals. But how so? Could it be that she – those artist folk – had shrewdness to know the reading of riddles so quaint and dubious? For him it was wholly a hopeless matter.

Wearied to death with the day's battles, he fell to a nodding sleep on a chair.

But with earliest dawn he sprang, the senility quite gone, raving at all things, himself most, and the foul murder he had done. He ran in disorder to the base-court, distraught of eye, stuttering and spluttering through a frantic clarion. Sixty men volunteered to follow him on a fresh sally, remembering the partial success of the day before, thinking his rashness knightly, rather than the demented rage of whom the god destroys. Caspar dissipating a random fury was among the first to fall, done to death by the sword of Fritz. When Swabian help before dawn of the next day at last arrived, the castle was a smoking desolation.

Fritz made a point of saving from the wreck his Madonna of Stephan, which later on somehow found its way to the Cathedral at Cologne. The Raphael cartoons flamed with the rest. It was so that Hohenschwangau was anticipatory of South Kensington; and thus did Albrecht Dürer's washed head, and its burning, become the undoing of a house.

About thirty years later a small new castle seems to have been built near the old site on the heights of the Schwanstein by some other branch of the Swabian ducal family. This was purchased by the late King Maximilian of Bavaria for a sum, I have heard, of about one hundred and fifty forms (fifteen pounds). It was then demolished, and a little yellow so-called "Schloss" erected in its place. The modern building is decorated throughout with paintings representing the life-turmoil of famed Lohengrin, the Swan-Knight. When the editor passed by it, it was used as the occasional *Residenz* of the somber and mysterious Ludwig, and his queen-mother. And to some such end it may still serve.

Vaila

E caddi come l'uome cui sonno piglia.

— Dante

A good many years ago, a young man, student in Paris, I was informally associated with the great Corot, and eyewitnessed by his side several of those cases of mind-malady, in the analysis of which he was a past master. I remember one little girl of the Marais, who, till the age of nine, in no way seemed to differ from her playmates. But one night, lying a-bed, she whispered into her mother's ear: "Maman, can you not hear the *sound of the world?*" It appears that her recently-begun study of geography had taught her that the earth flies, with an enormous velocity, on an orbit about the sun; and that *sound of the world* to which she referred was a faint (quite subjective) musical humming, like a shell-murmur, heard in the silence of night, and attributed by her fancy to the song of this high motion. Within six months the excess of lunacy possessed her.

I mentioned the incident to my friend, Haco Harfager, then occupying with me the solitude of an old place in S. Germain, shut in by a shrubbery and high wall from the street. He listened with singular interest, and for a day seemed wrapped in gloom.

Another case which I detailed produced a profound impression upon my friend. A young man, a toy-maker of S. Antoine, suffering from chronic congenital phthisis, attained in the ordinary way his twenty-fifth year. He was frugal, industrious, self-involved. On a winter's evening, returning to his lonely garret, he happened to purchase one of those vehemently factious sheets which circulate by night, like things of darkness, over the Boulevards. This simple act was the herald of his doom. He lay a-bed, and perused the *feuille*. He had never been a reader; knew little of the greater world, and the deep hum of its travail. But the next night he bought another leaf. Gradually he acquired interest in politics, the large movements, the roar of life. And this interest grew absorbing. Till late into the night, and every night, he lay poring over the furious mendacity, the turbulent wind, the printed passion. He would awake tired, spitting blood, but intense in spirit — and straightway purchased a morning leaf. His being lent itself to a retrograde evolution. The more his teeth gnashed, the less they ate. He became sloven, irregular at work, turning on his bed through the day. Rags overtook him. As the greater interest, and the vaster tumult, possessed his frail soul, so every lesser interest, tumult, died to him. There came an early day when he no longer cared for his own life; and another day, when his maniac fingers rent the hairs from his head.

As to this man, the great Corot said to me:

"Really, one does not know whether to laugh or weep over such a business. Observe, for one thing, how diversely men are made! Their are minds precisely so sensitive as a cupful of melted silver; *every* breath will roughen and darken them: and what of the simoon, tornado? And that is not a metaphor hut a simile. For such, this earth — I had almost said this universe — is clearly no fit habitation, but a Machine of Death, a baleful Vast. *Too* horrible to many is the running shriek of Being — they *cannot* bear the world. Let each look well to his own little whisk of life, say I, and leave the big fiery Automaton alone. Here in this poor toy-maker you have a case of the ear: it is only the neurosis, Oxyecoia. Splendid was that Greek myth of the Harpies: by *them* was this man snatched — or, say, caught by a limb in the wheels of the universe, and so perished. It is quite a grand exit, you know — translation in a chariot of flame. Only remember that the member first involved was *the pinna:* he bent *ear* to the howl of Europe, and ended by himself howling. Can a straw ride composedly on the primeval whirlwinds? Between chaos and our shoes wobbles, I tell you, the thinnest film! I knew a man who had this peculiarity of aural hyperæsthesia: that every sound brought him minute information of the matter causing the sound; that is to say, he had an ear bearing to the normal ear the relation which the spectroscope bears to the telescope. A rod, for instance, of mixed copper and iron impinging, in his hearing, upon a rod of mixed tin and lead, conveyed to him not merely the proportion of each metal in each rod, but some strange knowledge of the essential meaning and spirit, as it were, of copper, of iron, of tin, and of lead. Of course, he went mad; but, beforehand, told me this singular thing: that precisely such a sense as his was, according to his *certain* intuition, employed by the Supreme Being in his permeation of space to apprehend the nature and movements of mind and matter. And he went on to add that Sin — what we call *sin* — is only the movement of matter or mind into such places, or in such a way, as to give offence or pain to this delicate diplacusis (so

I must call it) of the Creator; so that the 'Law' of Revelation became, in his eyes, edicts promulgated by their Maker merely in self-protection from aural pain; and divine punishment for, say murder, nothing more than retaliation for unease caused to the divine aural consciousness by the matter in a particular dirk or bullet lodged, at a particular moment, in a non-intended place! Him, too, I say, did the Harpies whisk aloft."

My recital of these cases to my friend, Harfager, I have mentioned. I was surprised, not so much at his acute interest — for he was interested in all knowledge — as at the obvious pains which he took to conceal that interest. He hurriedly turned the leaves of a volume, but could not hide his panting nostrils.

From first days when we happened to attend the same seminary in Stockholm, a tacit intimacy had sprung between us. I loved him greatly; that he so loved me I knew. But it was an intimacy not accompanied by many of the usual interchanges of close friendships. Harfager was the shyest, most isolated, insulated, of beings. Though our joint *ménage* (brought about by a chance meeting at a midnight *séance* in Paris) had now lasted some months, I knew nothing of his plans, motives. Through the day we pursued our intense readings together, he rapt quite back into the past, I equally engrossed upon the present; late at night we reclined on couches within the vast cave of an old fireplace Louis Onze, and smoked to the dying flame in a silence of wormwood and terebinth. Occasionally a *soirée* or lecture might draw me from the house; except once, I never understood that Harfager left it. I was, on that occasion, returning home at a point of the Rue St. Honoré where a rush of continuous traffic rattled over the old coarse pavements retained there, when I came suddenly upon him. In this tumult he stood abstracted on the trottoir in a listening attitude, and for a moment seemed not to recognize me when I touched him.

Even as a boy I had discerned in my friend the genuine Noble, the inveterate patrician. One saw that in him. Not at all that his personality gave an impression of any species of loftiness, opulence; on the contrary. He did, however, give an impression of incalculable *ancientness*. He suggested the last moment of an æon. No nobleman have I seen who so bore in his wan aspect the assurance of the inevitable aristocrat, the essential prince, whose pale blossom is of yesterday, and will perish tomorrow, but whose root fills the ages. This much I knew of Harfager; also that on one or other of the bleak islands of his patrimony north of Zetland lived his mother and a paternal aunt; that he was somewhat deaf; but liable to transports of pain or delight at variously-combined musical sounds, the creak of a door, the note of a bird. More I cannot say that I then knew.

He was rather below the middle height, and gave some promise of stoutness. His nose rose highly aquiline from that species of forehead called by phrenologists "the musical," that is to say, flanked by temples which incline *outward* to the cheekbones, making breadth for the base of the brain; while the direction of the heavy-lidded, faded-blue eyes, and of the eyebrows, was a downward *droop* from the nose of their outer extremities. He wore a thin chin-beard. But the astonishing feature of his face were the ears: they were nearly circular, very small, and flat, being devoid of that outer volution known as the *helix*. The two tiny discs of cartilage had always the effect of making me think of the little ancient round shields, without rims, called *clipeus* and *peltè*. I came to understand that this was a peculiarity which had subsisted among the members of his race for some centuries. Over the whole white face of my friend was stamped a look of woeful inability, utter gravity of sorrow. One said "Sardanapalus," frail last of the great line of Nimrod.

After a year I found it necessary to mention to Harfager my intention of leaving Paris. We reclined by night in our accustomed nooks within the fireplace. To my announcement he answered with a merely polite "Indeed!" and continued to gloat upon the flame; but after an hour turned upon me, and said:

"Well, it seems to be a hard and selfish world."

Truisms uttered with just such an air of new discovery I had occasionally heard from him; but the earnest gaze of eyes, and plaint of voice, and despondency of shaken head, with which he now spoke shocked me to surprise.

"*À propos* of what?" I asked.

"My friend, do not leave me!"

He spread his arms. His utterance choked.

I learned that he was the object of a devilish malice; that he was the prey of a hellish temptation. That a lure, a becking hand, a lurking lust, which it was the effort of his life to eschew (and to which he was especially liable in solitude), continually enticed him; and that thus it had been almost from the day when, at time age of five, he had been sent by his father from his desolate home in time sea.

And whose was this malice?

He told me his mother's and aunt's.

And what was this temptation?

He said it was the temptation to return — to fly with the very frenzy of longing — back to that dim home.

I asked with what motives, and in what particulars, the malice of his mother and aunt manifested itself. He replied that there was, he believed, no specific motive, but only a determined malevolence, involuntary and fated; and that the respect in which it manifested itself was to be found in the multiplied prayers and commands with which, for years, they had importuned him to seek again the far hold of his ancestors.

All this I could in no way comprehend, and plainly said as much. In what consisted this horrible magnetism, and equally horrible peril, of his home? To this question Harfager did not reply, but rose from his seat, disappeared behind the drawn curtains of the hearth, and left the room. He presently returned with a quarto tome bound in hide. It proved to be Hugh Gascoigne's *Chronicle of Norse Families*, executed in English black-letter. The passage to which he pointed I read as follows:

"Nowe, of thise two brethrene, tholder (the elder), Harold, beying of seemely personage and prowesse, did goe pilgrimage into Danemarke, wher from he repayred againward boom to Hjaltlande (Zetland), and wyth hym fette (fetched) the amiabil Thronda for hyss wyf, which was a doughter of the sank (blood) royall of danemark. And his yonger brothir, Sweyne, that was sad amid debonayre, but far surmounted the other in cunnying, receyued him with all good chere. Butte eftsones (soon after) fel sweyne sick for alle his lust that he hadde of Thronda his brothir's wyfe. And whiles the worthy Harold, with the grenehede (greenness) and foyle of yowthe, ministred a bisy cure aboute the bedde wher Sweyne lay sick, lo, sweyne fastened on him a violent stroke with swerde, and with no lenger taryinge enclosed his hands in bondes, and cast him in the botme of a depe holde. And by cause harold wold not benumb (deprive) hymself of the gouernance of Thronda his wif, Sweyne cutte off boeth his ere[s], and putte out one of his iyes, and after diverse sike tormentes was preste (ready) to slee (slay) hym. But on a daye, the valiant Harold, breking hys bondes, and embracinge his aduersary, did by the sleight of wrastlyng ouerthrowe him, and escaped. Natwith- standyng, he foltred whan he came to the Somburgh Hed not ferre (far) fro the Castell, and al-be-it that he was swifte-foote, couth ne farder renne (run) by reson that he was faynte with the longe plag[u]es of hyss brothir. And whiles he ther lay in a sound (swoon) did Sweyne come sle (sly) and softe up on hym, and whan he had striken him with a darte, caste him fro Samburgh Hede in to the See.

"Nat longe hereafterward did the lady Thronda (tho she knew nat the manere of her lordes deth, ne, veryly, yf he was dead or on live) receyve Sweyne in to gree (favor), and with grete gaudying and blowinge of beamous (trumpets) did gon to his bed. And right soo they two wente thennes (thence) to soiourn in ferre partes.

"Now, it befel that sweyne was mynded by a dreme to let bild him a grete maunsion in Hialtland for the hoom-cominge of the ladye Thronda; where for he called to hym a cunninge Maistre-worckman, and sente him hye (in haste) to englond to gather thrals for the bilding of this lusty Houss, but hym-self soiourned wyth his ladye at Rome. Thenne came his worckman to london, but passinge thennes to Hialtland, was drent (drowned) he, and his feers (mates), and his shippe, alle and some. And after two yeres, which was the tyme assygned, Sweyne harfager sente lettres to Hialtlande to vnderstonde how his grete Houss did, for he knew not the drenchynge of the Architecte; and eftsones he receiued answer that the Houss *did wel*, and was bildinge on the Ile of Vaila; but that ne was the Ile wher-on Sweyne had appoynted the bilding to be; and he was aferd, and nere fel doun ded for drede, by cause that, in the lettres, he saw before him the mannere of wrytyng of his brothir Harold. And he sayed in this fourme: 'Surely Harolde is on lyue (alive), elles (else) ben thise a lettres writ with gostlye hande.' And he was wo many dayes, seeing that this was a dedely stroke. Ther-after, he took him-selfe back to Hjalt-land to know how the matere was, and ther the old Castell on Somburgh Hede was brek doun to the erthe. Thenn Sweyne was wode-worthe, and cryed, 'Jhesu mercy, where is al the grete Hous of my faders becomen? allas! thys wycked day of desteynye.' And one of the peple tolde him that a hoost of worckmen fro fer partes hadde brek it doun. And he sayd: 'who hath bidde them?' but that couth none answer. Thenne he sayd agayn; 'nis (is not) my brothir harold on-lyne? for I haue biholde his writinge'; and that, to, colde none answer. Soo he wente to Vaila, and saw there a grete Houss stonde, and wharm he looked on hyt, he saye[d]: 'this, sooth, was y-bild by my brothir Harolde, be he ded, or bee he on-lyue.' And ther he dwelte, and his ladye, and his sones and hys sones sones vntyl nowe. For that the Houss is rewthelesse (ruthless) and withoute pite; where-for tis seyed that up on al who dwel thcre faleth a wycked madncss and a lecherous agonie; and that by waye of the eres doe they drinck the cuppe of the furie of the erelesse Harolde, til the tyme of the Houss bee ended."

I read the narrative half-aloud, and smiled.
"This, Harfager," I said, "is very tolerable romance on the part of the good Gascoigne; but has the look of indifferent history."
"It is, nevertheless, genuine *history*," he replied.
"You believe that?"
"The house still stands solidly on Vaila."
"The brothers Sweyn and Harold were literary for their age, I think?"

"No member of my race," he replied, with, a suspicion of hauteur, "has been illiterate."

"But, at least, you do not believe that mediæval ghosts superintend the building of their family mansions?"

"Gascoigne nowhere says that; for to be stabbed is not necessarily to die; nor, if he did say it, would it he true to assert that I have any knowledge on the subject."

"And what, Harfager, is the nature of that 'wicked madness,' that 'lecherous agonie,' of which Gascoigne speaks?"

"Do you ask me?" He spread his arms. "What do I know? I know nothing! I was banished from the place at the age of five. Yet the cry of it still reverberates in my soul. And have I not *told* you of agonies — even within myself — of inherited longing and loathing . . ."

But, at any rate, I answered, my journey to Heidelberg was just then indispensable. I would compromise by making absence short, and rejoin him quickly, if he would wait a few weeks for me. His moody silence I took to mean consent, and soon afterward left him.

But I was unavoidably detained; and when I returned to our old quarters, found them empty. Harfager had vanished.

It was only after twelve years that a letter was forwarded me — a rather wild letter, an excessively long one — in the well-remembered hand of my friend. It was dated at Vaila. From the character of the writing I conjectured that it had been penned *with furious haste*, so that I was all the more astonished at the very trivial nature of the voluminous contents. On the first half page he spoke of our old friendship, and asked if, in memory of that, I would see his mother who was dying; the rest of the epistle, sheet upon sheet, consisted of a tedious analysis of his mother's genealogical tree, the apparent aim being to prove that she was a genuine Harfager, and a cousin of his father. He then went on to comment on the extreme prolificness of his race, asserting that since the fourteenth century, over four millions of its members had lived and died in various parts of the world; three only of them, he believed, being now left. That determined, the letter ended.

Influenced by this communication, I traveled northward; reached Caithness; passed the stormy Orkneys; reached Lerwick; and from Unst, the most bleak and northerly of the Zetlands, contrived, by dint of bribes to pit the weather-worthiness of a lug-sailed 'sixern' (said to be identical with the 'langschips' of the Vikings) against a flowing sea and a darkly-brooding heaven. The voyage, I was warned, was, at such a time, of some risk. It was the Cimmerian December of those interboreal latitudes. The weather here, they said, though never cold, is hardly ever other than tempestuous. A dense and dank sea-born haze now lay, in spite of vapid breezes, high along the waters enclosing the boat in a vague domed cavern of doleful twilight and sullen swell. The region of the considerable islands was past, and there was a spectral something in the unreal aspect of silent sea and sunless dismalness of sky which produced upon my nerves the impression of a voyage *out* of nature, a cruise *beyond* the world. Occasionally, however, we careered past one of those solitary 'skerries,' or sea-stacks, whose craggy sea-walls, cannonaded and disintegrated by the inter-shock of the tidal wave and the torrent currents of the German Ocean, wore, even at some distance, an appearance of frightful ruin and havoc. Three only of these I saw, for before the dim day had well run half its course, sudden blackness of night was upon us, and with it one of those tempests, of which the winter of this semi-polar sea is, throughout, an ever-varying succession. During the haggard and dolorous crepuscule of the next brief day, the rain did not cease; but before darkness had quite supervened, my helmsman, who talked continuously to a mate of seal-maidens, and waterhorses, and *grülies,* paused to point to a mound of gloomier grey in the weather-bow, which was, he assured me, Vaila.

Vaila, he added, was the center of quite a system of those *rösts* (dangerous eddies) and crosscurrents, which the action of the tidal wave hurls hurrying with complicated and corroding swirl among the islands; in the neighborhood of Vaila, said the mariner, they hurtled with more than usual precipitancy, owing to the palisade of lofty sea-crags which barbicaned the place about; approach was, therefore, at all times difficult, and by night fool-hardy. With a running sea, however, we came sufficiently near to discern the mane of surf which bristled high along the beetling coast-wall. Its shock, according to the man's account, had oft-times more than all the efficiency of a bombing of real artillery, slinging tons of rock to heights of several hundred feet upon the main island.

When the sun next feebly climbed above the horizon to totter with marred visage through a wan low segment of funereal murk, we had closely approached the coast; and it was then for the first time that the impression of some *spinning* motion in the island (born no doubt of the circular movement of the water) was produced upon me. We effected a landing at a small *voe,* or seaarm, on the western side; the eastern, though the point of my aim, being, on account of the swell, out of the question for that purpose. Here I found in two feal-thatched *skeoes* (or sheds), which crouched beneath the shelter of a far overhanging hill, five or six poor peasant-seamen, whose livelihood no doubt consisted in periodically trading for the necessaries of the great house on the east. Beside these there were no dwellers on Vaila; but with one of them for guide, I soon began the ascent and transit of the island. Through the night in the boat I had been strangely aware of an oppressive booming in the ears, for which even the roar of the sea round all the coast seemed quite insufficient to account. This now, as we advanced, became fearfully intensified, and with it, once more, the unaccountable conviction within me of *spinning* motions to which I have referred. Vaila I discovered to be a land of hill and precipice, made of fine granite and flaggy gneiss; at about the center, however, we came upon a high table-land sloping gradually from west to east, and covered by a series of lochs, which sullenly and continuously flowed one into the other. To this chain of somber, black-gleaming water I could see no terminating shore, and by dint of shouting to my companion, and bending close ear to his answering shout, I came to know that there *was* no such shore: I say *shout*, for nothing less could have prevailed over the steady bellowing as of ten thousand bisons, which now resounded on every hand. A certain tremblement, too, of the earth became distinct. In vain did the eye seek in its dreary purview a single trace of tree or shrub; for, as a matter of course, no kind of vegetation, save peat, could brave, even for a day, that perennial agony of the tempest which makes of this turbid and benighted zone its arena. Darkness, an hour after noon, commenced to overshadow us; and it was shortly afterward that my guide, pointing down a precipitous defile near the eastern coast, hurriedly set forth upon the way he had come. I frantically howled a question after him as he went; but at this point the human voice had ceased to be in the faintest degree audible.

Down this defile, with a sinking of the heart, and a most singular feeling of giddiness, I passed. Having reached the end, I emerged upon a wide ledge which shuddered to the immediate onsets of the sea. But all this portion of the island was, in addition, subject to a sharp continuous ague evidently not due to the heavy ordnance of the ocean. Hugging a point of cliff for steadiness from the wind, I looked forth upon a spectacle of weirdly morne, of dismal wildness. The opening lines of *Hecuba,* or some drear district of the *Inferno,* seemed realized before me. Three black 'skerries,' encompassed by a fantastic series of stacks, crooked as a witch's forefinger, and giving herbergage to shrill routs of osprey and scart, to seal and walrus, lay at some fathoms' distance; and from its race and rage among them, the sea, in arrogance of white, tumultuous, but inaudible wrath, ramped terrible as an army with banners toward the land. Leaving my place, I staggered some distance to the left: and now, all at once, a vast amphitheater opened before me, and there burst upon my gaze a panorama of such heart-appalling sublimity, as imagination could never have conceived, nor can now utterly recall.

"A vast amphitheater" I have said; yet it was rather the shape of a round-Gothic (or Norman) doorway which I beheld. Let the reader picture such a door-frame, nearly a mile in breadth, laid flat upon the ground, the curved portion farthest from the sea; and round it let a perfectly smooth and even wall of rock tower in perpendicular regularity to an altitude not unworthy the vulture's aerie; and now, down the depth of this Gothic shape, and *over all its extent,* let bawling oceans dash themselves triumphing in spendthrift cataclysm of emerald and hoary fury, — and the stupor of awe with which I looked, and then the shrinking fear, and then the instinct of instant flight, will find easy comprehension.

This was the thrilling disemboguement of the lochs of Vaila.

And within the arch of this Gothic cataract, volumed in the world of its smoky torment and far-excursive spray, stood a palace of brass . . . circular in shape . . . huge in dimension.

The last gleam of the ineffectual day had now almost passed, but I could yet discern, in spite of the perpetual rain-fall which bleakly nimbused it as in a halo of tears, that the building was low in proportion to the vastness of its circumference; that it was roofed with a shallow dome; and that about it ran two serried rows of shuttered Norman windows, the upper row being of smaller size than the lower. Certain indications led me to assume that the house had been built upon a vast natural bed of rock which lay, circular and detached, within the arch of the cataract; but this did not quite emerge above the flood, for the whole ground-area upon which I looked dashed a deep and incense-reeking river to the beachless sea; so that passage would have been impossible, were it not that, from a point near me, a massive bridge, thick with algæ, rose above the tide, and led to the mansion. Descending from my ledge, I passed along it, now drenched in spray. As I came nearer, I could see that the house, too, was to half its height more thickly bearded than an old hull with barnacles and every variety of brilliant seaweed; and — what was very surprising that from many points near the top of the brazen wall huge iron chains, slimily barbarous with the trailing tresses of ages, reached out in symmetrical divergent rays to points on the ground hidden by the flood: the fabric had thus the look of a many-anchored ark; but without pausing for minute observation, I pushed forward, and dashing through the smooth circular waterfall which poured all round from the eaves, by one of its many small projecting porches, entered the dwelling.

Darkness now was around me — and sound. I seemed to stand in the very throat of some yelling planet. An infinite sadness descended upon me; I was near to the abandonment of tears. "Here," I said, "is Kohreb, and the limits of weeping; not elsewhere is the valley of sighing." The tumult resembled the continuous volleying of many thousands of cannon, mingled with strange crashing and bursting uproars. I passed forward through a succession of halls, and was wondering as to my further course, when a hideous figure, bearing a lamp, stalked rapidly towards me. I shrank aghast. It seemed the skeleton of a tall man, wrapped in a winding-sheet. The glitter of a tiny eye, however, and a sere film of skin over part of the face, quickly reassured me. Of ears, he showed no sign. He was, I afterwards learned, Aith; and the singularity of his appearance was partially explained by his pretence — whether true or false — that he had once suffered *burning*, almost to the cinder-stage, but had miraculously recovered. With an expression of malignity, and strange excited gestures, he led the way to a chamber on the upper stage, where having struck light to a vesta, he pointed to a spread table and left me.

For a long time I sat in solitude. The earthquake of the mansion was intense; but all sense seemed swallowed up and confounded in the one impression of sound. Water, water, was the world — nightmare on my chest, a horror in my ears, an intolerable tingling on my nerves. The feeling of being infinitely drowned and ruined in the all-obliterating deluge — the impulse to gasp for breath — overwhelmed me. I rose and paced; but suddenly stopped, angry, I scarce knew why, with myself. I had, in fact, found myself walking with a certain *hurry*, not usual with me, not natural to me. The feeling of giddiness, too, had abnormally increased. I forced myself to stand and take note of the hall. It was of great size, and damp with mists, so that the tattered, but rich, mediæval furniture seemed lost in its extent: its center was occupied by a broad low marble tomb bearing the name of a Harfager of the fifteenth century; its walls were old brown panels of oak. Having drearily observed these things, I waited on with an intolerable consciousness of loneliness; but a little after midnight the tapestry parted, and Harfager with hurried stride, approached me.

In twelve years my friend had grown old. He showed, it is true, a tendency to corpulence; yet, to a knowing eye, he was, in reality, tabid, ill-nourished. And his neck protruded from his body; and his lower back had quite the forward curve of age; and his hair floated about his face and shoulders in a disarray of awful whiteness. A chin-beard hung grey to his chest. His attire was a simple robe of bauge, which, as he went, waved aflaunt from his bare and hirsute shins, and he was shod in those soft slippers called *rivlins*.

To my surprise, he spoke. When I passionately shouted that I could gather no fragment of sound from his moving lips, he clapped both palms to his ears, and thereupon renewed a vehement siege to mine: but again without result. And now, with a seemingly angry fling of the hand, he caught up the taper, and swiftly strode from the chamber.

There was something singularly unnatural in his manner — something which irresistibly reminded me of the skeleton, Aith: an excess of zeal, a fever, a rage, a *loudness,* an eagerness of walk, a wild extravagance of gesture. His hand constantly dashed the hair-whiffs from his face. Though his countenance was of the saffron of death, the eyes were turgid and red with blood — heavy-lidded eyes, fixed in a downward and sideward intentness of gaze. He presently returned with a folio of ivory and a stylus of graphite hanging from a cord about his garment.

He rapidly wrote a petition that I would, if not too tired, take part with him in the funeral obsequies of his mother. I shouted assent.

Once more he clapped palms to ears; then wrote: "Do not shout: no whisper in any part of the building is inaudible to me."

I remembered that, in early life, he had seemed slightly *deaf.*

We passed together through many apartments, he shading the taper with his hand. This was necessary; for, as I quickly discovered, in no part of the shivering fabric was the air in a state of rest, but seemed forever commoved by a curious agitation, a faint windiness, like the echo of a storm, which communicated a gentle universal trouble to the tapestries. Everywhere I was confronted with the same past richness, present raggedness of decay. In many of the chambers were old marble tombs; one was a museum piled with bronzes, urns; but broken, imbedded in fungoids, dripping wide with moisture. It was as if the mansion, in ardor of travail, sweated. An odor of decomposition was heavy on the swaying air. With difficulty I followed Harfager through the labyrinth of his headlong passage. Once only he stopped short, and with face madly wild above the glare of the light, heaved up his hand, and uttered a single word. From the shaping of the lips, I conjectured the word, "Hark!"

Presently we entered a very long black hall wherein, on chairs beside a bed near the center, rested a deep coffin, flanked by a row of tall candlesticks of ebony. It had, I noticed, this singularity, that the footpiece was absent, so that the soles of the corpse were visible as we approached. I beheld, too, three upright rods secured to the coffin-side, each fitted at its summit with a small silver bell of the kind called *morrice* pendent from a flexible steel spring. At the head of the bed, Aith, with an appearance of irascibility, stamped to and fro within a small area. Harfager, having rapidly traversed the apartment to the coffin, deposited the taper upon a stone table near, and stood poring with crazy intentness upon the body. I too, looking, stood. Death so rigorous, Gorgon, I had not seen. The coffin seemed full of tangled grey hair. The lady was, it was clear, of great age, osseous, scimitar-nosed. Her head shook with solemn continuity to the vibration of the house. From each ear trickled a black streamlet; the mouth was ridged with froth. I observed that over the corpse had been set three thin laminæ of polished wood, resembling in position, and shape, the bridge of a violin. Their sides fitted into groves in the coffin-sides, and their top was of a shape to exactly fit the inclination of the two coffin-lids when closed. One of these laminæ passed over the knees of the dead lady; another bridged the abdomen; the third the region of the neck. In each of them was a small circular hole. Across each of the three holes passed vertically a tense cord from the morrice-bell nearest to it; the three holes being thus divided by the three cords into six vertical semicircles. Before I could conjecture the significance of this arrangement, Harfager closed the folding coffin-lid, which in the center had tiny intervals for the passage of the cords. He then turned the key in the lock, and uttered a word, which I took to be, "Come."

At his summons, Aith, approaching, took hold of the handle at the head; and from the dark recesses of the hall a lady, in black, moved forward. She was very tall, pallid, and of noble aspect. From the curvature of the nose, and her circular ears, I conjectured the lady Swertha, aunt of Harfager. Her eyes were red, but if with weeping I could not determine.

Harfager and I, taking each a handle near the coffin-foot, and the lady bearing before us one of the candlesticks, the procession began. As we came to the doorway, I noticed standing in a corner yet two coffins, inscribed with the names of Harfager and his aunt. We passed at length down a wide-curving stairway to the lower stage; and descending thence still lower by narrow brazen steps, came to a portal of metal, at which the lady, depositing the candlestick, left us.

The chamber of death into which we now bore the coffin had for its outer wall the brazen outer wall of the whole house at a point where this approached nearest the cataract, and must have been deep washed by the infuriate caldron without. The earthquake here was, indeed, intense. On every side the vast extent of surface was piled with coffins, rotted or rotting, ranged upon tiers of wooden shelves. The floor, I was surprised to see, was of brass. From the wide scampering that ensued on our entrance, the place was, it was clear, the abode of hordes of water-rats. As it was inconceivable that these could have corroded a way through sixteen brazen feet, I assumed that some fruitful pair must have found in the house, on its building, an ark from the waters; though even this hypothesis seemed wild. Harfager, however, afterwards confided to me his suspicion, that they had, for some purpose, been *placed* there by the original architect.

Upon a stone bench in the middle we deposited our burden, whereupon Aith made haste to depart. Harfager then rapidly and repeatedly walked from end to end of the long sepulcher, examining with many an eager stoop and peer, and upward strain, the shelves and their props. Could he, I was led to wonder, have any doubts as to their security? Damp, indeed, and decay pervaded all. A piece of woodwork which I handled softened into powder between my fingers.

He presently beckoned to me, and with yet one halt and uttered "Hark!" from him, we traversed the house to my chamber. Here, left alone, I paced long about, fretted with a strange vagueness of anger; then, weary, tumbled to a horror of sleep.

In the far interior of the mansion even the bleared day of this land of heaviness never rose upon our settled gloom. I was able however, to regulate my *levées* by a clock which stood in my chamber. With Harfager, in a startlingly short time, I renewed more than all our former intimacy. That I should say *more*, is itself startling, considering that an interval of twelve years stretched between us. But so, in fact, it was; and this was proved by the circumstances that we grew to take, and to pardon, freedoms of expression and manner which, as two persons of more than usual reserve, we had once never dreamed of permitting to ourselves in reference to each other. Down corridors that vanished either way in darkness and length of perspective remoteness we linked ourselves in perambulations of purposeless urgency. Once he wrote that my step was excruciatingly deliberate. I replied that it was just such a step as fitted my then mood. He wrote: "You have developed an aptitude to *fret.*" I was profoundly offended, and replied: "There are at least more fingers than one in the universe which *that* ring will wed."

Something of the secret of the unhuman sensitiveness of his hearing I quickly surmised. I, too, to my dismay, began, as time passed, to catch hints of loudly-uttered words. The reason might he found, I suggested, in an increased excitability of the auditory nerve, which, if the cataract were absent, the roar of the ocean, and bombast of the incessant tempest about us, would by themselves be sufficient to cause; in which case, his own aural interior must, I said, be inflamed to an exquisite pitch of hyperpyrexial fever. The affection I named to him as the Paracusis Willisii. He frowned dissent, but I, undeterred, callously proceeded to recite the case, occurring within my own experience, of a very deaf lady who could hear the fall of a pin in a rapidly moving railway-train.[*] To this he only replied: "Of ignorant persons I am accustomed to consider the mere scientist as the most profoundly ignorant."

Yet that he should affect darkness as to the highly morbid condition of his hearing I regarded as simply far-fetched. Himself, indeed, confided to me his own, Aith's, and his aunt's proneness to violent paroxysms of *vertigo*. I was startled; for I had myself shortly before been twice roused from sleep by sensations of reeling and nausea, and a conviction that the chamber furiously spun with me in a direction from right to left. The impression passed away, and I attributed it, perhaps hastily (though on well-known pathological grounds), to some disturbance in the nerve-endings of the "labyrinth," or inner ear. In Harfager, however, the conviction of wheeling motions in the house, in the world, attained so horrible a degree of certainty, that its effects sometimes resembled those of lunacy or energumenal possession. Never, he said, was the sensation of giddiness wholly absent; seldom the feeling that he stared with stretched-out arms over the verge of abysmal voids which wildly wooed his half-consenting foot. Once, as we went, he was hurled, as by unseen powers, to the ground; and there for an hour sprawled, cold in a flow of sweat, with distraught bedazzlement and amaze in eyes that watched the racing house. He was constantly racked, moreover, with the consciousness of sounds so very peculiar in their nature, that I could account for them upon no other hypothesis than that of *tinnitus* highly exaggerated. Through the heaped-up roar, there sometimes visited him, he said, the high lucid warbling of some Orphic bird, from the pitch of whose impassioned madrigals he had the inner consciousness that it came from a far country, was of the whiteness of snow, and crested with a comb of mauve. Else he was aware of accumulated human voices, remotely articulate, contending in volubility, and finally melting into chaotic musical tones. Or, anon, he was stunned by an infinite and imminent crashing, like the huge crackling of a universe of glass about his ears. He said, too, that he could often see, rather than hear, the parti-colored whorls of a mazy sphere-music deep, deep, within the black dark of the cataract's roar. These impressions, which I ardently protested *must* be purely entotic, had sometimes upon him a pleasing effect, and long would he stand and listen with raised hand to their seduction; others again inflamed him to the verge of angry madness. I guessed that they were the origin of those irascibly uttered "Harks!" which at intervals of about an hour did not fail to break from him. In this I was wrong: and it was with a thrill of dismay that I shortly came to know the truth.

---

† Such cases are known, or at least easily comprehensible, to every medical man. The concussion on the deaf nerves is said to be the cause of the acquired sensitiveness. Nor is there any *limit* to such sensitiveness when the concussion is abnormally increased.

For, as once we passed together by an iron door on the lower stage, he stopped, and for several minutes stood, listening with an expression most keen and cunning. Presently the cry "Hark!" escaped him; and he then turned to me, and wrote upon the tablet: "You did not hear?" I had heard nothing but the monotonous roar. He shouted into my ear in accents now audible to me as an echo heard far off in dreams: "You shall see."

He lifted the candlestick; produced from the pocket of his garment a key; unlocked the door. We entered a chamber, circular, very loftily domed in proportion to its extent, and apparently empty, save that a pair of ladder-steps leaned against its wall. Its flooring was of marble, and in its center gloomed a pool, resembling the impluvium of Roman atriums, but round in shape; a pool evidently deep, full of an unctuous miasmal water. I was greatly startled by its present aspect; for as the light burned upon its jet-black surface, I could see that this had been quite recently *disturbed*, in a manner for which the shivering of the house could not account, inasmuch as *ripples* of slimy ink sullenly rounded from the center toward its marble brink. I glanced at Harfager for explanation. He signed to me to wait, and for about an hour, with arms in their accustomed fold behind his back, perambulated. At the end of that time he stopped, and standing together by the margin, we gazed into the water. Suddenly his clutch tightened upon my arm, and I saw, not without a thrill of honor, a tiny ball, doubtless of lead, but smeared blood-red by some chymical pigment, fall from the direction of the roof and disappear into the center of the black depths. It hissed, on contact with the water, a thin puff of vapor.

"In the name of all that is sinister!" I cried, "what thing is this you show me?"

Again he made me a busy and confident sign to wait; snatched then the ladder-steps toward the pool; handed me the taper. I, mounting, held high the flame, and saw hanging from the misty center of the dome a form — a sphere of tarnished old copper, lengthened out into balloon-shape by a down-looking neck, at the end of which I thought I could discern a tiny orifice. Painted across the bulge was barely visible in faded red characters the hieroglyph:

"HARFAGER-HOUS: 1389-188"

Something — I know not what — of *eldritch* in the combined aspect of spotted globe, and gloomy pool, and contrivance of hourly hissing ball, gave expedition to my feet as I slipped down the ladder.

"But the meaning?"

"Did you see the writing?"

"Yes. The meaning?"

He wrote: "By comparing Gascoigne with Thrunster, I find that the mansion was *built* about 1389."

"But the final figures?"

"After the last 8," he replied, "there is another figure, nearly, but not quite, obliterated by a tarnish-spot."

"What figure?"

"It cannot be read, but may be surmised. The year 1888 is now all but passed. It can only be the figure 9."

"You are *horribly* depraved in mind!" I cried, flaring into anger. "You assume — you dare to *state* — in a manner which no mind trained to base its conclusions upon fact could hear with patience."

"And you, on the other hand, are simply absurd," he wrote.

"You are not, I presume, ignorant of the common formula of Archimedes by which, the diameter of a sphere being known, its volume may be determined. Now, the diameter of the sphere in the dome there I have ascertained to be four and a half feet; and the diameter of the leaden balls about the third of an inch. Supposing then that 1389 was the year in which the sphere was full of balls, you may readily calculate that not many fellows of the four million and odd which have since dropped at the rate of one an hour are now left within it. It could not, in fact, have contained many more. The fall of balls *cannot* persist another year. The figure 9 is therefore forced upon us."

"But you assume, Harfager," I cried, "most wildly you assume! Believe me, my friend, this is the very wantonness of wickedness! By what algebra of despair do you know that the last date *must* be such, was intended to be such, as to correspond with the stoppage of the horologe? And, even if so, what is the significance of the whole. It has — it can have — no *significance!* Was the contriver of this dwelling, of all the gnomes, think you, a being pulsing with omniscience?"

"Do you seek to madden me?" he shouted. Then furiously writing: "I know — I swear that I know — nothing of its significance! But is it not evident to you that the work is a stupendous hourglass, intended to record the hours not of a day, but of a cycle? and of a cycle of five hundred years?"

"But the whole thing," I passionately cried, "is a baleful phantasm of our brains! an evil impossibility! How is the fall of the balls regulated? Ah, my friend, you wander — your mind is debauched in this bacchanal of tumult."

"I have not ascertained," he replied, "by what internal mechanism, or viscous medium, or spiral coil, dependent no doubt for its action upon the vibration of the house, the balls are retarded in their fall; that is a matter well within the cunning of the mediæval artisan, the inventor of the watch; but this at least is clear, that one element of their retardation is the minuteness of the aperture through which they have to pass; that this element, by known, though recondite, statical laws, will cease to operate when no more than three balls remain; and that, consequently, the last three will fall at nearly the same moment."

"In God's name!" I exclaimed, careless what folly I poured out, "but your mother is *dead*, Harfager! You dare not deny that there remain but you and the lady Swertha!"

A contemptuous glance was all the reply he then vouchsafed me.

But he confided to me a day or two later that the leaden balls were a constant bane to his ears; that from hour to hour his life was a keen waiting for their fall; that even from his brief slumbers he infallibly startled into wakefulness at each descent; that, in whatever part of the mansion he happened to be, they failed not to find him out with a clamorous and insistent *loudness;* and that every drop wrung him with a twinge of physical anguish in the inner ear. I was therefore appalled at his declaration that these droppings had now become to him as the life of life; had acquired an intimacy so close with the hue of his mind, that their cessation might even mean for him the shattering of reason. Convulsed, he stood then, face wrapped in arms, leaning against a pillar. The paroxysm past, I asked him if it was out of the question that he should once and for all cast off the fascination of the horologe, and fly with me from the place. He wrote in mysterious reply: "A *threefold* cord is not easily broken" I started. How threefold? He wrote with bitterest smile: "To be enamored of pain — to pine after aching — to dote upon Marah — is not that a wicked madness?" I was overwhelmed. Unconsciously he had quoted Gascoigne: a wycked madness! a lecherous agonie! "You have seen the face of my aunt," he proceeded; "your eyes were dim if you did not there behold an impious calm, the glee of a blasphemous patience, a grin behind her daring smile." He then spoke of a prospect, at the infinite terror of which his whole nature trembled, yet which sometimes laughed in his heart in the aspect of a maniac *hope.* It was the prospect of any considerable increase in the volume of sound about him. At *that,* he said, the brain must totter. On the night of my arrival the noise of my booted tread, and, since then, my occasionally raised voice, had caused him acute unease. To a sensibility such as this, I understood him further to say, the luxury of torture involved in a large sound-increase in his environment was an allurement from which no human strength could turn; and when I expressed my powerlessness even to conceive such an increase, much less the means by which it could be effected, he produced from the archives of the house some annals, kept by the successive heads of his race. From these it appeared that the tempests which continually harried the lonely latitude of Vaila did not fail to give place, at periodic intervals of some years, to one sovereign *ouragan* — one Sirius among the suns — one *ultimate* lyssa of elemental atrocity. At such periods the rains descended — and the floods came — even as in the first world-deluge; those *rösts*, or eddies, which at all times encompassed Vaila, spurning then the bands of lateral space, shrieked themselves aloft into a multitudinous death-dance of waterspouts, and like snaky Deinotheria, or say towering monolithic in a stonehenge of columned and cyclopean awe, thronged about the little land, upon which, with converging *débâcle*, they discharged their momentous waters; and the loebs to which the cataract was due thus redoubled their volume, and fell with redoubled tumult. It was, said Harfager, like a miracle that for twenty years no such great event had transacted itself at Vaila.

And what, I asked, was the third strand of that threefold cord of which he had spoken?

He took me to a circular hall, which, he told me, he had ascertained to be the geometrical center of the circular mansion. It was a very great hall — so great as I think I never saw — so great that the amount of segment illumined at any one time by the taper seemed nearly flat. And nearly the whole of its space from floor to roof was occupied by a pillar of brass, the space between wall and cylinder being only such as to admit of a stretched-out arm.

"This cylinder, which seems to be solid," wrote Harfager, "ascends to the dome and passes beyond it; it descends hence to the floor of the lower stage, and passes through that; it descends thence to the brazen flooring of the vaults, and *passes through that* into the rock of the ground. Under each floor it spreads out laterally into a vast capital, helping to support the floor. What is the precise quality of the impression which I have made upon your mind by this description?"

"I do not know!" I answered, turning from him; "propound me none of your questions, Harfager. I feel a giddiness . . ."

"Nevertheless you shall answer me," he proceeded; "consider the *strangeness* of that brazen lowest floor, which I have discovered to be some ten feet thick, and whose under-surface, I have reason to believe, is somewhat above the level of the ground; remember that the fabric is at no point *fastened* to the cylinder; think of the *chains* that ray out from the outer walls, seeming to anchor the house to the ground. Tell me, what impression have I *now* made?"

"And is it for this you wait?" I cried — "for *this?* Yet there may have been no malevolent intention! You jump at conclusions! Any human dwelling, if solidly based upon earth, would be at all times liable to overthrow on such a land, in such a situation, as this, by some superlative tempest! What if it were the intention of the architect that in such eventuality the chains should break, and the house, by yielding, be saved?"

"You have no lack of charity at least," he replied; and we returned to the book we then read together.

He had not wholly lost the old habit of study, but could no longer constrain himself to sit to read. With a volume, often tossed down and resumed, he walked to and fro within the radius of the lamp-light; or I, unconscious of my voice, read to him. By a strange whim of his mood, the few books which now lay within the limits of his patience had all for their motive something of the *picaresque*, or the foppishly speculative: Quevedo's *Tacaño;* or the mundane system of Tycho Brahe; above all, George Hakewill's *Power and Providence of God*. One day, however, as I read, he interrupted me with the sentence, seemingly *à propos* of nothing: "What I *cannot* understand is that you, a scientist, should believe that the physical life ceases with the cessation of the breath" — and from that moment the tone of our reading changed. He led me to the crypts of the library in the lowest part of the building, and hour after hour, with a certain *furore* of triumph, overwhelmed me with volumes evidencing the longevity of man after "death." A sentence of Haller had rooted itself in his mind; he repeated, insisted upon it: "sapientia denique consilia dat quibus longævitas obtineri queat, nitro, opio, purgationibus subinde repetitis . . ."; and as opium was the elixir of long-drawn life, so death itself, he said, was that opium, whose more potent nepenthe lullabied the body to a peace not all-insentient, far within the gates of the gardens of dream. From the *Dhammapada* of the Buddhist canon, to Zwinger's *Theatrum,* to Bacomi's *Historia Vitæ et Mortis,* he ranged to find me heaped-up certainty of his faith. What, he asked, was my opinion of Baron Verulam's account of the dead man who was heard to utter words of prayer; or of the leaping bowels o' the dead *condamné?* On my expressing incredulity, be seemed surprised, and reminded me of the writhings of dead serpents, of the *visible* beating of a frog's heart many hours after "death." "She is not dead," he quoted, "but *sleepeth."* The whim of Bacon and Paracelsus that the principle of life resides in a subtle spirit or fluid which pervades the organism he coerced into elaborate proof that such a spirit must, from its very nature, be incapable of any *sudden* annihilation, so long as the organs which it permeates remain connected and integral. I asked what limit he then set to the persistence of sensibility in the physical organism. He replied that when slow decay had so far advanced that the nerves could no longer be called nerves, or their cell-origins cell-origins, or the brain a brain — or when by artificial means the brain had for any length of time been disconnected at the cervical region from the body — *then* was the king of terrors king indeed, and the body was as though it had not been. With an indiscretion strange to me before my residence at Vaila, I blurted the question whether all this *Aberglaube* could have any reference, in his mind, to the body of his mother. For a while he stood thoughtful, then wrote: "Had I not reason to believe that my own and my aunt's life in some way hinged upon the final cessation of hers, I should still have taken precautions to ascertain the progress of the destroyer upon her mortal frame; as it is, I shall not lack even the minutest information." He then explained that the rodents which swarmed in the sepulcher would, in the course of time, do their full work upon her; but would be unable to penetrate to the region of the throat without first gnawing their way through the three cords stretched across the holes of the laminæ within the coffin, and thus, one by one, liberating the three morrisco bells to a tinkling agitation.

The winter solstice had passed; another year opened. I slept a deep sleep by night when Harfager entered my chamber, and shook me. His face was ghastly in the taper-light. A transformation within a few hours had occurred upon him. He was not the same. He resembled some poor wight into whose unexpecting eyes — at midnight — have glared the sudden eye-balls of Terrour.

He informed me that he was aware of singular intermittent straining and creaking sounds, which gave him the sensation of hanging in aërial spaces by a thread which must shortly snap to his weight. He asked if, for God's sake, I would accompany him to the sepulcher. We passed together through the house, he craven, shivering, his step for the first time laggard. In the chamber of the dead he stole to and fro examining the shelves, furtively intent. His eyes were sunken, his face drawn like death. From the footless coffin of the dowager trembling on its bench of stone, I saw an old water-rat creep. As Harfager passed beneath one of the shortest of the shelves which bore a single coffin, it suddenly fell from a height with its burden into fragments at his feet. He screamed the cry of a frightened creature, and tottered to my support. I bore him back to the upper house.

He sat with hidden face in the corner of a small room doddering, overcome, as it were, with the extremity of age. He no longer marked with his usual "Hark!" the fall of the leaden drops. To my remonstrances he answered only with the words, So soon! so soon! Whenever I sought I found him there. His manhood had collapsed in an ague of trepidancy.

I do not think that during this time he slept.

On the second night, as I approached him, he sprang suddenly straight with the furious outcry: "The first bell tinkles!"

And he had hardly larynxed the wild words when, from some great distance, a faint wail, which at its origin must have been a most piercing shriek, reached my now feverishly sensitive ears. Harfager at the sound clapped hands to ears, and dashed insensate from his place, I following in hot pursuit through the black breadth of the mansion. We ran until we reached a mound chamber, containing a candelabrum, and arrased in faded red. In an alcove at the furthest circumference was a bed. On the floor lay in swoon the lady Swertha. Her dark-grey hair in disarray wrapped her like an angry sea, and many tufts of it lay scattered wide, torn from the roots. About her throat were livid prints of strangling fingers. We bore her to the bed, and, having discovered some tincture in a cabinet, I administered it between her fixed teeth. In the rapt and dreaming face I saw that death was not, and, as I found something appalling in her aspect, shortly afterwards left her to Harfager.

When I next saw him his manner had assumed a species of change which I can only describe as hideous. It resembled the officious self-importance seen in a person of weak intellect, incapable of affairs, who goads himself with the exhortation, "to business! the time is short — I must even bestir myself!" His walk sickened me with a suggestion of *ataxie locomotrice*. I asked him as to the lady, as to the meaning of the marks of violence on her body. Bending ear to his deep and unctuous heard, "A stealthy attempt has been made upon her the skeleton, Aith."

My unfeigned astonishment at this announcement he seemed not to share. To my questions, repeatedly pressed upon him, as to the reason for retaining such a domestic in the house, as to the origin of his service, he could give no lucid answer. Aith, he informed me, had been admitted into the mansion during the period of his own long absence in youth. He knew little of the fact that he was of extraordinary physical strength. *Whence* he had come, or how, no living being except Swertha had knowledge; and she, it seems, feared, or at least persistently declined, to admit him into the mystery. He added that, as a matter of fact, the lady, from the day of his return to Vaila, had for some reason imposed upon herself a silence upon all subjects, which he had never once known her to break except by an occasional note.

With a curious, irrelevant *impressement*, with an intensely voluntary, ataxic strenuousness, always with the air of a drunken man constraining himself to ordered action, Harfager now set himself to the ostentatious adjustment of a host of insignificant matters. He collected chronicles and arranged them in order of date. He tied and ticketed bundles of documents. He insisted upon my help in turning the faces of portraits to the wall. He was, however, now constantly interrupted by paroxysms of vertigo; six times in a single day he was hurled to the ground. Blood occasionally gushed from his ears. He complained to me in a voice of piteous wail of the clear luting of a silver *piccolo*, which did not cease to invite him. As he bent sweating upon his momentous futilities, his hands fluttered like shaken reeds. I noted the movements of his muttering and whimpering lips, the rheum of his far-sunken eyes. The decrepitude of dotage had overtaken his youth.

On a day he cast it utterly off, and was young again. He entered my chamber, roused me from sleep; I saw the mad *gaudium* in his eyes, heard the wild hiss of his cry in my ear: "Up! It is sublime. The *storm!*"

Ah! I had known it — in the spinning nightmare of my sleep. I felt it in the tormented air of the chamber. It had come, then. I saw it lurid by the lamplight on the hell of Harfager's distorted visage.

I glanced at the face of the clock. It was nine — in the morning. A sardonic glee burst at once into being within me. I sprang from the couch. Harfager, with the naked stalk of some maniac old prophet, had already rapt himself away. I set out in pursuit. A clear deepening was manifest in the quivering of the edifice; sometimes for a second it paused still, as if, breathlessly, to listen. Occasionally there visited me, as it were, the faint dirge of some far-off lamentation and voice in Ramah; but if this was subjective, or the screaming of the storm, I could not say. Else I heard the distinct note of an organ's peal. The air of the mansion was agitated by a vaguely puffy unease. About noon I sighted Harfager, lamp in hand, running along a corridor. His feet were bare. As we met he looked at me, but hardly with recognition, and passed by; stopped, however, returned, and howled into my ear the question: "Would you *see?*" He beckoned before me. I followed to a very small window in the outer wall closed with a slab of iron. As he lifted a latch the metal flew inward with instant impetuosity and swung him far, while a blast of the storm, braying and booming through the aperture with buccal and reboant bravura, caught and pinned me against an angle of the wall. Down the corridor a long crashing *bouleversement* of pictures and furniture ensued. I nevertheless contrived to push my way, crawling on the belly, to the opening. Hence the sea should have been visible. My senses, however, were met by nothing but a reeling vision of tumbled blackness, and a general impression of the letter O. The sun of Vaila had gone out. In a moment of opportunity our united efforts prevailed to close the slab.

"Come" — he had obtained fresh light, and beckoned before me — "let us see how the dead fare in the midst of the great desolation and *dies iræ!*" Running, we had hardly reached the middle of the stairway, when I was thrilled by the consciousness of a momentous shock, the bass of a dull and far-reverberating thud, which nothing conceivable save the huge simultaneous thumping to the ground of the whole piled mass of the coffins of the sepulcher could have occasioned. I turned to Harfager, and for an instant beheld him, panic flying in his scuttling feet, headlong on the way he had come, with stopped ears and wide mouth. Then, indeed, fear overtook me — a tremor in the midst of the exultant daring of my heart — a thought that *now* at least I must desert him in his extremity, now work out my own salvation. Yet it was with a most strange hesitancy that I turned to seek him for the last time — a hesitancy which I fully felt to be selfish and diseased. I wandered through the midnight house in search of light, and having happened upon a lamp, proceeded to hunt for Harfager. Several hours passed in this way. It became clear from the state of the atmosphere that the violence about me was being abnormally intensified. Sounds as of distant screams — unreal, like the screamings of spirits — broke now upon my ear. As the time of evening drew on, I began to detect in the vastly augmented baritone of the cataract something new — a shrillness — the whistle of an ecstasy — a malice — the menace of a rabies blind and deaf. It must have been at about the hour of six that I found Harfager. He sat in an obscure apartment with bowed head, hands on knees. His face was covered with hair, and blood from the ears. The right sleeve of his garment had been rent away in some renewed attempt, as I imagined, to manipulate a window; the slightly-bruised arm hung lank from the shoulder. For some time I stood and watched the mouthing of his mumblings. Now that I had found him I said nothing of departure. Presently he looked sharply up with the cry "Hark!" — then with imperious impatience, "Hark! Hark!" — then with rapturous shout, "The second bell!" And *again,* in instant sequence upon his cry, there sounded a wail, vague but unmistakably real, through the house. Harfager at the moment dropped reeling with vertigo; but I, snatching a lamp, hasted forth, trembling, but eager. For some time the high wailing continued, either actually, or by reflex action of my ear. As I ran toward the lady's apartment, I saw, separated from it by the breadth of a corridor, the open door of an armory, into which I passed, and seized a battle-axe; and, thus armed, was about to enter to her aid, when Aith, with blazing eye, rushed from her chamber by a further door. I raised my weapon, and, shouting, flew forward to fell him; but by some chance the lamp dropped from me, and before I knew aught, the axe leapt from my grasp, myself hurled far backward. There was, however, sufficiency of light from the chamber to show that the skeleton had dashed into a door of the armory: that near me, by which I had procured the axe, I instantly slammed and locked; and hasting to the other, similarly secured it. Aith was thus a prisoner. I then entered the lady's room. She lay halfway across the bed in the alcove, and to my bent ear loudly croaked the *râles* of death. A glance at the mangled throat convinced me that her last hours were surely come. I placed her supine upon the bed; curtained her utterly from sight within the loosened festoons of the hangings of black, and inhumanly turned from the fearfulness of her sight. On an *escritoire* near I saw a note, intended apparently for Harfager: "I mean to defy, and fly. Think not from fear — but for the glow of the Defiance itself. *Can* you come?" Taking a flame from the candelabrum, I hastily left her to solitude, and the ultimate throes of her agony.

I had passed some distance backward when I was startled by a singular sound — a clash — resembling in *timbre* the clash of a tambourine, I heard it rather loudly, and that I should *now* hear it at all, proceeding as it did from a distance, implied the employment of some prodigious energy. I waited, and in two minutes it again broke, and thenceforth at like regular intervals. It had somehow an effect of pain upon me. The conviction grew gradually that Aith had unhung two of the old brazen shields from their pegs; and that, holding them by their handles, and smiting them viciously together, he thus expressed the frenzy which had now overtaken him. I found my way back to Harfager, in whom the very nerve of anguish now seemed to stamp and stalk about the chamber. He bent his head; shook it like a hail-tormented horse; with his deprecating hand brushed and barred from his hearing each recurrent clash of the brazen shields. "Au, when — when — when —" he hoarsely groaned into my ear, "will that rattle of hell choke in her throat? I will myself, I tell you — *with my own hand!* — Oh God . . ." Since the morning his auditory inflammation (as, indeed, my own also) seemed to have heightened in steady proportion with the roaring and screaming chaos round; and the *râles* of the lady hideously filled for him the measured intervals of the grisly cymbaling of Aith. He presently hurled twinkling fingers into the air, and with wide arms rushed swiftly into the darkness.

And again I sought him, and long again in vain. As the hours passed, and the slow Tartarean day deepened toward its baleful midnight, the cry of the now redoubled cataract, mixed with the throng and majesty of the now climactic tempest, assumed too definite and intentional a *shriek* to be longer tolerable to any mortal reason. My own mind escaped my governance, and went its way. Here, in the hot-bed of fever, I was fevered; among the children of wrath, was strong with the strength, and weak with the feebleness of delirium. I wandered from chamber to chamber, precipitate, bemused, giddy on the up-buoyance of a joy. "As a man upon whom sleep seizes," so had I fallen. Even yet, as I approached the region of the armory, the noisy ecstasies of Aith did not fail to clash faintly upon my ear. Harfager I did not see, for he too, doubtless, roamed a headlong Ahasuerus in the round world of the house. At about midnight, however, observing light shine from a door on the lower stage, I entered and found him there. It was the chamber of the dropping horologe. He half-sat, swaying self-hugged, on the ladder-steps, and stared at the blackness of the pool. The last flicker of the riot of the day seemed dying in his eyes. He cast no glance as I approached. His hands, his bare right arm, were red with new-shed blood; but of this, too, he appeared unconscious. His mouth gaped wide to his pantings. As I looked, he leapt suddenly high, smiting hands, with the yell, "The last bell tinkles!" and galloped forth, a-rave. He therefore did not see (though he may have understood by hearing) the spectacle which, with cowering awe, I immediately thereupon beheld: for from the horologe there slipped with hiss of vapor a ball into the torpid pool: and while the clock once ticked, another! and while the clock yet ticked, another! and the vapor of the first had not *utterly* passed, when the vapor of the third, intermingling, floated with it into grey tenuity aloft. Understanding that the sands of the house were run, I, too, flinging maniac arms, rushed from the spot. I was, however, suddenly stopped in my career by the instinct of some stupendous doom emptying its vials upon the mansion; and was quickly made aware, by the musketry of a shrill crackling from aloft, and the imminent downpour of a world of waters, that a water-spout had, wholly or partly, hurled the catastrophe of its broken floods upon us, and crashed ruining through the dome of the building. At that moment I beheld Harfager running toward me, hands buried in hair. As he flew past, I seized him. "Harfager! save yourself!" I cried — "the very fountains, man, — by the living God, Harfager" — I hissed it into his inmost ear — *"the very fountains of the Great Deep. . . !"* Stupid, he glared at me, and passed on his way. I, whisking myself into a room, slammed the door. Here for some time, with smiting knees, I waited; but the impatience of my frenzy urged me, and I again stepped forth. The corridors were everywhere thigh-deep with water. Rags of the storm, irrageous by way of the orifice in the shattered dome, now blustered with hoiden wantonness through the house. My light was at once extinguished; and immediately I was startled by the presence of *another* light — most ghostly, gloomy, bluish — most soft, yet wild, phosphorescent — which now perfused the whole building. For this I could in no way account. But as I stood in wonder, a gust of greater vehemence romped through the house, and I was instantly conscious of the harsh *snap* of something near me. There was a minute's breathless pause — and then — quick, quick — ever quicker — came the throb, and the snap, and the pop, in vastly wide circular succession, of the anchoring chains of the mansion before the urgent shoulder of the hurricane. And *again* a second of eternal calm — and then — deliberately — its hour came — the ponderous palace *moved.* My flesh writhed like the glutinous flesh of a serpent. Slowly moved, and stopped: — then was a sweep — and a swirl — and a pause! then a swirl — and a sweep — and a pause! — then steady industry of labor on the monstrous brazen axis, as the husbandman plods by the plow; then increase of zest, assuetude of a fledgling to the wing — then intensity — then the last light ecstasy of flight. And now, once again, as staggering and plunging I spun, the thought of escape for a moment visited me: but this time I shook an impious fist. "No, but God, no, no," I cried, "I will no more wander hence, my God! I will even perish with Harfager! Here let me waltzing pass, in this Ball of the Vortices, Anarchie of the Thunders! Did not the great Corot call it translation in a chariot of flame? But this is gaudier than that! redder than that! This is jaunting on the scoriac tempests and reeling bullions of hell! It is baptism in a sun!" Recollection gropes in a dimmer gloaming as to all that followed. I struggled up the stairway now flowing a steep river, and for a long time ran staggering and plunging, full of wild words, about, amid the downfall of ceilings and the wide ruin of tumbling walls. The air was thick with splashes, the whole roof now, save three rafters, snatched by the wind away. In that blue sepulchral moonlight, the tapestries flapped and trailed wildly out after the flying house like the streaming hair of some ranting fakeer stung gyratory by the gadflies and tarantulas of distraction. The flooring gradually assumed a slant like the deck of a sailing ship, its covering waters flowing all to accumulation in one direction. At one point, where the largest of the porticoes projected, the mansion began at every revolution to bump with horrid shiverings against some obstruction. It bumped, and while the lips said one-two-three, it three times bumped again. It was the levity of hugeness! it was the mænadism of mass! Swift — ever swifter, swifter — in ague of urgency, it reeled and raced, every portico a sail to the storm, vexing and wracking its tremendous frame to fragments. I, chancing by the door of a room littered with the *débris* of a fallen wall, saw through that wan and livid light Harfager sitting on a tomb. A large drum was beside him, upon which, club grasped in bloody hand, he feebly and persistently beat. The velocity of the leaning house had now attained the *sleeping* stage, that ultimate energy of the spinning-top. Harfager sat, head sunk to chest; suddenly he dashed the hairy wrappings from his face; sprang; stretched horizontal arms; and began to spin — dizzily! — in the same direction as the mansion! — nor less sleep-embathed! — with floating hair, and quivering cheeks, and the starting eye-balls of horror, and tongue that lolled like a panting wolf's from his bawling degenerate mouth. From such a sight I turned with the retching of loathing, and taking to my heels, staggering and plunging, presently found myself on the lower stage opposite a porch. An outer door crashed to my feet, and the breath of the storm smote freshly upon me. An *élan*, part of madness, more of heavenly sanity, spurred in my brain. I rushed through the doorway, and was tossed far into the limbo without.

The river at once swept me deep-drowned toward the sea. Even here, a momentary shrill din like the splitting asunder of a world reached my ears. It had hardly passed, when my body collided in its course upon one of the basalt piers, thick-cushioned by seaweed, of the not all-demolished bridge. Nor had I utterly lost consciousness. A clutch freed my head from the surge, and I finally drew and heaved myself to the level of a timber. Hence to the ledge of rock by which I had come, the bridge was intact. I rowed myself feebly on the belly beneath the poundings of the wind. The rain was a steep rushing, like a shimmering of silk, through the air. Observing the same wild glow about me which had blushed through the broken dome into the mansion, I glanced backward — and saw that the dwelling of the Harfagers was a memory of the past; then upward — and lo, the whole northern sky, to the zenith, burned one tumbled and fickly undulating ocean of gaudy flames. It was the *aurora borealis* which, throeing at every aspen instant into rays and columns, cones and obelisks, of vivid vermeil and violet and rose, was fairly whiffed and flustered by the storm into a vast silken oriflamme of tresses and swathes and breezes of glamour; whilst, low-bridging the horizon, the flushed beams of 'the polar light assembled into a changeless boreal corona of bedazzling candor. At the augustness of this great phenomenon I was affected to blessed tears. And with them, the dream broke! — the infatuation passed! — a hand skimmed back from my brain the blind films and media of delusion; and sobbing on my knees, I jerked to heaven the arms of grateful oblation for my surpassing Rephidim, and marvel of deliverance from all the temptation — and the tribulation — and the tragedy — of Vaila.

Premier and Maker

Give him the Nectar!
Pour out for the Poet,
Hebe, pour free!
Quicken his eyes with celestial dew,
That Styx the detested no more he may view,
And like one of us Gods may conceit him to be,
Thanks, Hebe! I quaff it! Io Pæan! I cry.
  The wine of the immortal
  Forbids me to die.

— COLERIDGE *(Imitation of Schiller)*

My friend, Mr. O'Malley Phipps, is a young man of good principles and ancient family, but one who, owing to his indolent habits, and an incurable weakness for dispensing among the poor munificences wildly disproportionate to his "means," seems to live at perpetual loggerheads with Fortuna on the Money Question. It is to his profound, and apparently quite unaffected, contempt for "public opinion" that I owe permission to publish the following piece. Having lately made a small essay of perceptible, but (as I must think) somewhat crude, genius, he thought fit to dispatch a copy thereof to the then Prime Minister, together with the following extraordinary note:

"My Lord, —

"I herewith send you a copy of my little book, *Life and the Poppy*, which, if you can read at all so well as I can write, will not fail to renovate and translate you. I have, my Lord, many designs half peeping within me — hair-tearings, delights — which it may not be *so* well for England if I do not utter. But I am, my Lord, impecunious — 'without cattle'; certain aspre-minded persons, exquisitely called 'gentle,' having usurped all the lands on which one might feed one's possible cattle; and these things, my Lord, I have not

even the slightest intention of uttering for England (which, as you know, depends upon her Celtic and Celticized population for her great and half-great men), if England do not, to begin with, grant me reasonable ease and leisure for that purpose. If you care, however, to offer me a sine-cure, I might possibly be content to accept it. I have always fancied, my Lord, that between your destiny and mine subsisted some affinity, since the day on which you formally opened the street now known as X—— Avenue; that day was my birthday, the 21st of July, which, as you perceive, is the Third Seventh day of the Seventh month; in that street I then resided. This, however, has nothing to do with the case. —
"I am, my Lord, your sincere,
"O. O'Malley Phipps"

A month later, when Mr. Phipps pretends to have quite forgotten the fact of this letter, he received the following reply:

"Sir, —
"I am instructed by Lord X—— to acknowledge the receipt of your letter of the 7th ult., together with a copy of your book, *Life and the Poppy*. This work his Lordship now directs me to say he has read with very considerable interest; and if you will be good enough to call at his Lordship's town residence, No. 11A. M—— St., W., at 11 A.M. on Wednesday next, the 7th inst., his Lordship will be glad of a few hours' private converse with you. — I am, Sir,
"Your obd^t. Servt.,
"E—— L——,
"*Private Secy*"

On Wednesday at 11 A.M., London was black with fog. Mr. Phipps was, however, punctual in presenting himself at the Premier's residence, where, in spite of the menial's surprise at the rather shabby character of his attire, lank hair, four-cornered coif of threadbare velvet, and a general appearance of the mediæval poor-scholar, he was at once led forward and ushered into an inmost chamber, the center of a labyrinth, in which, hardly aided by the glow of two tapers made, like Zobeide's, of aloes-wood and ambergris, he could at first discern nothing. He presently perceived, however, that the room was Moorish, full of small tables of woods ivory-inlaid, and liberal with crystal, porcelain, mirrors, stuffs of Mecca, shawls of India, and a profusion of cushions; the tapestries being paneled in colored velvets embroidered with sentences from the poet Sadi; also that, with an arm leaning on the plush of an ottoman near, and the other held out in greeting, the Premier squatted sartorial at one end of a rug on the floor. His Lordship wore a dressing gown of crocus satin, widely-cylindrical pantaloons of cerulean silk, slippers which curled high at the toes, and a close gold-wrought cap for calpac and turban. His shaven face, though ruddy, looked not un-Moorish in the dimness. After indicating a similar robe, he motioned Mr. Phipps to occupy the cushion at the other end of the rug, upon which the author accordingly proceeded to deposit himself in like Turkish fashion. Silence reigned. On two tripods of tortoise-shell stood sherbet of orange in ice; and from one of the crystals his Lordship, laying down the stem of his hookah, took occasional lazy sips. Mr. Phipps also, finding a narghil at his elbow, rosily drew through rose-water the smoke of the tobacco of Philippi. No sound was in the room, but the faint stuttering of a distant grate. Presently an Oriental person imported three dishes containing almond patties and two creams of pomegranate, one fennel-yellow, one light pink, freckled each with spices; followed by another with tiny white-china cups of Mocha coffee, yellow-black, boiled with cloves and saffron. The attendants having made a salaam, retired backwards.

No sound was in the room. An hour passed. As a bitter pelican broods solitary on a mid-sea crag at even-fall, so gravity was fathomful in the contemplation of the two: you would have said that, through the closed lids of a death stiff between them, they gazed into the vague orbits of eternity. Once only the premier, looking up, nodded sagely to the maker, a salutation which Mr. Phipps returned in kind. It was only after yet half-an-hour that the minister, as if surging from nirvana, waved high fluctuant the flag of his left eyebrow, and, sighing, said:

"What can you *do*?"

"I can write a shorthand."

"What else?"

"I can write decent Monk-Latin; think in the best Attic Greek."

"Proceed."

"I can swim in water."

"Let not your voice sink in air."

"I can read in many sciences, algebras, calculi."

"My ear is a hostelry."

"I can trample to death a short distance with the toes of an extremely rapid run."

"Spurt on."

"I can read the Hebrew Scriptures; which, in my case, more or less implies the Arabic, Syriac, Æthiopic, and Samaritan."

"My ear cerumenously waters."

"I can make women and children obey me."

"My ear is a word-perceiving Eye which never shuts in sleep."

"I can delight them with whimsies, and histories, and conceited anomalies."

"I am swallowed by my middle ear."

"I can discourse tolerably on English, Celtic, French, German, Spanish, Portuguese, Italian, Danish, Anglo-Saxon, old Hoch-Deutsch, old Icelandic, Rabbinical, Basque and Norse literatures."

"My ear is an only half-filled museum."

"I can ride a horse."

"Trot on."

"I can make very pretty pictures with black-lead pencil and Chinese white on tinted paper."

"My ear is a pit of receptiveness."

"I can pick out the 'The Heavens are Telling' with my right forefinger on the harpsichord."

"Stump on."

"I can write a book on the *rationale* of musical laws, in which I should have three quite new theories to propound; and a relation to demonstrate between the nature of the mind and a new species of rhyme."

"Proceed."

"I can make a boy to hate vileness; to love culture and goodness."

"My ear is a miser's purse.

"I can exactly tune an embrace or a conversation to the momentary temperament of a woman: I am of the same height as she at every altitude."

"My ear opens like a flower-calyx to the breeze of your mouth."

"I can govern this kingdom wisely and humanly."

"You?"

"I here. I can frame a fabric of law upon the foundations of the universe —"

"What can you *not* do?"

"I cannot spin a top."

"Proceed."

"I cannot add up rows of figures, nor comprehend the money columns in the newspapers.

"My ear is a word-trap."

"I cannot, in some moods, understand why Odysseus did not abide immortal with Calypso, or at the Ææan Isle."

"Proceed."

"I cannot conceive, though they appear in all the MSS., that Sophocles really wrote the words '*akestera chalinon*' (the *healing* bridle): the expression seems complex, Hebraic, for a Greek."

"My ear proves the pangs of a longing woman."

"I cannot remember the British being who wrote of 'the haughty Romans and the insolent Greeks' without an itching energy in my hide-bound ends."

"How so?"

"Because the Greeks were not insolent."

"No?"

"And because, if he had ransacked the lexicons of language, he would have met no adjective half so libelous upon a people with whom to be suave and kind and simple and joyous was religion."

"Do not lengthen speech. What else?"

"I cannot understand how a woman can live from year to year without hearing me. How forlorn that poor man who grows old and never loved me!"

"Your mouth is an ear-syringe, sedatively expressive of warm jets of language."

"I cannot sleep at night."

"Is 't so! Then there *is* some affin —"

"Do not mention it. It becomes too obvious."

"When *can* you sleep?"

"At noon: when some matter leans upon vigilance."

"When else?"

"At morn: when tappings rhyme *reveille.*"

"Proceed."

"When summer has me: and falling water droops a red pennant to the breathless sunset."

"Persist."

"When sermons thump and thunder: so Napoleon slumbered on the battlefield."

"You attend divine service?"

"I have done so a boy."

"What distinguished thing have you since achieved?"

"I have written a Book,"

"Everyone has. I myself."

"Not everyone: I know two."

"What are they?"

"Novelists."

"What restrains them?"

"Self-respect, and a morbid craving for distinction."

"You have achieved what else?"

"I have sighed at *Don Quixote* and *Le Tartuffe;* I have laughed at *Cato* and *Polyeucte.*"

"Proceed."

"I have taught a dog to spare a mouse — to reverence and love it."

"My ear is the sponge of eloquence."

"I have said to broad-faced Jove: 'Abnormal! Appear now before me, and I will push a spear —'"

"Why did you so speak?"

"At sunset I had an opaline opium-dream; through the long night I paced, racking remembrance; at daybreak my worn brain grew impious, and I cried: 'Abnormal! appear now —'"

"He did not appear?"

"He knows what a pillow is my bosom for his head — and he knew that I had no spear."

"You had other weapons."

"You cannot attack the immortals with a quill."

"The challenge was quixotic. He is Spirit."

"Yet, by night, in a lonely upper chamber by the sea, I have *seen.*"

"So? And what did you?"

"I *wept*. His hair dripped a dew, and his beard, new-drenched with the storms of Saturn. He is more beautiful, I say to you, than a palace of margarita pillowed upon rainbows in mid-air, and from every ranked window there becks a wine-stained concubine of Sibmah. I, shrinking self-loathed from the long kisses of his mouth, sobbed:

'Oh that I knew how I might bind thee to my posts, and load thee with fetters in my chamber!'

I wept till I was water."

"Did you speak?"

"There was long familiarity of talk. I said:

"How went it with Sirius last night? And was it well with Aldebaran? Does old Neptune still retch those old belches of hell? or has a moon of Vega, swift-wheeling as the clay, slipped exorbitant of late from the treadled wheel of thy pottering? Which of the tribes of thy pasture lacks forgotten grain of thee this night, and for this whisp of me, too, can it be verily so that thou thinkest? At that he glanced the reproach of Love, and for a moment our hearts burst and flowed together: there was no division between us. He said I was not such a very whisp as I thought, because cubic bulk is nothing at all, and a soul casts a sweller shadow than a planet, the measure of things being the amount of spirit they contain. He told me I was not to trouble about Mr. Matthew Arnold and those people, at heart, most of them, philosophers; because philosophers are always wrong, and all men wrong, except one man only – the Poet! the Music-maker! right he in his errors. He assured me that he *is* 'a magnified non-natural man in the clouds' – and more – and elsewhere; but at least that and there, so that those who have thought so of him were *not wrong!* The Egyptians symbolized him by the cat, and he said he is that, too – and more; and a lark, and a lion – and more; and Thoth, and Pasht, and Phthah – and Nisroch and Adramalech – and whatsoever shape of Ape, or soaring Hippogriff or sideway-rearing Ram, or crouching Mixoparthenon, our whim can lend to him – and more. He told me then to call him not so much 'Not-Myself which makes for righteousness,' as, Abh, and Nurse, and Aïtas; for that when a human male, with eyes drowning like some strong swimmer, surnames him *so,* that soft-soaps and overcomes him; and it is as though one stroked an infinite cat; the universe goes *purring* for comfort. And many killing things he said of men. He told me that he had noticed with interest my little efforts to produce beautiful things, and that if I persevered in my passion for goodness, I should yet make one little great work of high perfectness, which should be recognized as such, not only by myself and him, but by five other cultivated persons now living; also that he had appointed a place where he would meet with me when I am older, and there open me a secret, by the knowledge of which the mystery involved in certain weird discords of the Harp would cease to be a mystery to me."

"You are prolix."

"I am precise."

"You have achieved what else?"

"I have 'invented' three mechanical puzzles for children."

"Proceed."

"I have given my last actual and foreseen six-pence to a street-lass for toffee."

"And dreamed yourself vastly magnificent, no doubt!"

"It was magnificent. It was as grandly dissolute as the economics of Jesus or Shelley. I dreamed it so."

"The ear is feminine: the mouth is masculine: I lie naked and wanton to your aggressions."

"I have discovered an altogether novel *raison d'être* for serpent-worship; also for the serpent being represented by the autochthones as yoked to the car of Demeter and Triptolemus; also that Microbius was quite wrong in thinking the serpent-limbs of the giants typical of their debased emotions."

"I am like a corn-field bending ears to the wide-whispered breaths of summer."

"I have discovered that if Mr. Ruskin, and I, and Mr. Gladstone, and you, and Mr. Balfour, and the Harcourt sirship, all died suddenly on the same day, considerable were thereby the disaster to England; but *less* than the disaster caused by the birth into England of one unhealthy child."

"My ear is a weighing-machine."

"I have gone forth to see the world: and I saw the wrong that was done: the hand of the murderer was stained; the harlot glanced behind her; by night intruded the thief. And this, having returned to my chamber, I said: In the period of the universe is a day for every dark, and in the breadth of its paradise a herb for every hurt; but the strong man who, for three running days, oppresses a weak, is an exile from Grace."

"My ear is the Gothic door of a gloomy hermit's vault, ajar for every pilgrim."

"I have invented a New Commandment, which, for the next two hundred years I wish to take precedence of all the commands of all the law-givers; for it includes them all, and more."

"What is it?"

"It is hard to understand *now*; yet *will* be understood."

"But what is it?"

"Thou shalt be a good Citizen."

"There is no thoroughfare between my ears; all words attempting to pass undergo arrest."

"I have kissed a lovely Nun."

"My ear is the belly of vacuity!"

"I have seen three women bathe in a lakelet, and their beauty like a soul was born again in the inverted baptism of the water."

"You interest me strangely!"

"I perceive it."

"Tell me! where were you?"

"I was behind the oval copse that lipped the lake."

"And you peered? You really saw?"

"I saw."

"Did they look like nymphs at Tempe?"

"They resembled British women."

"Tell me! what did they?"

"The water hissed and spurted. There was hoop-hoop and laughter."

"Did they see you?"

"They sniffed me – on the morning breeze. Have you observed the startled herd of antelopes, instinct wide in their darting eyes?"

"By the Prophet! – were they ladies?"

"One was a young viscountess — all, for the moment, were washerwomen."

"You are a democrat."

"I am a *revolutionnaire* — a thing it may be ordained that *you* shall yet be."

"You answer everything."

"You spoke."

"In the multitude of words is folly."

"But a close-fitting answer is like a plaster to the broken skin, or stays to the pappy mammæe."

"You are a *revolutionnaire*, then. What else?"

"A philosopher."

"Proceed."

"A poet."

"Persist."

"A Puritan Don Juan."

"Define 'Puritan.'"

"A sane miser."

"Define 'Don Juan.'"

"A body-genius."

"Define 'genius' the man."

"He is humanity in the kettle-spout: as steam to water to ice, so he to mankind to the brute."

"Define 'genius' the thing."

"Tertiary diplopia of the brain."

"Why tertiary?"

"'All life is disease' — optic-nerve-obliquity. In the brute it is primary, in mankind secondary, in genius tertiary."

"You are what else?"

"A pantheist."

"Define 'pantheist.'"

"A believer in God."

"You are what else?"

"A humanist."

"Define 'humanist.'"

"A Christian."

"Define Christianity."

"It is the success of the attempt of which modern Gothic art is the woeful failure: it is the idealization of the commonplace."

"True; but I fancy trite."

"It is the apotheosis of the courtesan: Phryne made a constellation no less than Helen; Nana star-throned amid the galaxies no less than

Stella Mans."

"You are apt."

"I am curiously felicitous."

"You are self-opinionated."

"To be felicitous is easy. To be curiously felicitous is extremely difficult."

"I am also curiously felicitous."

"What do you do for a living?"

"I make works of fine art."

"What is a work of fine art?"

"A self-consciously-wise product of the pure imagination."

"What is imagination?"

"It is Euclid grown Orphic, it is winged Reason, it is the mathematics of fancy."

"Explain yourself."

"I might have said *mathesis:* it is fancy grown *précieux,* purposeful, architectural, nay, self-creative. In this last function it greatly resembles, or is, that divine Essence by which the worlds stood forth; so that a man *so* engaged may, for the moment, without presumption, call himself God and Elohim.

"And what is fancy?"

"The adventure-luck *(Abenteuer-Glück)* of the touring soul."

"What else do you?"

"I make works of gross art."

"What is a work of gross art?"

"A self-consciously-wise product of the observation, more or less assisted by the fancy; or (in some branches of art) of the fancy alone."

"Not of the observation alone?"

"I cannot imagine such a thing 'self-consciously-wise.' A blue book is not a work of art."

"But when the fancy alone is thus wise, is it not then imagination?"

"I cannot answer you both shortly and convincingly. But this I will say: I have looked at a work and decided definitely in myself: this is only fancy, not imagination; dream, not apocalypse; and yet it is self-consciously-wise. *Gulliver* is an instance."

"Of the two kinds I need not ask which you consider the highest."

"They are not comparable: one is high as height itself: the other no higher than shoe-clouting (which also is high)."

"The highest is, of course, the hardest."

"They are not comparable: one is the hardest of the possible matters upon which the spirit of a man may engage: it is the snatching of flame from the heavenly gods: premiering, for instance, being a trifling business in comparison. The other, to the practiced, is, or should be, cheaper than — matches.

"Do not spread your answers. To distinguish between the two kinds, you should first of all define art in general. Is it definable?"

"Those mustachio slippers — the gleaming of yonder tapers — are not so cleanly definable."

"It is not then a vague something, the precise nature of which nobody (or only a few mysteriously sage persons) quite knows?"

"Its precise nature has over and over again been well known to everybody then living."

"What then is it?"

"As the etymology of the word betokens, it is simply a 'fitting-together.'"

"So if I adjust this stem in my hookah, and thus effect a fitting-together, that is art?"

"Yes, that is art; if, in doing so, you have, and accomplish, a specific purpose other than smoking."

"Well, define it. My ear is a barren old womb."

"Art, then, is the production, by elaborate new contrivance, of intended effects upon intended minds."

"That is your inclusive-exclusive definition?"

"It is."

"It is short."

"It is exhaustive. It swaddles the universe. And it is the Greek radical conception."

"The notion of fitting-together is, I presume, contained in your word 'contrivance?'"

"Yes. But I apologize for 'elaborate.' I do not quite mean what I say. I do not, for example, mean 'complex.' By 'elaborate' I half mean elaborate and half deliberate. Perhaps 'labored' would be better; yet I somehow prefer 'elaborate.'"

"You speak of *intended* minds."

"Yes; for though the scarecrow was a work of art, it is not one for wingless me; Peterborough would affect a Tahitian, or a Tahitianlike Englishman, but not produce the effect intended by the architect; while *The Creation* would produce no effect at all except a humming bewilderment. So a friend of mine writes tales only for persons who are drunk, and to such his works accordingly give great delight; and I have myself written a piece which no one uninfluenced by the sulfate of morphia could fully appreciate. You know, too, how the highest kind of poetry, the Greek myths for instance, seems simply silly to unpoetical people. So, too, there are passages in Milton and Euripides which, from a certain lack of humor or time-spiritedness, could be poetry to no living person, and yet, I think, are good art: poetry to some of their contemporaries."

"You speak of *intended* effects."

"Yes; for a work may produce an admirable effect, yet if not the effect intended by the maker, or if he had no precise intention on planning the work, then the work is clearly not a work of *art,* but of something else."

"Your definition is exclusive: thus we speak of the Physician's Art, the Art of War."

"We speak wrongly. Art is the production of effects upon *minds.* The steam-engine is not a work of art; but the scarecrow is."

"But if a general causes the enemy to think him in one place when he is in another?"

"That is art — if his contrivance be new."

"Or if by his conduct, he strike terror into the foe, or inspire his own troops?"

"That is art — if his conduct be purposeful of those effects."

"Alexander at the Hydaspes annihilated with a wretched army the masses of Porus and his elephants."

"Supposing Arrian exact, that was one part art, and nine parts mechanical ingenuity. Jay Gould or Mr. Edison could have done it — or nine parts of it."

"You speak of *new* contrivance."

"Yes; for it is clear that, though the inventor of the three-card trick (whatever that be) was a genuine artist, no one would call the *second* operator by such a name."

"But suppose someone now invents a similarly wise new fraud with *cards?*"

"He indeed. I do not, of course, mean that the whole paraphernalia of an art-work must be new. The second man who painted a picture was not *altogether* novel."

"What then do you mean?"

"Only that the chain of thought, starting from a knowledge of the mind to be acted upon, which precedes the execution of the work, must in the main be new; must be not such as has, in the main, been previously welded in one's own or another's mind."

"And now for fine art and gross art; how are they known?"

"By their effects."

"Explain."

"The effect of one is fine; the effects of the other are gross."

"What are fine effects? what gross?"

"The child on being born, weeps, and laughs, is afraid, scratches himself, and physically lusts. He needs no work to teach him these things. Nor does any such work add at all to his *culture*. To Fear, Laughter, etc., were temples at Sparta — but not at Athens."

"Proceed. My ear —"

"The characteristic of a gross work of art is this: that though its contrivance is new, its effects are old. It merely reincites in the man emotions the same as, or similar to, those which arose spontaneously in the child. Broadly speaking, its ultimate effects are muscular, rather than nervous. It never wins the mind into a state it dreamed not of before; into the doing of a thing it did not before."

"Laughter, tears, horror, lust, etc., you call gross: and yet some of our highest artists, our Dickens, and Thackeray and Zola —"

"*Ne me citez pas ces gens-là!*"

"You are angry."

"Two know better. For the third hot knowledge waits."

"You believe in a Lake —"

"No. But I believe that a man, or a nation, cannot take a fluent, or haphazard, or vulgar book, and say: I will go lounge and complacently dram-drink this for titillation: it will do me no good: it can work me no harm. In truth, it will work harm. It is ordained that the man, the nation, shall be more fluent, more haphazard, vulgar."

"And you think that the person who *writes* such in large quantities —"

"Does a big thing! σχέτλια ἔργα! If there are pains and penalties reserved, they are for him."

"But people are not compelled to read —"

"Yes. Mr. Matthew Arnold, indeed, has told them to read 'only the best'; and that, as you know, is one of those lucky sayings whose unexpected wisdom does not fail to surprise one the longer one thinks of it: wise — but quite futile: until this other counsel be added: See, somehow, that nothing but the best be *written* in your nation. For Mr. Arnold might just as well have said: 'Drink nothing but mountain-lymph,' to a people upon whom the gin-shop presses omnipresent from birth, for all the world like a law of nature. The people, of course, will *not* drink mountain-lymph, until you close the shop-doors — with a bang, too, of such crude fanatic violence, that it shall go sounding through the nations, and reach the very throne of Heaven, giving pleasure *there*. Now, a person who, knowing that there are too many, keeps open an *old* shop, is, of course, a bad citizen but how of him who opens a *new* one? he, surely, is a great criminal. And with regard to books, I say this: That you will never persuade Lord Tom and Mr. Dick really to study Dante (who will make them cultured), until you find means to induce, or compel, M. Zola (who makes them fallow) to write — for the love of God – no more. And if I seem to you to speak strongly, it is not that I speak strongly, but that you do not suffer from a weakness of which I, by no effort, can rid myself: the weakness of dearly loving Tom and Dick, and of cordially detesting the foolish or knavish person who, for his own pleasures, does them hurt."

"By 'fluent' do you mean 'wordy?'"

"That, and if there is anything worse, then that: cataclysmic incontinence, salivation, letter-writing literature, pen-talk. The *tongue*, you know, was made for talking; the pen, on the other hand, is the modern substitute for the graver on stone, and, in literature, should be used with the same agony of curiosity. The Ten Commandments did not, you know, fill many Minerva volumes, for each letter was the work of a day. But how, says Thackeray, do the thoughts, unsuspected before, flow to us when once we take pen in hand! Notice the insolent *us*. *Us*, one hopes, meant only self, Dickens, and crew; for being a reader of Greek and Hebrew books, he must have known that some of *us* know very well what we must say long before we take the pen in hand, and know too that any addition of 'happy thoughts' to that will mean the hopeless ruin of our clean undertaking."

"But 'Shabby-genteel People' is certainly very pleasant rea –"

"Do not speak in that way. 'Sitting at the feet of Jesus, clothed, and in his right mind;' take that phrase, whoever made it, as a model of good writing, and believe that all art-writing which essentially differs from it is more or less base. Here you have agonized reticence – and with it, 'opium' enough, halo, – the few (twelve) words producing a *super*-abundant impression, expressing, as it were, vastly more than they say. They paint a picture, not for the mind's-eye, but for the *inner* mind's-eye of fantasy; are not really picturesque at all (as I think Coleridge said of Milton), but *musical;* related, that is, less to the art of painting than to the art of sounds, and so are directed to the mind's *ear;* or say again, are not a word-picture but a word-aria. Which of your 'happy-thought' men, forgetful of the denunciation against spoken idle words (aimed how much more against written?), but would have whelmed the world with a chapter of vulgar incident and small-talk, or the deluge of half a volume, to produce the complete effect of that one word 'clothed?'"

"But you are severe –"

"Not, you mean. Have you considered the significance of the fact that not one of the really decent minds of our century, the Carlyles, etc., will have anything to do with prose fine art, ashamed and scared from any species of association with the singular crew who purport to practice it? In consequence of which, the word 'novelist' or 'fictionist' has now got to carry with it a certain slight social opprobrium, like the words 'coroner' 'butcher,' 'lord-mayor,' 'policeman;' so that *you*, for instance, now think somewhat less of a gentleman after hearing that he is a person of that trade than before hearing. I at least do. Thus have we debased the Holy of Holies; and to such a point brought it with our floods of words. Says Plutarch: We are pleased with perfumes and purple, while dyers and perfumers appear in the light of mean mechanics. And Hosea: Because thou hast rejected knowledge, therefore have I rejected thee that thou be no priest to *Me*. You know, too, how one at least of the men you have mentioned thought it nothing odd to go about proclaiming, with a species of city-clerk pride, his innocence of — *Greek!*"

"But we hardly still consider that inability fatal —"

"It is, however. Imagine a Christian preacher who had never heard of the Bible! Greek art is, of course, the Bible of artists; in so much that some people could not string a dozen decent English sentences on the same day on which they had not read some sort of Greek writing. So, too, you are a Prime Minister: is it likely that you will effect the supreme in statecraft, if you have not soaked yourself with the supremest done in that line from the beginning? Except indeed you be a man of altogether stupendous intellect."

"But I notice you prolix. You are long-winded in your answers."

"Not willingly. You force me by your dullness."

"Dull me no dullness."

"Long-wind me no long-windedness."

"Let us proceed. We have now spoken of gross art and its gross effects; what are the fine effects of fine art?"

"Its effect is always uniform."

"You surprise me."

"Uniform, I mean, as to genus, not as to species. The genus of the effects produced by two beautiful women is the same; their species different."

"What is the uniform genus of its effect?"

"An effect of Beauty."

"This cream of pomegranate appears beautiful to my senses: is my *chef* then a fine artist in reference to me?"

"No. The beauty of the custard lacks two qualities which, did it possess them, would prove your *chef* a fine artist."

"So that not *any* beauty will do for the fine artist? but only a certain special beauty having two invariable qualities?"

"That is so."

"What then are they?"

"Novelty (or Uniqueness); and Infinity."

"Novelty. That then makes yet a difference between the work of gross and of fine art? For whereas the gross is novel in its contrivance, but old in its effects; the fine is novel both in its contrivance, and the species of its effect. Is 't so?"

"You are observant and exact."

"Why *must* the gross be novel in its contrivance?"

"By definition and three-card illustration: otherwise it were not art."

"And now Infinity. What *do* you mean?"

"Only that the task of the better kind of artist is not to create 'new forms of beauty'; but to create new forms of *such* beauty as shall suggest, in *some* manner, at *some* point, were it but for a moment, what includes, and is more than, the *allgemein,* that is to say, the Infinite."

"But I do not understand this of Infinity. I am practical. You are vague."

"Earth is of the same hue as the skies, though a taint of yellow infects her azure to terrestrial green; yet, even so, the *sea,* you know, regains the celestial chrome. Or say again: Man is but a little lower than the angels; the veil that divides them may, here a little, there a little, be lifted. The hint, then, of every great art-work is this: Homo is, or may be made to suggest, a tremendous fellow — a head higher than his collar! — important to the gods! He *looks* most absurdly small, but only unbosom your tape and try the *shadow* of him athwart the abysms. His body is more than raiment, his life is more than breakfast-table Autocracies, genialities! And if you want *certain* proof of the very high humor that is in him, just cast a glance at this very woof which I, a man, have been weaving here! That, I think, is what the Greek tragedies wanted to say, and said, and could not utterly say."

"Do you make Fine Art a kind of 'handmaid to religion?'"

"Nonsense. It is religion itself."

"You consider *De Rerum Naturâ* and *Queen Mab* religious?"

"Quite infinitely."

"Explain yourself." "If *laborare* is *orare,* how much more is *elaborare?*"

"I begin to see."

"'Operosa parvus carmina lingo.' — I, little chiel, potter my toilsome songs. Is not that religion? How humble, haughty. Suppose your *chef* sits him down, and, meekly believing that there dwells in man an infinite spirit, shall so build upon his knowledge of your nature a fabric of deliberate reasoning, that he shall thereby evolve a novel custard, of which *you,* tricked, shall exclaim: This, of a surety, is none other than own sister to that ambrosia of the *heavens,* which, if a man eat, he shall never die! then is he a fine artist. Fail not to sinecure *him.* He has made you a cultured man, he has saved your soul alive."

"I see. And this, you say, is an effect only to be wrought by imagination."

"Only so, when it is a genuine art-effect. But it may also be wrought by inspiration."

"Why may it not be wrought by observation?"

"Because one invariable element of all high beauty is, as has so often been said, a certain divine 'strangeness.' We do not, you know, kiss a hand to the sun at noon: but to the White-One, walking in shining? and to her, *because* she is queer-eyed, and disheveled, and lunatic. And the *midnight* sun again? And that furious world, the sunset? And that most weird ænigma of Mrs. Langtry's charitoblepharous eyes? Of *such* is the Kingdom of Heaven. Have you observed the very singular character of the landscape in Burne-Jones's 'Looking-glass?' Or those 'Golden Stairs' which never curved on earth. . . ? Now, let it be admitted at once that there is nothing more 'strange' than the commonplace — a sphinx not a whit more than a cat: only, the commonplace cannot by any goading be made to *seem* strange, and since art is the production of seemings, that is why you find *all* the great art of the ages concerned with sphinxes, and never at all with cats. A cat it certainly is, you know, and not a sphinx, which Thackeray would have set up at the Pyramids; and he would have made a monstrous big one, too, and a very knowing-looking one, to the whiskers; just such a one as he one day *chanced* to see on some Dowager's lap; so that people would have flocked, crying: 'See now, how like a real cat, and how startling a cat-knower have we with us, subtil to catch in stone the very simper of dowager-cats!' The Egyptians, however, though not themselves the greatest artists, yet immeasurably greater than Thackeray, thought differently, and gave to the world what you know. So you see that he who reports his observations must necessarily report the antithesis of the 'strange,' that is to say, the commonplace; and even when his selection of the things reported is most scrupulous and wise, he will fail to produce an impression of true loveliness, since all, or nearly all, his parts being of one *genre*, his whole cannot be of another."

"Why cannot such an effect be wrought by fancy?"

"Because another invariable element of all high beauty is a certain accuracy, an *exact* justice of its parts: and this impression can only be produced by a faculty *mathematical* in its operations — possessing a delicate *conscience* of error and fitness. A square moon, or Hermes with the beard of Jove, would be still beautiful, but no longer divinely so. In reading *Gulliver,* people say: 'This is good, yet had I written it, I had written it different; and better.' But no one ever studied, the earlier books of the Odyssey without a feeling that they different were they spoiled;

they seem, in fact, as minutely just as the intergravitation of the planets, and have all the look of construction by a being half machine, half man, and half — something higher."

"He was thus a Homer and a half."

"His third was his 'better half': it was that spirit of loveliness to which he was wed."

"And this, you say, is an effect only to be wrought by the pure imagination? Yet the Odyssey, at least, undoubtedly contains much that was once 'commonplace,' and so must have been partly a work of 'observation.'"

"You are wrong. The subject of Art is not Man, but his shadow. Homer makes all *his* fine artists *blind, incapable* of contemporary ocular observation; was himself blind. 'Blind Thamyris, blind Mæonides, and Teirisias and Phineus, prophets old.' Similarly every fine artist must be blind; having 'converted' eyes, — 'dead' or blind to the earthly vulgar, and 'alive' or seeing to the heavenly lovely."

"But *why?* The Aphrodite of Praxiteles was a work 'infinite' in beauty, producing an intense degree of 'novel' rapture upon the 'intended' minds:* a product therefore of the pure imagination. Yet the statue stands upon two legs, not upon one nor three. Was not this due to the fact that the artist had 'observed' that women in general have two legs?"

"You seek to puzzle me: that is clear. Better seek to gyve the whirlwind with withes. You cannot, you know, instill into the wild zebra the love of poppy; nor teach the tossing limbs of ocean to swear allegiance to mandrake."

"But do not the waves yield to the homely sense of a little paraffin?"

"The oil must be genuine mineral; bilge-water will not do. And if you are not wrong as to all this, you are at least wrong-headed. Imagination, from its very nature, is a faculty which does not work in collaboration with another. It is sole. Its attitude is, if anything, one of *hostile* superiority to nature. Herr God made cold meat, Mrs. Lazenby pickles. I praise both, but give the apple to the lady. But there is *one* little bit of

---

* If I remember right, people ran agape from all over cultured Greece to see this stone. Yet Mr. Ruskin says that there was nothing specially "beautiful" in Greek sculpture, and thence infers that there are people now living lovelier than the loveliest of the Greeks. It would be weird if this were so. But Mr. Ruskin confutes himself when he proceeds to assert that body is only the expression of mind; for if this be true, then an average Greek must have been as much lovelier than the loveliest of moderns, as Euclid or Archimedes (to say nothing of Plato) was more radically cunning than Mr. Ruskin. I say *average,* for not mind, but body, seems to have been the sphere of their highest development. It is, in fact, almost certain that they were lovelier than they were mental; and everybody, except Dryden, knows that they were mentaler than the mentalest.

nature to which imagination pays devoutest homage: the nature, namely, of the mind which it seeks to influence. Now, it is a principle of this mind that in animal-figures it shall perceive the highest beauty when the animal has two legs, not more, nor less. And to the artist's consciousness of *this* fact, not to his observation that women have two legs, was due the shape of the Aphrodite. Nor must you think this a mere quibble, the result being the same, anyway; for, on the contrary, here you have the very *radix* of the difference between gross art and fine; and oftentimes the result is far from being the same, anyway; inasmuch as not all things that we see are utterly fit, as is the number of a woman's legs. And if the Creator had made the mistake of giving to her three legs, or, still worse, only one, be sure that Praxiteles, whatever Giotto might have done, would have detected the slip, and given to his Aphrodite two. Nay, even where the arrangement of nature *is* utterly fit, imagination sometimes does not hesitate, in attacking the mind on some of its sides, to take the law into its own hands, and with victorious masterfulness bid total defiance to nature: thus Homer gave to Odysseus two eyes, but to the Cyclops only one; nor must you think either more triumphant, credible, deep-rooted, than the other. In the relief at Ellora, too, of the beauteous Parvati and Siva, the latter has four arms, not two. And *this* one gets to feel to be right."

"But has not George Eliot said something about the duty of the artist to reproduce the world as it stands; to see life 'without opium?'"

"Yes, she seems to have been a lightsome hen, that lady. Imagine Gounod writing a Serenade, Shakespeare a *Winter's Tale*, Euripides a *Hippolytus*, without opium! Stockbrokers, you know, see life 'without opium'; doctors, jurymen, prime ministers; and see it, from birth, without opium, because without effort. The artist, *sacer vates*, or whatever you call him, used to consider himself greater than all these, because to him alone of men was granted force to scale Olympus, to descend even into the dim house of Aides, in order, as if by fire, to come at some little opium: so remotely shy a thing is opium; so difficult to be sure that one has not, after all one's trouble, clutched nothing but the mere thin nauseating ghost of it."

"You advocate, then, the 'opium-traffic?'"

"Human life were impossible without it. Richly (in places) has it been used by the Arch-Poet in his plan of the world. You know very well what your wife is, what Helen was: a mass of gore and livery carrion — glamoured over with a pink skin. Not that the skin was *really* pink, or the sky blue, or that there is any sky there: but only pink, and there, and blue to *our* eyes. Nay, that very skin, I now hear, was full of worms, and little objectionable creatures living at ease, but so cunningly adapted to the opiated eyes of Paris, that sacred Troy has fallen, and to you life becomes possible and even musical. Putrescence, then, if we abolish that too languishing traffic."

"Imagination, by your suggestions, must be uncommon among men?"

"In England, a reviewing gentleman tells me, there are now published annually hundreds of fiction-works and pictures, which are bad all through; in which, he means, there is not *anything* richly good (a new product of human industry, I fancy, for the sun to see), and in everyone of these, if you look, you will probably find traces of imagination – a certain impotent imagination, unconscious of itself."

"The faculty is common then?"

"If every man has it not, then nearly every man."

"What then is precious?"

"Poetical imagination: imagination so freely, yet fastidiously imaginative, that its product becomes poetical, *musical (μουσίκος)* in its effect. One sort amuses, 'gives pleasure' to vulgar people, and refined people in low moods; the other bemuses, gives translation to refined people."

"Illustrate yourself."

"Contrast *Don Quixote* with *Round the World in Eighty Days;* contrast *L'Homme Qui Rit* with *Dr. Jekyll and Mr. Hyde; Astarte Syriaca* with Leighton's *Solitude* or someone's *Doctor;* the Doge's Palace with the Tour Eiffel!"

"And that higher imagination is, you say, rare?"

"It is always rarer than platinum; it is generally rarer than rubidium; it is sometimes as rare as the dodo."

"But is not this imagination that you call 'impotent,' or 'non-poetical' or 'non-musical' closely akin to mere unyoked fancy?"

"You are right. They are, in fact, hardly distinguishable. And yet, by looking into myself, I feel certain they are distinct."

"And now tell me: what is the reason of the scarcity, if they are scarce, of these 'fine effects' of which you speak among us?"

"There are many. The age is iron, art-infidel, *Assyrian.*[*]

---

[*] Very curious, in truth, is the resemblance between, say, the modern novel, and the sculptures of Nineveh; nor could anyone to whom it was once pointed out fail to notice it; the crude, and revolting (because absolute) fidelity to life in the hinder parts of the winged bulls especially, and the fingers of the kings, is very instructive. Add to the lifelikeness of the bulls the raw instinctive reaction against mere imitation of nature indicated by the *incoherent* fancy of their *wings,* and you have the modern novel. It seems, however, that a certain indefinable supremacy of vulgarity was reserved by the ages for the contemporaries of M. Zola.

"That is vague."

"The Greeks, I have said, were gentle and joyous, and *kind*. Their hearts were most simple, sensitive, religious. With all their dreadful tragedies, they could not bear a murder on the stage. When Telemachus sneezed (horrid was the hoop-hoop!) Penelope *laughed*. Only such people are fancy-free: and fancy is the raw material of fine art."

"Another."

"We, artists and nation, think more of a hundred pound *avoir-du-poids*, and the gold of Paz and Kharûts, than of an all-wifely adjective, or a wraithly metaphor, or the symmetry of a right tale, or the flight of a continent curve; love money and *éclat* better than the perfection of beauty. The Greeks confessedly loved money and *éclat*."

"That is so. Most corn-eating men. But if you see no world of difference between their love and ours, you are a bad reader, and your instincts are awry."

"Another."

"Partly, I suppose, owing to the character of our thoughts, the nations have not yet attained to a high degree of physical beauty. From childhood our senses grow hardened to *all* forms of terrestrial poverties, cruelties, horrors."

"Proceed."

"The audience of our fine artists is small — few and hardly fit. They work only for a 'tenth' — and the only unimportant tenth — of mankind. The mass, who, in the end, might possibly be stern and right critics, do not study such work for two reasons."

"What?"

"They are still too poor; and still too rude."

"Do they not read and understand Dickens? Jan van Beers?"

"But not Tennyson and Rossetti; they appreciate the 'music hall'; Beethoven is the buzzoozing sea-shell to their ear. The Greek proletariat, on the contrary, seems to have appreciated to the full the very highest art."

"'Buzz-zoozing' is *beau*. It is nicely onomatopoetic without being nonsense, like the 'shattering' trumpet. Is it original?"

"Yes. It deserves a permanent place in the memory of man. But do not suppose that nonsense makes 'shattering' less beautiful. Both words are absolute, right. They depend for their production upon faculties far finer and more venerable than those which won Austerlitz, or invented the phonograph. They are more precious than the corals of P'ninim, or the ruby of Sultan Giamschid, or the collars of Mahmood's —"

"Let another man praise thee, and not thy own mouth!"

"But if you want a thing well done, you must do it yourself: you must not leave it to others. For maxim, you see, I wreak you maxim, for parable, parable. Besides, you must not think me weak enough to praise myself: it is Homer that I praise, the poet, the party of God."

"Another reason."

"Women, now first in history, attack in large numbers high-art subjects. This must degrade not only women, but art."

"But! — I strongly differ from you. Why so?"

"If you are going to differ from me, you should cease your questioning. You cannot suppose that I would willfully mislead you, and you may well give me credit for knowing the rudimentary facts of a subject, the inner secrets of which I might be supposed to know for certain."

"Yet you make two statements: prove them. Why does it degrade *woman?*"

"The Maker, in his making, was not *often* an artist: the sun, quinine, cat's-meat, for instance, he made not so much for the admiration of the eyes which perceive them as for vastly other reasons. Occasionally, however, he said: Come now, we will do something for the Nerve! And *then*, the thing produced was so *excessively* effective, that a danger of *lunacy*, moon-sickness, overtook the intended beholder. Now, of such kind was our weaving dear, the loaf-giver; the penumbra of this place of shadow; our hint of light; a work of fine art — 'unique' — 'infinite.' Here, certainly, the Artist outdid himself. He blushed shame for his crude tinkering upon the seraphs when he saw completed Woman. So far he overshot, that man found it necessary to *veil* her glory, to her very face in some countries, lest at her nakedness the world rush into frenzy of admiration; and to this day, if a young man meet a maid in the lanes of spring, broad-faced Jove, where he sits, pondering upon the sum of things, knows what is pending. He smiles. The father of gods and men is not without a sense of humor. He says: 'That old sex-idea of mine, though far-fetched-seeming at first, has turned out a fine success, after all, and still works. I shall now watch those two into the glades of the forest, and see what shall there grow up.' Now, this I say: that when woman produces to the utmost this complex fine-art effect upon the world, as does not fail whenever her functioning is pure womanly and intended, then is she at her supremest, fulfilling the law of her being; and that it is pure womanly and intended when it is *felt* to be so by the intended minds, and when not felt to be so, not so; but if she subtract at all from herself, you get an effect of hair-cutting; and if she add at all to herself, you get an effect of *rouge;* and it is as though one added to, or subtracted from, the Odyssey — the result, anyway, degradation."

"Why does the art of woman degrade *art?*"

"Because it can only have the effect of causing the proportion of low-class work to vastly preponderate over the high: always a great calamity when it occurs in a nation."

"But that surely is not a final answer. For what reason *must* their work be low?"

"Every work of art is a new, self-sure experiment — nothing fundamentally resembling it was yet seen. And this from the very meaning of the word *Art*. That is to say, art is more inventive than the son of Maia, it is more aggressive than war, than piracy. And women are, by structure, non-aggressive, non-inventive."

"That is opinion. You cannot prove it."

"Not opinion as to aggressiveness, surely? but aggressiveness is one element of inventiveness: and a thing cannot exist without all its elements. Nor do I even mean that women are *never* aggressive: for I see daily that they are somewhat so, and Moses would contradict me with one too fearful example: but only that she is not naturally so: that if she step forward alone, she will, by some sure instinct, do it with a certain ataxic *gaucherie,* as when she throws a stone; that her aggression is transgression. Milton makes our general mother plunge her leg into a deepish vacuum by taking a morning walk alone, I think? Makes her, you know, *more* aggressive than our general ancestor, goody Adam; but whereas it is she who hits upon the idea of eating the wrong pulp, it is he who invents right clothes. Not rightly aggressive then, not rightly inventive. And I can prove, at any rate, that to this hour a woman has not invented anything — not even the needle, not the distaff, not the pot. And this, if you look into yourself, you will find that you know *by instinct*. Miriam and 'all the women' went out with timbrels and with dances; but we know that the timbrels were the invention of a man; and, if the dances were very good, then the dances."

"Sappho and her sapphics?"

"Do not refer to that poor lady — she pined for *me,* and I was long in being born; hence these tears and sapphics. I have a fancy (though one knows little of Sappho) that you would hit nearer the mark if you said crude Emily Brontë, or even narcotic Jane Porter. But every savage knows that the world's hardest work, its fighting, and plowing, and prophesying, must be done by men; and *we,* too, know it, and instinctively decide that women lack force to make good premiers: and if premiers, how much more high artists? And *this* last fact also we should know, were it not for a radical misconception in our nineteenth-century minds as to the awful venerableness and difficulty of fine art. If you cannot, however long you try, produce so great a poem, or new-musical-thing-made, as 'Il Penseroso' or 'Lewti,' you may be sure that the reason is that Milton and Coleridge were better premiers than you: for from their very decent flying, you may conclude their admirable running, and their all-surpassing walking. So when I tell you that I cannot spin a top, nor add up figures, I want you to understand that I can spin and add them much better than Lord Tom or Mr. Dick — if I could be persuaded to try. Now this I say of Sappho and her sapphics: that the Almighty has ordained that there shall be one thing *impossible* for a man, possible for a woman: to gestate, to bear; and, in compensation, one thing impossible for a woman, possible for a man: to beget, create; the outward structure, to the very skull-shape, thigh-bone, being, in each case, an expression of the inner. Of course, you may have mental, as you have physical, hermaphrodites; but the characteristic of such a being is not, you know, that it performs *both* the male and female functions equally well; but that, on the whole, it performs *neither* well; being, in truth, a neutrality, or No Thing."

"But —"

"Why, after all, 'but' me? You must know that what I say is true; and if you do not know it, read too-didactic Milton and the rest of them; and if you gashly think that you know better than *He*, then neither will you be persuaded though one rose from the dead."

"But do you not then consider that women should be professional persons, doctors, and the like?"

"That question takes me beyond the sphere of my special knowledge. I am not sure. But does not Mr. Ruskin, who seems to be an expert in ladies, point out that Helen, Circe, etc., were excellent druggists? They did not, indeed, *sell* their knowledge of drugs, for they were genuine ladies, or loaf-*givers*; but if you can once get over your objection to a lady of your family selling herself, I should think that women, with their preternatural powers of observation, quick brains, and infallible little peepy wisdom, might make splendid scientists, and discoverers in science. But she cannot beget a child; she cannot make a new thing."

"But do not women write excellent novels?"

"*You* are right. And the mere fact that *so* many women write *such* excellent novels, should be an indication to a waking *mind* that there is something fearfully and wonderfully wrong with the *novel;* that it is not, in fact, a true art-form; or, in any case, has long since ceased to be novel, or capable of novelty. The idea of presenting a picture of contemporary life in book-shape, though a good historical or scientific *motif*, was not at any time, in my opinion, a good *art-motif* — especially when that contemporary life happened to be the last possibility in the way of hideousness; but, at any rate, the idea once contained this great art-element — that it was *new:* and that this was its chief merit in the eyes of its inventor and his contemporaries is proved by the name 'novel,' which they gave to its product. But when this *motif* had been used for the second, the tenth time? Why then, its only merit had vanished, and with it the thing's reason for existence. And as a matter of fact, so base a century as the eighteenth (for you cannot count *Belphegor* and the like) could not have been expected to produce an art-form at the same time new and good. So that he who would now be both fictionist and fine-artist must revert, like the Norwegian, to the old forms, or begin to cast about him for entirely new forms, or, at least, for characters and incidents of a wholly different kind, very much less lifelike — equally *alive* — very much more artificial, artistic."

"Unlifelike, and yet alive?"

"It is difficult, *because* high; but not, of course, impossible. I know a gentleman who is a great writer. He is well-to-do. He does not publish. But he causes to be made four copies of each of his productions, which he distributes to four friends who form his public. His aim in life is to produce five or six short pieces in prose which shall be in no way inferior to any of the works of God; and, in fact, those of his works which I have seen have all the self-assurance and *heiterkeit*, the coherence and profundity, of works of Nature. (They are inferior, of course, in mere bulk; but bulk is nothing at all: for if the world had been made orange-size, and all else in the universe to correspond, nothing would have been lost.) Now, this is his way: the name of each of his tales is a *place*-name with the word 'At' prefixed — the name of some conceived environment, or say rather, of some imagined world, which is never really *this* world, though it purports to be; nor are his characters really men, though they purport to be. They are more unlifelike than Lear, than Œdipus, and as alive, coherent, as Scott's crude Louis, or Plutarch's younger Cato: that is to say, are *creations* — makings out of *nothing:* words not *wholly* meaningless when applied to the operations of a divinely-gifted human spirit which thinks it not robbery to be equal with God. He is, indeed, a *disciple* of God, and imitates the methods of his Master, but does not copy his *work:* for why, he says, should that which is once done be twice done? As to the execution of his conceptions, everything is artificial, nice; a sentence, a detail, transposed from one piece to another would spoil both; he has no invariable 'style' of his own — and would regard with some contempt a critic who spoke of his 'style' — for each tale is written in a different 'literary manner' (itself sometimes an invention, or else borrowed from some Greek), the manner of all others, best suited to the hue of *that* particular world; nay, one part of one piece is written this way, another that: for here he is concise as a précis-writer, there all ordered flowers and fancies, anon he pretends to be bitingly philosophic, and yonder you find him bawling like hell. And the whole is the complete expression and impression of a new *mood;* that is to say, does what a piece of music does; and is, in fact, a piece of music; apparently as perfect, and certainly as unique, as Mars or Venus, a-singing *their* diverse 'angel-songs.'"

"Another reason."

"You cannot conceive how amusingly fast we all work. Olympus quivers with gay, immortal paunches; the very apes and turkey-cocks stutter merriment."

"The very *apes,* you say —"

"Yes. Agatharcus said: I dispatch my pictures without overtravail. Zeuxis replied: If I boast, it shall be of the long-drawn slowness with which I enter upon mine. The better sort of artist, at that time, not at all considering himself called upon to produce the good (which is easy), but to produce the best (which is nearly impossible)."

"Almost you persuade me."

"Do you remember the meaning of the contemptuous Greek word *autoschediastes?* No? It is a word well worth adoption into English. You should use it in a speech against someone. It means, *'one who speaks or works off-hand; a novice.'* Very well; that is what we are. Not trembling eremite fitters-together of things born and pining for approximation, and choicely culled by winged adventure from the four quarters of the searched universe — but happy-go-lucky ones — persons with notebooks (of all things) — trusters in the god of chance, and in that epidemic of most cheap appreciation which is now working the moral, artistic, and political hurt of Europe — content, and teaching the world contentment, with the approximate, the passable, and everywhere shooting the thin, plenteous excrement of our dysenteric brains — improvisers — naturists, not artists — *autoschediastæ.*"

"How do you prove all —"

"Consider only: almost anyone of our prominent fictionists probably produces more, numbering the words, in a year or two than one of the old fellows in a lifetime; and more in a lifetime than all the Greeks in *their* added lifetimes. The reason *may* be, of course, that we possess vastly more brain-power than they. Do *you* think that is the reason?"

"Ha! ha! ha! no."

"Ha! ha! ha!"

"Ha! ha! ha!"

"He! he! no — I agree with you — that can hardly be the reason."

"It seems alarming."

"It seems like the beginning of the end of something or other."

"But the Greeks wrote mostly rhythm?"

"And is rhythm then so much harder than prose? You cannot mean that. Its flight indeed is somewhat higher, but remember that they are both flight: for if prose be not flight, then what is it at all? and whyever is it written, except for scientific and news-giving purposes? And have you considered in what lies the special difficulty of rhythm? Milton says it must be 'simple, sensuous, and in trouble' (he used the word 'passionate,' but meant in trouble, or *empressé* there being no English 'passion' in the Odyssey, or in Milton's greatest: *P. Regained).* In a late age, however, it must be a fourth thing, as Milton well knew: it must be solemn or usual, or its effect will be a laugh; but it must also be novel, or it will not be art; and it is in the nice conciliation of these two hostile claims that the difficulty of the architectural part of modern poetry seems to lie. Our poets, I must say, appear to me to err on the side of usualness; on the other hand, in the personage Whitman, potentially one of the greatest of poets, but without cultivated intimacy with literature, and so without any notion of the difficulty of fine art in general and the need of solemnity in particular, you have a man aiming at being a music-maker, and succeeding indeed in being poetical or musical, but not in being a poet or maker at all. Now prose, almost freed from this conflict between solemnity, or usualness, and novelty, is yet all the more burdened with the necessity of being novel: and it is easier to be solemn than to be novel. Moreover, the temptation to fly loosely is always greater in prose, and since there is always pain in resisting temptation, that is an added hardship. But however all that be, it seems to me the merest axiom that the sum-total of a nation's art should be small in bulk, small and precious. If it is large, then you have a *proof* that the nation is vulgar; and you have a *cause* of ever accelerated vulgarity.

"Do you and your contemporaries call this voluminous work fine art?"

"I am not sure, but I fancy so. We sometimes even unbosom to the public papers, with exquisite lack of humor and dignity, yet with the darkly mysterious unbendings of hierophants, the precise way in which we do our thaumaturgies. One illustrious, as by some chance I have read, avows that, about to 'invent' a work, he sits crouched over a fire, smoking a pipe, 'for a few hours, thinking *hard;*' rises then, victory sitting on his brow, crying, 'I have done it!' Can fancy frame you a more droll, yet pathetic figure than that poor carle sitting there, unable to answer the question: *why?* yet bent, islanded in smoke, with eye stern, hair revert, mindless, yet thinking *'hard,'* miraculously believing in his light cube-root of a heart that he is doing *'it?' It,* mind you — not something which has been done many times before *ad nauseam,* and which there is not the slightest necessity to do again, if it be not to fill the illustrious man's own unamiable void places. It cannot, you know, be a very light matter to give a new impression to Mr. Gladstone after his eighty years of art-gluttony: yet that is what 'it' has got to do (or have reasonable hopes of doing), or *strictly* speaking, it is an 'idle word,' and has no right to appear in a world already piled with the perfect fine art of ages, from Moses to Tennyson; a world, too, in which land longs (or ought to) for the plower, and leather cries out (or ought to) for the awl of the stitcher.'

"But you are too —"

"Not at all. Sometimes, I am told, a great personage will even fanfare that he is accomplishing more than one undertaking at *the same time.* I have even heard of three together, six. Now, if Pallas and Apollo do not laugh at that, then, like the fool, I am prepared to say that there is *no* Pallas and Apollo. A pregnant ecstatic hen, conceiving the notion that the universe perished for lack of tiny eggs, went gashly cackling her resolve to lay, at her next visitation, not one large egg, but six equivalent small ones — and to do that very thing, or *die!* In the end she did neither. Six putrid spurts, not having any resemblance to small eggs, was the limit assigned by nature to *her* success."

"Did not the six monstra sell?"

"I am pretty certain that they sold. But eggs or books are not successful when they sell, but when God knows that they are very good."

"I am myself flotsam on the current of that opinion. But what, think you, is the root of all this rank blossoming?"

"The *root* is this: the existence of an artist-class who live only or mostly upon the proceeds of their art. I cannot think that in a well-ordered state such an arrangement would be tolerated. At any rate, where, in a crowded age, you have such a class, you get base art."

"Can you prove that?"

"It seems to me so obvious. Men are such, that if you say to a man: 'Do this, and I will give you fame, and a hundred pound *avoir-du-poids,*' he will not do it so well as if you say to him: 'Do this, and I will give you infamy and death; albeit you will benefit your race.' And this I say not of your Newtons, great men, of whom it is obvious, but of common Lord Tom and Mr. Dick, if uncorrupted by bad institutions. I mean that a man *cannot* work divinely well for wages. Precious things must be given away, or sold only for a wreath of wild olives, or something of that sort."

"But I notice you apt to substitute opinion for argument. All that is mere —"

"*Proof* is easy. For when you have a class living by their art, the question arises: Of what kind must my art be, so that I may live *well?*

And the answer is always uniform: It must be voluminous, and such as to give 'pleasure.' The giving of 'pleasure,' then, becomes the chief aim of art. Now, it is *easy* to give 'pleasure,' because men and women are so made, that it is, in general, a positive pain for them to sit still and do absolutely nothing; and into the hand of a person so sitting, if you put a straw, a cigarette, a French novel, a mirror, *anything* that is not hot, it will give 'pleasure.' And if you want certain evidence that much of modern art *has,* in fact, become easy, you have only to consider two things; first, that it is largely photographic, and secondly, that of all trades the photographer's is *by far* the easiest to acquire and practice; whereupon the reason of the 'success' in, say literature, (the second hardest of the arts) of every foolish young woman, crass and unenchanted, who chooses to take pen in hand, will become clear to you. Where, therefore, is such a class, art becomes easy; and I might go on to show that when it is easy it is necessarily base, but this is perhaps so axiomatic from the very constitution of the world that I need not do so. Where, therefore, is such a class, art is, or rapidly becomes, base; and instead of a noble, Rechabite band of artists, eaten up with a holy, self-forgetful zeal for art, and belief in the *possibility* of art, you are apt to get a mere chance rabble of little blind mouths, bitterly stale citizens of Clapham and Monte Video, happy *yahoos,* with hardly more genuine *mother-*wit, *radical* ingenuity, and no more genuine cark for the well-being of mankind, than that other rabble which fills your prisons."

"But by a principle of weeding-out, and survival of the fittest, do you not always get *some* few —"

"Do not repeat that poor old scientific catchword. It is not true. Among individual men, at any rate, the general rule of Nature, so far, seems to be the survival of the unfittest. I cannot understand in what way Paris was fitter than Hector — except 'fit' means 'flexible,' cartilaginous, and so inorganic, base: yet Hector dies, Paris thrives; Jesus dies, Barabbas thrives; Agis, Gracchus, Cato die, Sulla and Newcastle thrive; Chatterton, Poe, Keats, Byron die, and die scornfully, triumphantly; Monsieur Zola and Mr. H. R. Haggard thrive. That is survival of the fittest after a *piquant* fashion, I think?"

"But tell me — how, think you, came that six-work man by his notion that Art is easy? It surely never used to be considered so."

"I cannot even guess. The opinion has somehow arisen. Thackeray, you know, in one of his books says that the painter's business is a *'delightfully easy'* one. In *his* case the superstition, I fancy, arose from the fact that *he* found the *writer's* (and the illustrator's!) craft so unexpectedly easy. Both, however, are hard. On a leaf picked up in the street, I find the following put into the mouth of a primitive artist by Mr. R. Kipling, a well-known writer of this century: 'Take this wisdom for your use, which I learned when deer and moose nightly roared where Paris roars tonight: there are nine and thirty ways of composing tribal lays, *and every single one of them is right!*' Now, this species of raw optimism, as of a man deep in the wine-cup at midnight, lends itself, one must admit, to very genial jingle in the hand of the writer — if only the mind could resist the suspicion that it is meant not at all for jingle, but for *'wisdom'* whereupon it cannot be kept from exclaiming: How! every *single* one of those thirty-nine ways right? Not one wrong? And Mr. Kipling's fortieth, too? and my forty-first? It needs a scribbler of this century to believe it! I, on the other hand, without having seen any of the forty, am bold to say that not one *single* one of those forty-one ways is right — or if one right, then only one — the best way, namely — the canonical way — but probably all wrong; it being understood that that way is wrong in art, which, if different, would be better for its purpose, and only that right, which, if different, would be not so good. So that I say: Not easy! as elephantine old Carlyle has it, but 'hard' — even for the most gifted; the world being so made — so framed and fenced about, — that nothing greatly good shall be smuggled into it, from a healthy child, to a Roman race, to a perfect song, without travail most sore — throe on throe — and 'pangs that wrung me till I *could* have shrieked, but would not.'"

"Is that your own experience?"

"Do not ask. I wish that I could even split dead on the rack of aspiration — but the cold clay, and the 'burning marl' — alternate Eros, and the opium-dream — But for this at least you may give me credit, that until I *do* thole such pangs, I shall never permit myself to be deluded, either by myself or others, into the notion that I have done anything worth two perfect pennies. For this advantage I have over delightfully-easy, four-eyed Thackeray: that I have been to the Mint, and there seen that the pennies, anyway, are the product of brisk thumps, headstrong forces; and I have also stood and watched the grinning teeth of a woman's trouble, and there learned how close a thing is genuine Birth in a world not made of soap-suds and New Suppurations, Humors; but of something else. By all which I only mean to say that what we call Art is either toying and trifling, or it is not: if it is (as Thackeray and Herr Nordau, rare twinity, say and illustrate), then it is a shame that strong, two-handed men should spend their parasite lives in practicing it; if it is not (as Goethe and *his* kind say and illustrate), then it must be very difficult indeed, and a thing to be handled only by consecrated hands."

"But that old Presbyterian idea of being 'called' to a business has now been ousted by the rush of our modern life. You can hardly expect it to survive alone among painters, scribblers and the like?"

"It should, however — because they, surely, and not the bishops, are the oracle of God. If they be silent, indeed, no harm is done, the world being already full of the finest art which *their* inferior work keeps somebody or other from studying: but if they speak and speak basely, of earth, and not of heaven, then much, or all, as they say in France yonder, is, for the moment, base and earthly. But how if you hear one old artist saying to another not so old: Do not 'waste' all your good 'ideas' upon short pieces: be more 'economical' — draw them out, and make *Books* of them! In other words, do not consider, with agony of a thousand doubts, knowing that the history of literature somewhat depends upon your decision, what is the ideally right form of drama, lyric, *conte*, in which to cast your special 'idea' (such as it is — to begin with an 'idea' at all being to begin at the wrong easy end); but consider how you may make most pounds and fame by it; or again, do not serve God in your little attempt at writing; serve Mammon! or lastly, if you insist upon serving God, as most decent people do, then do it not with a single eye to *his* glory, but with a triple eye to your own weighing-machine and soon-dying *éclat* also. There you have that Presbyterian idea in a somewhat astral state, I fancy."

"But have we, then, in your opinion, absolutely no perfect art among us today, except —"

"Do you say *perfect?*"

"Yes."

"Plenty of *that.*"

"Give an example."

"A London penny novelette — most Sunday morning sermons — a novel of Zola — a Sardou or Adelphi melodrama — many advertisements —"

"You surprise me! Can you really mean that these productions are art-works as near perfection as the *Odyssey* or *Œdipus Coloneus?*"

"Nearer perhaps. You must not suppose, because it is *easy* to write such, that this has any the least relation to their claim to be called either art or the perfection of art. It was not, for instant, *difficult* to make a scarecrow, which, you know, is perfect art."

"What, then, is your test of perfection?"

"Have you not observed some poor citizen's advertisement of '*pink* pills for *pale* people?' That, if it was deliberate, and not merely a 'happy thought,' is perfect art. (Notice the suasiveness, *epieikeia*, then the contrast, then the alliteration, and the combination of these.) Here you have nicest adaptation, fitting-together, between an object and the eyes that see it; in other words, you have an object producing in a high degree the very effect it was intended to produce upon the very minds intended. If upon me and you these things produce no effect but one of seasickness, remember that they were not made for me and you. Servant-girls really *weep* — with the genuine *art-frenzy* — over the novelette; country-defenders blubber and roar at the melodrama. If, then, they are art at all, I say their perfection is more emphatic and definite than that of Œdipus."

"You say, '*if* they are art at all.'"

"I only mean that I am not quite sure whether the 'contrivance' — as, for example, the aristocratization of the characters in the novelette — is ever *now* sufficiently in the nature of a *novel* contrivance on the part of the writer to admit of the label 'art.' It certainly *once* was. Loosely speaking, they may still be called art. They are about as novel as Dickens."

"But it seems to me — do you not make art nothing more than mere artfulness directed toward a mind?"

"Quite so — nothing more. It never was anything more. Only, I hope you do not imagine that there is any higher thing possible to man, or angel, or final God, than this 'mere artfulness.' By mere artfulness was the earth seated, and, lo, He fastened the Heavens with Artfulness. Venerable is it to me, even when tellingly exhibited on the low plane of the common thief — and so, too, you remember, it was to the Greek. For mere artfulness, and ever more of it, till I tingle musical with it, rises day and night my prayer to Hermes."

"I take it, then, from what you have now said, that the production of genuine and perfect, though gross, art, may be a commonplace everyday affair?"

"Yes — except in the two highest branches of art, which, when genuine and serious, are never gross."

"Which is the highest?"

"Music."

"Why so?"

"Because it habits the highest æthers."

"That is vague."

"Because, of the three factors, observation, fancy, imagination, it does not employ the lowest. It is fanciful or imaginative. Its production has no relation to what is called 'life' (that is to say, to existing phenomena), except only to the existing nature of the mind which it influences."

"And am I to understand that in proportion as the other branches of art cease to be observational — that is, to be in close relation with actual 'life' — in that proportion they rise to the height of the highest, or music?"

"You are shrewd. That is just so."

"The art of music, then, you say, is of two kinds — fanciful or imaginative."

"I did not say the art of music."

"What did you say?"

"Music."

"Explain yourself."

"Think of Gounod's Serenade, and the Symphony in B Flat. If at first both seem to you like the *alalahs* of archangels, afterwards you *feel* a difference. One I call the highest imagination disporting itself in the highest element; the other I call fancy. One art; the other not. You cannot mean that painful Beethoven was not an artist?"

"I do mean something like that. The Pythoness, delirious with the waters of Cassotis, was not called by the Greeks an artist. Though her doomings rived her with hell-agonies, yet was she not an artist. Beethoven was a seer — drunk with God. A man who forgets his own name and address is not an artist, but a seraph. Inspiration is, of course, not art. Art is successful aspiration, right reasoning."

"Which is the highest: this inspired fancy, or the imagination of Gounod?"

"They are both infinitely, and therefore equally, dvine. One I call the working of Nature; one of Art. Turner, you know, was not less sublime than the sunset; Hugo than the hurricane. A tall man — on tiptoe — may be near the summit of God."

"You spoke of the *two* highest branches of art: which is the next highest?"

"The invention of new dances, times, measures, rhythms."

"Not a very prosperous art today, I think?"

"No. It is in abeyance. It dies at an iron age, as a ditty in the lanced throat. It lately found a fitting winding-sheet in the draperies of the 'serpentine' lime-lit cloud-compeller. It will reappear: and, I think, flourish above all others with the serious advent of a more social society."

"The next highest."

"Literature."

"Proceed."

"Then architecture, house-decoration, and landscape-disposition."

"Persist."

"Then drawing."

"My ear is holy."

"Painting."

"My ear is a watering mouth for the tit-bits of utterance."

"Sculpture."
"I lust."
"Play-acting."
"I pine."
"Dancing."
"My ear is Mahlström!
"Flirting."
"My body bursts into blossom with ears!"
"Piano-strumming, fiddling, singing, dress, cookery, jugglery, etc."
"But! – *what of Oratory?*"
"Forgive me for seeming to forget you."
"For seeming?"
"I only seemed. Oratory is a grosser literature, its pen flabby, its eye haliotoid. When at its best, its ultimate effects generally consist in the muscular actions of blowing the nose, or clapping the hands. Yet great, as you well know, is its power. So goody Cicero made Cæsar change a lachrymose mind."

"But state-craft is surely an art?"
"When its effects are directly mental, and are intended to be what they prove. It then comes under the head of flirting or jugglery; as does war, swindling,* etc."

"You include acting. Has that not been called into question?"
"Only by persons who have forgotten, or never knew, what art is."
"Prove your position."
"The mere fact that the same drama performed by two different companies will produce, *not* different effects indeed, but different intensities and tones of the same effect, should be sufficient to show that the actor has room for 'elaborate new contrivance,' and so may be an artist."

"The general effect is never, then, a new effect of the actor's own?"
"No."
"His is therefore a gross art."
"That, at least, goes without saying. He is fettered on every hand to the already existing facts of 'life': to the written play, the appropriate costume, the whole properties and paraphernalia of the stage. His work *must* be more or less 'observational.' It can never be so imaginative as to be *musical.*"

"Yet the acted drama undoubtedly produces 'fine' effects."

---

* It is, of course, highly illustrative of the Greek radical view of Art that Hermes, the first of artists, was also the prince of swindlers. There is also an Altheof (All-thief!) in Scandinavian mythology: but I do not know what his significance was. There may be some significance, however, in the fact that Jubal-Cain was the grandson of Cain, the inventor of sudden death in other people.

"They are, in every case, the effects of the play-architect; not of the play-actor."

"You are sure of that?"

"I could give you a hundred reasons why it must be so, if I had time. If you, a cultured person, read *Œdipus* or *Sardanapalus*, and then see it acted, this is what will happen to you: the work will enormously gain in vividness, but somewhat *lose* in ethereal fineness of effect. If you see *A Winter's Tale*, you weep more, laugh more — but sigh less, smile less. For this *loss* of musicalness the corporeal actor is responsible. So far is his art from being 'fine.'"

"You speak of his work being *more or less* observational."

"I only mean that he need not be a mere lens for photographing life, if original-minded: that the stage does afford him scope — though little — for doing something higher than holding a mirror up to nature; and that in proportion as he faithfully holds this mirror, so his art becomes more and more gross, if more and more vivid. When he holds it to perfection, he ceases, of course, to be an artist, and the dramatist is all in all."

"That is hardly Shakespeare's view."

"Powerful, uneducated people sometimes feel grandly, but never think exactly. Now, Shakespeare, rude-thinking, and not himself an artist, might be depended upon to go wrong on the theory of such a subject (just as he might be depended upon to go instinctively right in the practice of it). That he differed from me may therefore be taken as a rough proof that I am right. A mirror-holder is not an artist, but a mirror-holder. A blue-book is not an artwork."

"You ban boldly."

"Not boldly. Whoever supposes him an artist must have strange notions of word-meanings. Words, of course, *have* fixed meanings, which no amount of loose talk can alter. Will did not think that of himself. The nightingale is not an artist. Art is self-conscious; Will was luxuriously self-unconscious. He was a jolly, many-gifted fellow, full of high musics and instincts; resembling Beethoven. Goethe has partly shown how an artist would have constructed *Hamlet*. What Will showed was his real divinity in coasting, with sails filled by the voluntary afflatus of the heavens, so tremulously near the ideal artistic, *without* the careful oars of art."

"The *danseuse*, too, you make a gross artist."

"As genuine as the actor; but grosser; and gross for the same reasons."

"The daughter of Herodias, dancing, did so exalt the mind of Herod, that she seduced him to the sublimity of an oath. She, surely, was a fine artist?"

"Yes — if she invented her own dance. So is the wise actor if he writes his own fine drama; or the wise violinist if he writes his own fine music. If, on the contrary, her synthesis of motion was the invention of another, then what she really did was this: by her wise and novel presentment of the inventor's thought, she so incited an animal animation in the spectator — not a novel *effect*, you observe, but one already well known to Herod — that she thus became the means, in the end, of laying his whole being with the ethereal, and infinite, and novel effect intended by the inventor — an effect which culminated in the outburst of the oath."

"You are *very* prolix. Suppose the dance was impromptu?"

"In that case there was no 'deliberate contrivance,' and no art, gross or fine. The sylphs and the graces are not artists."

"I now clearly know all you think about art?"

"You know little that I think. You gather shells on the seashore." "I know something: I know that you make your living by gross art and fine art: and what these are. How else?"

"I 'invent' things."

"What?"

"Puzzles, toys, and witty articles."

"What have you thereby gained?"

"Fifteen shillings."

"What have you spent on patents, etc?"

"Forty-five pounds."

"You have lost then?"

"You are a budget-man: the problem is not insoluble to meditation."

"What else?"

"I prosecute people civilly."

"Proceed."

"I pawn Paphian pipes — for the sake of the alliteration."

"Persist."

"I act as shorthand writer and messenger-boy to myself; receiving a weekly stipend from myself."

"Are you regularly paid?"

"Payments are in arrear."

"You do not prosecute yourself civilly?"

"To prosecute Vacuity is to plunge into the Infinite: I am willing, but gravitation restrains me."

"What else?"

"I write magazine simplicities."

"Your words are honeybees; my ear their waxy cell."

"I keep a staff of rich wedded sisters."

"My ear resembles them, for like a staff, it understands you."
"I milk a maiden aunt."
"That is impossible."
"She yields a catarrh: I milk her 'through the nose.'"
"Proceed."
"I beg."
"Persist."
"I borrow."
"You do not steal?"
"I have stolen."
"How often?"
"Thrice."
"How much?"
"Two cigars, and a threepenny bit."
"What for?"
"The cigars to smoke; the bit to buy a war-ship."
"Who were your victims?"
"My father as to the cigars; my mother as to the bit."
"You were young."
"No. I was six."
"You speak willingly of children. You are fond of them?"
"I am myself a child. Everything that is simplex and azure I love."
"What else?"
"A sick dog."
"Proceed."
"The solitude of a grey cave by the seashore."
"My ear is a harbor-basin for the fleets of Yourmouth."
"A tall ship, nothing but a wide-winged whiteness: and, as the blue-eyed beck and nod elusive so she, lenient, trips and fawns and curtsies to the offing-breeze."
"You delight in the salt-water?"
"My father was a ship-owner. We dwelt on the summit of an island. He went often down from us. Nothing restrained him to the land. When he rarely returned, we said: He is come! One meeting another a-crag or a-field, said: How droll! he is here and you did not know it. Simple he was, sensuous too, passionate enough. Ocean heaved and billowed in his brain. If it lightened, he was sublime. If thunder cracked brittling through the heaven of heavens, battle-joy it was to drink the rich brool of his challenging cry. God was his turbulent friend. The full hurricane made him Prometheus."
"He is dead?"
"Yes — he fell a victim to the choragic exigencies of heaven."

"You love what else?"
"Anything that is drowning."
"Proceed."
"A young virgin."
"Persist."
"An old man."
"These above all?"
"Yes."
"Why so?"
"A young virgin, unlike the grown woman, or the boy, is quite whole and untarnished. An old man wonderfully knows. He has seen man and God. Do not suppose that tsar or shah is half so reverend as he. He is on the brink of promotion in the ranks of being. Much is not secret to him."
"You have known some?"
"I knew one. She was six. She came to my bedside in the early morning, bearing a message of illness. I had not seen her before. She stood, winter-gloved, wonderfully stout and neat. I said: *Who* are you? She replied: A little girl. I said: Where lurks the cabala of your surety? Her hung head simpered infinite things."
"You smiled?"
"I comprehended the world."
"Another."
"I knew another. He was ninety-five. Every Tuesday he received two shillings from the 'Parish.' He said: Is this relief-day? I replied: No — it is Saturday. He said: Well, really, I don't know *how* the Time is going; and spread his hands."
"You smiled?"
"I groveled and kissed his feet."
"He is dead?"
"They took him away to the workhouse: the same day he died."
"You wept?"
"I laughed."
"Another."
"Another translated Horace at eighty-six."
"That was great."
"It was *sweet*. It had upon me the effect of perfect fine art."
"What, the translation?"
"No: the translation was even poorer than the original so often is; but the knowledge that he translated."
"Another."
"Another — but time wears."

"Will you go?"
"I must go."
"I like you."
"You love me."
"You are Celtic, yet Greek; you are proud, yet meek; you are human, yet unique."
"Therein have you kneaded what is rare: a dough of both rhyme and reason.
"What sins do you commit?"
"No sins."
"You are perfect?"
"Yes. I may have coveted a neighbor's wife, or daughter, or maid-servant."
"But for that you would be perfect?"
"I am perfect in spite of that! The under-will is crystal! Argon is not so negative and simple. Strike me, and your tympanum shall tingle you testimony of a flawless gold. If I do a wrong, Jove reconsiders himself: he says: Well, the thing was right after all, for *he*, the poet, in his purity, has *done it*. Every time I find myself, and man, Well Makered."
"Well, I say that I like you."
"If you do not love me, it is that you do not understand me."
"You shall be my private secretary."
"The post is filled."
"The filler shall *filer.*"
"I dread his fillips."
"What sort of fillips?"
"His lipic fillips."
"Define 'lipic fillip.'"
"A Philippic."
"But you accept?"
"I am unused to steady labor."
"To what are you used?"
"Like Cato and Epictetus I permit myself to grow wedded to nothing — least of all to steady labor."
"The work shall be made erratic."
"I may nibble at it."
"You shall! You shall banquet at my table! You shall wed my daughter, Florrie!"
"I have said that, like Cato and Epictetus, I permit myself to grow wedded to nothing — least of all to steady —"
"Yet to my daughter, Florrie, shall you grow wedded!"
"Is she lovely?"

"She resembles me."
"Well — but how old is Florrie?"
"Seventeen."
"That is too old for me."
"You shall have Alexandrovna."
"How old?"
"Fifteen."
"Let the nuptials be hastened, then. Farewell."
"But you will come tomorrow?"
"I cannot subsist on cream of pomegranate. I must go write simplicities for my living: must work. I am not in the Cabinet."
"Do we not work in the Cabinet?"
"You perorate."
"We work."
"You attitudinize."
"We work!"
"You strut!"
"But you will come?"
"I may."
"Yes! Then shall we contemplate sherbet and Mocha, and rosily smoke upon vague discourse."
"Farewell, then!"
"Adieu!"
"*Salaam!*"*

---

* Note. — It is perhaps unnecessary to add, for the sake of Lord X———'s well-established reputation as a *connoisseur,* that all the details of this matter, except the mere personality and photograph of my friend, are *altogether* imaginary, or rather, not to give big adjectives to little things, nothing more, as Mr. Phipps himself would say, than the adventure-luck (or the adventure-bad-luck, surely) of my own touring soul.

Tulsah

Translation of a Scorched Hindu MS.

Most wonderful, I often think, must have been the dower of vitality originally vouchsafed me. The passage of one hundred and twenty years has not availed to bleach a single hair of these raven masses. My memory is still, as it was, almost more than that of men. Undimmed is my eye. Yet the end is surely near. A hundred and twenty was the age at which the great Boodh, prince of Oude, passed into unending muckut; at such age, too, died he whom they called my father, and, they say, *his* father also; and, for what I know — but such speculations are frivolous.

It is singular that none of my subjects ever heard of, or even suspected, the undoubted connection which exists between Boodh and my race. He was one of its sons, and one of its fathers. Here in the profundity and gloom of this subterrene, I now for the first time in modern days commit this tremendous secret to parchment.

I have spoken of my memory: yet on one side at least the tree is bare of blossom or leaf. All my first youth has passed from me as completely as though I never *had* a first youth. Many and many are the days which I have spent, unconscious of the universe, rapt in contemplation of this mystery. But no intensest effort could bring one ray of remembrance. I can recall, indeed, the circumstance of my awaking to self-knowledge; but as to all that preceded it, there is the blackness of darkness. In a chamber hollowed out of the face of the natural rock I opened my eyes. I lay on my back in a coffin of red stone. A reddish cloth, studded with jewels, enwrapped my body, but the convolutions extended far below my feet, as though the swaddling had been intended for one of much greater stature than I. The coffin itself was large enough to contain the body of a man. Long I lay, first in listless dream, then with the burgeoning consciousness of entity. I rose from the coffin; I cast off the cerements; I crawled from the chamber of rock. I looked at my limbs, the limbs of a well-grown boy, and saw that they were perfect, and withy, and beautifully brown. I could have exclaimed at all the marvel and delight. But the lion's voice broke upon my ear. I at once felt terror, understanding him an enemy. The sun was setting. I was in the midst of the jungle of the unfathomable forest.

I passed during the night through the million-fold life of the wild. I exulted when I eluded the mad elephant and the prowling tiger-cat by the sinuousness of my limbs; I looked without fear upon the ape and the untamed zebu; but when I saw the *serpent* — heinously leprous — then hatred and loathing thrilled me, and I climbed, breathless in panic, to the branches of a tree.

With the light of the morning I came, on the edge of the forest, to a stately town, full of aerie edifices, traceried light as vision; it lay in a valley enclosed by a circle of high blue mountains, down which brawled many a rill; the whole mirrored in an oval lake which nearly occupied the rest of the valley. It was at this sight that, so far as I can now remember, the conception of *Time* first arose in my brain: I went back æon upon æon, and connected this city with memories, penumbral but real, and old, it seemed, as the world. The town is situated in the center of Hindustan, is exceedingly ancient, a kingdom by itself, unvisited.

An aged priest met me on the outskirts. He looked with a quick intentness upon my face, and spoke some words to me. I did not understand, nor could I answer him. He led me to the temple where he ministered, and for three years concealed me in its recesses from the eyes of all. At the end of this time he made me lead him to the chamber of rock, and commanded me to point out the coffin in which I had opened my eyes. This satisfied him fully: it was the coffin of the maharajah of the city, who, he told me, had died a year before my awaking. The maharajah was then very old; he had acquired, it was said, the sum of human wisdom. His people had, by his own explicit directions, instead of burning the body, laid it to its rest in the sarcophagus, at the spot where conscious life, as far as I could recollect, was first born within me. Adjeebah, the Brahmin *guru* who had instructed me, announced me as the son, hidden by him till then, of the dead rajah. None could doubt it: to doubt would have been the insanity of unbelief: I was the living likeness of the dead! A day came when I mounted the throne of the palace as sovereign of Lovanah amid the acclamations of the people.

Among the first things I learned was that all my ancestors had been known and reverenced during life as men who had attained the holy calm of yug; that a long tradition had handed it down that, without exception, they had left the cares of durbar (or state) to their ministers, in order to muse in the interior palace upon the deep things of wisdom.

The same instinct rose spontaneously and irresistibly within me. I became a species of Yati, resolving to search out knowledge and the nature of things, if so be I might arrive at the comprehension of the ultimate mystery. The years fled rapidly. Many languages I learned; the wisdom of the Hellenes; the zoomorphism of the Egyptians; the heights of the pyramids of Chufu and Shafra. In intense meditations passed my leaden days. I read in the Hebrew scroll of that Melchisedec, King of Salem, priest of the Most High God, without father, without mother, having neither beginning of days minor-end of life. I learned how Boodh, too, who was of my kin, was delivered of his mother Maia in a manner most marvelous. I was convulsed at the thrilling secrets of the world; my tongue shuddered, my eye rolled, in ecstasy on ecstasy. I tracked the vanity and sublimity of Man to their hiding place; I sought out the meanings of religions, whence they come, whither they go.

I lighted, many years after my accession to the kingdom, upon a document, deep among the moldering archives, and yellow with the accumulation of ages. Having read it, I swooned upon the agate floor, and lay through the long day and night as dead. It was a narrative inscribed on biblion, and by it I learned the dark fate which befell the first of my race. He was called Obal, and went out from his home a century before ever that Abram, from whom the Hebrews sprang as the sands of the sea, had yet departed out of Haran. The object of his pilgrimage was to know wisdom, and learn the modes of men. He traveled onward till he reached Hur of the Chaldees, one of the first cities built by the hand of the mason and the smith. It was in Mesopotamia, which was called Naharaïm. Here dwelled the votaries of that Zabaism from which is derived the Parsee hierology. The doctrine has its origins deep in the roots of the universe. Loosely allied to it is phallic, and — very much more intimately — serpent, worship: for, inasmuch as the mist of constellations in the farthest heaven assumes the form of a *serpent* in its uneasy writhings, here have we a connection — profound enough, terrible enough — between Flame and the Serpent; and since Flame is torture, so is the Serpent the fit emblem of Hell. Hence the wisdom of the Hebrew serpent-myth of the temptation and fall of man; and hence, too, came it, that the Zabians, worshipping in the first instance the heavenly hosts of fire, were also worshippers of the snaky uncleanness. At Hur the heart of Obah was seduced by the specious beauty of Star and Moon: he became a devotee to the fire and the serpent. For many years he lived there a life of study and peace; not till he was a very old man did the consummation of Fate overtake him. In a forecourt of a temple of Ashtoreth he saw a maiden priestess whose loveliness kindled his sere heart. Her name was Tamar. She was vowed to chastity. How foul the crime to draw her from the service of the Goddess Obal knew. But he seems to have been a man of daring eye and headlong lust. He found occasion to speak with the maiden; the abomination of love became mutual between them; he wedded her. Had he not been a great man in Hur, he, with the apostate woman, would without doubt have been stoned to death. But they lived — so long, and so securely — that it seemed as though the heavens were oblivious of the sacrilege. At last Tamar died. Obal was full of years. On the night preceding her journey to the tomb, the patriarch slept by her side — for the last time — on the couch of ivory where she stiffly lay. He slept. In the morning his eunuchs, coming to the chamber, found him dead. His face, his staring eyes, were black with imprisoned blood. Around his throat had coiled itself a serpent, red of color, as though a flame perfused its veins. The body of Tamar was not seen.

I have said that I swooned upon the floor, and lay as dead. This was singular, for I had so far traveled upon the road of knowledge as to be aware of the ancientness and universality of superstition, manifesting itself always by a certain historical metabolism. The tendency of my mind was indeed toward the exact. While the Jookaja believes that nothing exists but knowledge, things being only the forms thereof; and the Medheemuck that both knowledge and things, are *sun,* or cipher, and the All itself but a visionary vesture half concealing the eternal Glare; I, admitting the seemliness of these syntheses of dogma, must say that my own mental trend was the other way, toward a full belief in matter, and the truthfulness of the senses. I was therefore more and more inclined to assert that no impression of life is explicable save by facts in their essence "natural." *And yet* this unauthenticated tale of the old and vanished world rent my soul, "like a veil," in twain. Let me not attempt to explain this mystery. Here is a secret too dark — too dark — for speech. The nations of the far West blab of a Deity who travails and travails and travails forever — just as though the bursting brain of a man could realize that thought and live! The yellow Brahmin, on the other hand, shaves his head, and with light heart full of craft, discusses a lazy Brimmah, omniscient, but clothed in inertia as in a mantle. I will say nothing. It is a subject *full* of fear. In the one doctrine at least is safety: in the other — could it be realized — is the frenzy eternal. Let me not therefore be understood to maintain this other: for who would believe if I say that *memory* was the secret of the effect which the tale of Obal wrought upon me? Would I not sputter the babblings of a maniac, did I assert that — vaguely, but really — afar off, but with no dubiety — I remembered — from beginning to end — ah! but at *this* mystery let silence cover with her hand the mouth of rashness!

I now set myself diligently to the study of the race of kings who had reigned since the beginnings of the over Lovanah. The facts which confronted me were startling. It was then that I first learned that the Boodh, who, like Obal, had left his home mad with the passion for wisdom, was of us. Of fifty kings in the direct line I found that all had lived to ages far beyond the ordinary span of human life; that more than half had taken as wives, not Hindus, but believers in the Zend-Avesta, followers of Zoroaster, *fire-worshippers;* that at least ten had deserted their kingdom, and wandered far over Asia — in obscurity, poor — hounded by the criminal lust of our race for the *cabala* of knowledge; that at least twenty-five — among them my own predecessor — had met their death by the stings of venomous serpents; that all of them had married; and that the death of not one of them had preceded in order of time the death of his consort.

It was when I had understood the sinister meaning of these things that, in the dim chamber which I had made my abode, I fell upon my face to the ground, and swore in my heart three oaths, to which I called every power of the Universe to witness; I would moderate, and, if necessary, quench, the zeal to know which inflamed me; I would never for any purpose wander abroad from the land, from the house in which I then found myself; no daughter of man would I ever espouse. This I swore, and thus did I resolve to break in my person the continuity of that destiny which hunted my race.

I called to my presence my *dewan* and two other ministers of state, and ordered them to publish abroad a proclamation offering a reward of ten rupees of silver to the slayer of every serpent within my dominion.

"Your father published the identical proclamation," answered the chief minister.

I started.

"And," said another, "its only visible result was an enormous increase in the number of serpents in the district."

"An increase," added the third, "which was above all conspicuous in the multiplication of an unknown species, distinguished by its very remarkable color, and extreme rancor."

These announcements did not fail to have their full effect upon me. I had then arrived at the age of perhaps fifty. From thenceforth I shut myself from mankind with even greaten-persistency than ever, and to lull into quiescence my too restive brain, I now abandoned my body to the delight of the lotus pipe, and the peace of the sleepy *bhang.* As the Jain, tangled in a mesh of religious frivolities, never slaying a living thing, seeks by strong crying to Parswanath, and the practice of self-torment, to enter forcibly into *nirvana;* so I, by another and a broader gate, entered the *nirvana* of vision. Thirty years passed over me as a watch in the night, opaline with vague prismic hues. I was a confirmed hermit: in a year hardly two of my servants saw my face: the active memory of me passed from men. I still studied — sought — thought — but over the intensity of research was shed the appeasing glamour of the long, long, trance, the hyperborean dream.

I walked one night in an out-court of the palace, and admired that "crooked serpent" which trails in everlasting length athwart the heaven. It was the first time for many years that I had passed from the gloom of my chamber. I was alone. The sound of voices in a neighboring field reached my ear. I walked pensive toward a gate, and chanced to see a concourse of people standing some little distance away. Long it was since I had mingled with my fellow: I walked quietly toward the crowd, and saw it grouped round a funeral-pile, on which lay stretched the body of a man. It was a *suttee*. In their midst stood a very young woman — most godlike tall — surpassing lovely — delirious with opiates; her body perfumed; her head sprinkled with sandal-powder; the wife of the dead maim, who had devoted herself to the flames which were to consume him. Tulsah! — dame of my life — sovereign mistress of my destiny — Tulsah! then first, under the moon, did my eye light upon that serpentine form, that iridescent grace! I beheld how with wavy ease she ascended the pyre — the imponderable limbs of spirit composed themselves beside the shape of the dead — her eyes closed; from a corner of the resinous pile I saw the red flame dart upward, upward! Already I was aged — but strong too, and lithe: I dashed forward — with victorious energy I tore her from the lick of the tongues of the fire, and to the murmuring mob I cried aloud:

"Back, fools — I am the Maharajah!"

I know not what extremity of change now accomplished itself within me. My disenchained spirit danced and danced in the ecstasy of a new youth. True, I had vowed — I had vowed. But Tulsah had that dear quality of the eyes to which the Greek artists gave the name το υγρον, 'liquidity.' This impression they produced in their statues by a slight raising of the underlid. Man is folly itself. Let this one fact only be considered: those same Greeks believed that they alone of the nations possessed the thing they called *philosophia* — the love of the subtleties of wisdom; and even while they were thus believing, the Vedic Hymns had been sung; the Brahmin had codified the intricate activities of the Attributes Sut, Raj, and Tum; and the Boodh had denied that Brahma, Vishnu, and Mahadeva were emanations of the Spirit of God. Such is the inborn vanity and shallowness of man.

And I, too, was vain and shallow! My oath I flung to the winds. The passions of a youth, intensified a million-fold, pulsated within my bosom. My zenana, so long tenantless, at last received an inmate — and her name was Tulsah!

Little cared I for the prejudices — deep, religious, though they were — of my uncultured people, who declared that I had robbed her from the dead. I loved to recline through the sluggish hours by her side, and watch the ichor that swelled and swelled her veins. Surely her skin was not the skin of the Hindus: but I cannot remember that I ever definitely learned her origin. I know only that Tulsah adored me. We passed our lives together in the twilight of a perfect and happy solitude; and never did I surfeit of her ethereal presence, or tire of gazing upon the strangely delicate streaks of reddish hue which mingled with her jet-black hair, or upon the torpidly-indolent and sinuous movements of her exquisitely soft, and supple, and undulating form.

In an evil hour one day, when, heavy with opiates, I lay in waking trance, by her side I revealed to her the history of the tragedy of the patriarch Obal.

She listened to the whole with agitation, with heaving bosom, and an intense alertness for which I could not account.

"He seduced her," she said after a long time, speaking bitingly, and gazing afar — "he seduced her from her devotion to the heavenly hosts —"

"Aye! — Tulsah! — he snatched her from her ministry upon the eternal flames —"

"And you —"

"I, my Tulsah? *I! I!*"

"Yes — you — *you* snatched me, a devotee to the flames, from the very flames themselves —" I folded her panting to my lean bosom.

"Angel! angel!" I shrieked, "yet does the Power not live whose craft could prevail to change thy dear perfection into the viper's tooth!"

In such manner we spent our life. The years multiplied themselves and passed. Tulsah approached the borders of age. Her beauty waned — markedly waned. As she grew older the sinuosity of her muscular and osseous systems became, I must say it, too pronounced to be longer fascinating. A singular affection of the skin covered her body with a multitude of regularly-shaped small dull-red erythemata. Her eyes reddened, uttering a rheumy mucus. I looked for the whitening of her hair. My disappointment was bitter. The heavy surges which, once black, billowed like a torrent to her feet, and wide overflowed the floor like the surf of a sea of ink, gradually at first — then rapidly — took on the gorgeous, and the *farouche,* and the unhuman semblance of a mantle of vivid flame.

She died. With my own hand I swaddled her corpse, and helped to place it upon the pyre. Death among our Eastern nations is surely never a comely sight: yet it was with sorrow rather than with loathing that I looked for the last time upon the wan face of my Tulsah.

We were alone together in a court of the palace. The fulsome gloat of moon and stars shone over and about us. I held a torch to the pile: a sheet of flame shot up, crackling, around the beloved sacrifice.

To this day I know not how it was: either the fire consumed its victim with a rapidity inconceivable, or a suspension of consciousness, due to the anodynes which I had that day freely imbibed, deprived me of sight: but from the moment when I applied the torch to the moment when I again looked at the pile was an interval which seemed so short as to be inappreciable; and yet within it, in sharp disproof of my estimate of its length, both the pyre and its occupant had passed, utterly consumed, from before my eyes.

I stood amazed, gazing at the column of blue smoke which rolled up from the very small heap of ashes into the air: and now a new impression — born perhaps of my own fantasy — or born of the despotism of drugs — or born of the more dread despotism of reality — an impression this the of absolute terror — forced itself upon my mind. I beheld, or thought so — the blue of the ascending reek turn to the sanguine hue of Sardius; and now with a spasmodic jerk the whole high and solid pillar of the reddened smoke split itself into innumerable dismemberment; and I saw every wreath, and curl, and tortured tendril stand apart in definite isolation, and shape itself into a changing snaky form, till the whole vast nest, coalescing, writhed together in infinite implication, with hollow eye, and extruded fang.

Aghast at the illusion, I hurried from the spot. I entered the palace. Through a secret corridor I passed to the chamber where Tulsah and I had spent the years of our love. A light shed itself from a vessel of oil in the ceiling. I sank doddering to a seat, and covered my face. Hours went by, and still I sat. All the past was around me — she herself. How like a dream the whole mystery of her coming, her abiding, her going! Tulsah! — I groaned her name. I lifted up my voice weeping. "Where now remote in some green sanctity of ocean cave or azure fold of space broods thy ethereal presence?" I rose to throw my despairs upon the couch where she had been wont to lie, when, in the gloom, I saw — within the palsy of horror saw — coiled thick upon the bed, with gorge erect above a foul vast base of clotted wreaths, and palpitant through all its mucous swelth, the fat and lazar loathliness of a monstrous Snake, whose ruby eyes regarded me.

I ran from the palace! A secret portal led me to the borders of the forest. Here I came upon the traces of a highway, the windings of which I followed. The rising sun of the next day found me still fugitive — hasting in wildest panic — already many a mile from the towers of Lovanah.

I had thus broken the second of my vows, which bound me to my home. It was not till long afterwards that this thought occurred to me. But there remained the third: never, by my own seeking, to penetrate the ultimate secret of the world: and by this I have faithfully abided.

*T*en years passed and left me, as they found me, vagabond over India. I journeyed from city to city, meditating on the manners of men, and begging my bread from the charitable. I have wandered in the streets of that Benares to which Boodh first retired from the world; I have stood beneath the great granite mosque of Jumna Musjid at Delhi; and through all the cities of the north I have passed.

But my pilgrimage was very far from purposeless. I sought with intense scrupulousness — as for hid treasures — after something. I hoped to find a retreat in which, with absolute security from the designs of destiny, I might lay me down, and die the natural death of the rest of men.

I came at last, in the vale of Cashmere, to a lonely Hindu temple — one of the great vihâras — consisting of a long oblong chamber. The roof was supported by two rows of huge stone pillars connected by vaulted architraves, and at the farthest end, semicircular in shape, stood a colossus of the seated Boodh. The temple had been chiseled out of the base of the Himalaya.

Through a burning lamp hung from a pillar, the sanctuary seemed deserted. I entered, and passed up the broad central nave. At the extremity, near the statue, where the vihâra might be expected to end, I happened to find an open door. I walked through it, and descended a long stairway which brought me to a second temple; all was now the intensity of darkness; but happening to meet with another door-way, I descended still farther — down and down — until, in this way, I had traversed six stair-ways of equal descent. I must by this time have traveled a very considerable distance both into the interior of the mountain and the depths of the earth.

Yet another series of steps, and I came to a passage, at the end of which was a circular apartment: here was clearly the termination of this great excavation. From its roof hung a lamp which distilled a vermilion light. I could see from the appearance of the chamber that it had been unvisited perhaps for ages, and I was unable to conjecture by what means the lamp was kept alive, except it were by means of feeding pipes from the far outermost temple of all; but, at any rate, it showed me that the key-contrivance of the door of the chamber was *on the outside.* With the deliberate purpose of there ending my days, I passed into the apartment, and pulled the door toward me. I heard with joy the click of the fastening which sealed my fate.

In the room is a small stone table and a stool. I had brought with me parchment, and the materials for writing. This history, as far as it has now gone, has by these means been recorded. I shall leave it to molder beside my bones. As the half-pleasurable pangs of hunger, and the languor of coming disease, invade my body, I may add yet a phrase or two.

I have now observed that this chamber is not of stone, as far at least as its interior lining is concerned. It is certainly extraordinary; but there can be no doubt that the flooring and ceiling are of wood, and that the circular sides are of old iron-plate paneled at regular intervals with narrow wooden laminæ. The faintness of the lamp's scarlet glow doubtless prevented me from noticing this singularity from the first.

I have brought with me a quantity of opium. On the lap of an ocean of rainbows will I embark when the great hour comes.

*T*he opium works well in stanching the current of the blood, and in overdriving the spent heart to its final throbbings. It will thus quicken the action of the hunger. The past five or six hours I have spent in a coma full of luxuriousness.

*S*pare me! Spare me! frail man that I am! This chamber, in which — with my own hand — I have imprisoned myself, *is the nethermost hell itself!* Happening to rise from my seat, I saw — in the shadow thrown by the table — a sight! the skeleton of a man; having a burned appearance; old as the mountain; dismembered now in the lower limbs, the ribs in fragments; but the cervical vertebræ still cohering, and around them — coiled — in perfect preservation, in hideous symmetry, the vertebræ of a great — No! not that word again! I dashed my body against the door of my prison; for a full hour of frenzy beat my life against its adamant: then fell to the ground.

*A*s I lay on the floor, my senses having returned to me, I seemed to hear a very faint sound, proceeding apparently from beneath the casing of wood. I bent down my ear. It was a gentle crepitant sound, as though a rat gnawed the wood.

But this it could hardly have been which made me leap up with an alacrity so frantic. The action was involuntary; but I soon recognized its reason. On placing the palm of my hand upon the boarding, a marked degree of *warmth* communicated itself to my skin. I have also touched the iron casing of the chamber all round, and find the same condition.

This apartment must be at a great depth in the bowels of the earth. Can it be that huge geologic forces, volcanic in character, are tumbling in Acherontic travail around me? The heat of the floor and walls slowly but steadily increases.

*S*eventy years ago I made a threefold vow. Forty years ago I broke the first, and wedded. Ten years ago I broke the second, and left my home. Three days ago I broke, thou seeing God, the third, when, within my own hand, I closed upon me this tomb of woe. For now — at last! — I know — with clear precision — the ultimate, the flaming, the maddening secret of being.

It is old: it has been heard from the beginning; but heard as an incredible tale. Upon no heart of man has its intolerable incubus ever rested as now it rests upon mine; no eyeball has its excess of light so scorched and blasted into ashes. And this I say in foolish and feeble words; that there is knowledge, and there may be things; but gibbering specters of this One Thing only: *an Eye that glares and glares forever!* And wise are they who call it Hammon, Brimmah, Zeu-Ya, and Ra, and Allah; but wiser they who say *Saranyû (i.e.* "Eninyes," Counteraction).

I will write even to the bitter and fiery end.

*

The scraping and gnawing sound has multiplied itself a million-fold, amid is now clamorous and constant. At every point beneath the flooring — along the length of every wooden panel — over all the wooden ceiling, it is heard. An army of creatures boring, *boring* their invincible way to reach me....

*T*he floor I can no longer touch with my feet; the table of stone itself grows hot; the iron casing of the chamber, even under the scarlet gleam of the lamp, now emits the redding glow of heated metal....

Tulsah! — that name again! — the fiery furnace of intensest hell — ah bitter, *bitter* love! to the center it blazes. And now — ah now — from a thousand apertures — around, above, beneath — a thousand small and crimson serpent-heads extrude! convulsive — O bile of God! — in ecstasy — they expel and retract their salamandrine necks! Crimson, crimson, is their name! But what a Babel of hissing! Once, in sleep, did I not see her tongue loll black and long — And now — wage, wage of lawless love! — now — O Majesty — they come — that flaming fault in worms — now — ten thousand forked and jagged (three words of doubtful meaning follow).

The Serpent-Ship

*"O that I knew where I might find Him!
that I might even come into His presence!"*

"My help!"
the Emperor called,
"the bard!
    With teaching touch
    who toucheth the harp,
    and teacheth the heart,
    to harp."

Nor long:
a rhapsody brave
of song:
    A hive of breath;
    and busy amongst,
    the lyrical buzz
    and throng: —

"Good-bye!"
the Viking his Gerd-
-a pressed:
    Two sobs that kiss —
    then life is a sail —
    then life is a-blurr,
    and mist.

Ten years:
the consequent times
revolved:
    But Hrolf, in Logres,

with Heracles moils,
was making the world
for God.

"That night,"
so, spinning, to Gurth,
the churl,
 The lady glozed,
 "how fine was his calm,
 when Hakon besieged
 the burg!"

And Gurth:
"but that was a day,
at Dvaiss!
 I wounded fell,
 pernicious as Thor,
 he hewed me a lane,
 and saved."

So she:
"he loved thee at heart,
poor Gurth!
 A heart, though strong,
 yet kingly infirm
 with fatherly lodes,
 and throes."

And Gurth:
"but where can his Sail
be spread?
 His Bones where white?
 or plies he till now
 his continent rage
 with men?"

She laughed:
"reblooms in the night
a gourd!
 He, thrilling plumb,
 like shuttlecocks falls;
 recurs like the moons

his Sword!

"What Bones!
I know that my warr-
-ior lives!
    Yet O, that Nord
    would wing me with winds,
    their wings to the winds
    who gives!"

At last
a rumor from God
has vogue:
    A myth, a breath:
    at Thanet he lies,
    his wounds unaneled,
    unmoaned.

Nor long:
a schip from the burg-
-bay runs:
    Her sixty oars
    unanimous troop,
    voluminous hoops
    her lug.

In vain!
at Thanet was void,
and ah:
    One knew — one thought —
    he'd fared for the Franks
    he'd passed to the Picts —
    afar!

"No more?
and *will* he no more
be *kind?*
    Then Gurth," she cries,
    "the wave be my world,
    though waste be its ways,
    and wild!"

She cruised:
at London is naught,
but germ:
    At Hythe no news —
    at Wyht he has stormed —
    at Dwyght he was yet
      — to storm.

When Day —
his cyclops inflamed
enlaved:
    When fairy Night,
    in lazuli grot,
    her lamp-lit bazaar
    unveiled;

Till dawn,
the swarm of her wake
she notes:
    Her sea-bitch hunts,
    a-hunt is the moon,
    and solves in gavottes
    the coast.

"How droll!"
so, pious and boon,
she taled:
    "On Triss, my mare,
    when tipsy one day,
    his feet on the ground
    he trailed."

And Gurth:
"but that was a day,
at Fahl!
    Our *yolle* capsized,
    and there was his head,
    like echoes and claps
    a-laugh!"

So she:
"you men in his train

were rich!
    The world, and woes,
    were made for his sake,
    to furnish with realm
    a prince."

And Gurth:
"but where can his sword
be groans?
    Or south, or north,
    with Logresman or Scot,
    or rolls with the flood
    his Bones?"

She smiled:
"he wounds, but himself
is Balm!
    'Tis said, you know,
    the hair of a hound,
    though bitter the bite,
    can salve.

I wait
a Silence through things
is spun:
    The first of men
    was made in the night,
    and skipped when he saw
    the sun."

Three years:
the seas with her oars
were thronged:
    But Hrolf, returned,
    in haven was heaved,
    and home-sick at home
    was strong.

Then four:
the voluble times
returned:
    A fame had steered

to Zetland her helm:
at Zetland was void,
and dearth.

He mourned:
all patient, adult,
arrived:
    His glance was worth,*
    and expert his heart,
    and chaste from the rods
    of Time.

He mourned:
a warrior crowned,
and trite:
    His hair was hoar,
    his warrings were o'er,
    his war-gear he wore
    and died.

And rich —
with breastplate of gold,
and targe,
    And broidered zone, —
    his mort they propose,
    sublime on his poop,
    and huge.

All day,
like mourners with griefs
a-rave,
    The crooning surfs
    to funeral troop,
    and funerals taint
    the rain.

At eve:
his rovers the shore
bethrong:
    The torch they use,

---

* Weorthan = werden, *become.*

the moorings they loose,
the holocaust moves,
is gone!

How grand!
thou mariners' Nurse,
though wet,
    Berock him now!
    with languidest waft
    they hail him a last
    Fare-well!

Afar,
the desert a Sign
acclaims:
    Between the hills
    a Pillar of Cloud,
    with banner of blue,
    her sail.

A-rave,
up sun-smears in oils
she glides:
    The buxom swell
    she glibly excels,
    a Pillar of Flame
    she rides.

But lo! —
by flurry applied,
her flame —
    the billows' bursts
    and cataracts quench:
    her peril she slips,
    though scathed.

* * *

'Twas night:
and Gerda from Zet-
-land works:
    The sea-room's lurch

her governing oar,
andante her cords,
beskirl.

It chanced —
when Imbrifer sets*
in murk,
 And sea, and sky,
 with dribbly rheums
 and equinox squalls,
 conturbs.

She fronts,
sedate on the deck,
the storm:
 The spoil of hope,
 though foundered in night,
 instinctive of light,
 her orbs.

And thus,
inclining her head,
to Gurth:
 "I saw, one night,
 a mist in his eye,
 when Dagmar, the scald,
 rehearsed."

And Gurth:
"but that was a day,
at Voss!
 He felled an oak,
 which fell on a thrall,
 and fell on the trunk,
 and sobbed."

So she:
"a typical man,
and tall!
 His social woe —

---

*   In October.

>   his musical weird . . .
> but talk not of oaks
>   — that fall."

And Gurth:
"but who shall his Se-
-cret guess?
>   Or far, or near,
>   his Dragon he steers,
>   or broads to the kites
>   his Breast?"

She wept:
"the world is its own
redress!
>   Its orb, though dark,
>   is starlight afar,
>   and smiles like a bride
>   a death.

"The past,
like throeings and growth,
we slight;
>   The future dark
>   may, dazzling dark,
>   be dark with excess
>   of bright.

"And say:
that sockets for eyes
he keep:
>   And worst be truth:
>   an outcome's innate;
>   from deathbeds a babe
>   may creep.

'Twas morn:
a sail through the squall
they spy:
>   Some pirate keel?
>   upon them he bears!
>   she, thoral below,

bids fly.

He looms —
a "serpent-schip" lank,
and high:
>But slighter she —
>and ruffling in stays,
>she yaws on the yeast,
>and flies.

And now —
with sea-winds my tale
I wet:
>In down-hill glee,
>each following threat
>she wins to her use,
>adept.

Their flow
with melting reserves
she rides:
>By noon he's air:
>they breathe from the oars:
>a westering blotch
>he hides.

Away!
affairé on Ahs
the Vault:
>The self-sick sea
>its bosom bespues:
>unearthly the world,
>and salt.

The prow
its dissolute Ghost
— out-pants!
>The eddies pair
>in scampering reel
>the regiment stalks,
>and tramps.

And bleak, —
comes brooding the dark,
like doom:
    A rift remains,
    and darkling bleak,
    that wraith through the rift
    relooms.

One eve —
(the Dead-sea terrasse
I roamed) —
    I saw a form,
    and still as I fled,
    a presence that form
    I found;

So they:
and plies them a name-
less cark!
    He steadfast drifts,
    and rudderless steers,
    an Argonaut blind,
    his bark.

* * *

There is —
engraved in the deep —
a place,
    With eddies vext,
    a caldron morose,
    all ringstraked with froths,
    that race

And midst,
circumference vast,
— it yawns!
    And harab dark,
    that staggering void,
    and wails from its whorls
    a swan.

To this —
for foul was the night, —
they drive:
>   To this that ship,
>   as sheep-dogs the sheep's,
>   had shiftily shaped
>   their flight.

As bent —
his jennet some flag-
rant steed
>   Pursues a-marsh,
>   with scattery scamp,
>   rotatory tramp,
>   a-ramp.

And soon —
that influence wild
involves:
>   She twists, she shoots, —
>   a mænad of death,
>   she planets, remote,
>   that orb.

He too:
to lightning my tale
I link!
>   A-keel they wing,
>   and fluttering poised,
>   with shuddering joys,
>   they wing.

As hunts —
a drake his unwife-
-ly bird,
>   (Their heads are far, —
>   — and half on the lake —
>   — and half on the wing —
>   they churn.)

So he:
a cable-length late,

he throes:
>   And round, and round,
>   in mizmazy rote,
>   in blackness secerned,
>   they roam.

When lo!
in rufous she bursts
the tomb!
>   Some shattered lamp —
>   in Tophet is dawn;
>   pregnated he, too,
>   — up-blooms!

But yet —
not *yet* does she dream
him nigh —
>   (As round, and round,
>   in narrowing whorls,
>   in volutes of lame,
>   they fly.)

Till now —
That chiseled extreme
they reach;
>   (Those satin depths
>   with shimmering shafts,
>   like Seraphim swords,
>   they parch.)

Then first!
then first does she dream
him close!
>   His streaming flag
>   — with wondering awe —
>   — his bulk on the pyre —
>   she notes.

As when —
some chymist his drugs
combines:
>   He waits, he frowns,

the menstruum fails;
but rallies the world,
he smiles:

So she —
dismays from her eyes
dismay,
 As trance of dawn
 at sunset arrests
 the withering eye
 of day.

'Tis Hrolf!
Reclaimant! how deep!
and strange!"
 (He *whispers dumb,*
 and Gorgon he smiles;
 surmising her heart,
 and sage.)

And swift!
she runs the blockade
of reek —
 With poising arms,
 like tottering bairns,
 her prow she attains
 — and leaps.

Nor fails:
for courtly he holds
his poop:
 Bonanza rare!
 She falls on his Length!
 and down to the skies
 they swoop.

* * *

He ceased:
but silence with song
was rife:
 The world's a star!

more stringèd a psalm
than trills on the ear,
its life.

Phorfor

Αι! αι! ταυ Κυθεραν!

They reckon ill who leave *Me* out!
   When me they fly — I am the Wings!
I am the Doubter and the Doubt;
   And I the hymn the Brahmin sings.

                             — R. W. Emerson

At that more somber season called Opora, which fills the interval between the rising of Sirius and the rising of Arcturus, when the cycled year dying as the phœnix, forest-leaves glow redreflective of the conflagration, and birds fly migratory from the world-wide majesty of the pyre — I passed on horse-back over the blue and high-surging undulations of the Orchat Mountains, whose broad swell is as the Eastern heave of a jeweled bosom; thence through lowerlying slopes, and delicious groves of citron, almond, and maple; and thence through a seine of streams, overwaved by that bulbous Nile-lily which the Greeks called "lotus"; till, entering the domain of Phorfor, I drew up, as night fell, at the entrance of the far-reaching castle by the sea.

    The ancient home! I had worn its dark forests as an easy old garment; listened through the whole dead summer-day by its brook-banks to the abstracted talk of my cousins Sergius and Areta, children then like me; splashed in the waters of its day. But a sudden pride, quickened by another's malice, impelled me to wide wanderings over the world, from which, after too many years, I now returned with little won — a knowledge of constitutions, modes, of the swellings of cities, artfulness of art; and a longing beyond language for heavenly message of the eyes of Areta, and the benign wisdom of the lips of Sergius.

    A letter of announcement had preceded me by some days. An old serving-man waited me at the entrance. I recognized him well, but to my smile he returned no answering smile. In silence he led the way, doddering with prone neck and angled knees, through a series of lofty glooms, till in the recesses he stopped before a high, embossed, and arched brazen gateway, to the curtained wicket of which he pointed, bowed, and retired.

I passed inwards. Here sight groped with somewhat more surety; though a thick odor of the smoke of myrrh smothered out the atmosphere. On a cushion on the ground I saw Areta sit: an easel before her. On the easel a square of ivory, in the center of which, by medium of *coccus,* the scarlet dye of the kermes-berry, she stained a small head. The brush was between her fingers. Wide and wild over the marble *dalles* of the flooring were spent the light purplish largesses of her main. Her back was towards me.

"Areta!"

Eagerly she painted. But she was conscious of my voice, for, without turning, she said in a thick, hurried murmur:

"You are come, then. See — *your* work."

She pointed with the handle, and continued her task.

I, looking, saw in misty distances of the chamber — a bed. But how *my* work? I drew gently near it. It was strewed with splinters of fragrant agalloch-wood. I saw a noble, cold forehead. The body was robed in splendid volutions of cloth-of-gold; the red lamp of a ruby glowed large at his breast; the head was crowned with daphne: an expression all this, as I knew, of Count Zinzendorf's whim, that death, so far from being the chill passage through any valley of any shadow, is, without metaphor, a jubilant bursting from sleep at day-break. But how *my* work? Wherein was *I* guilty? That question I asked myself. A coffin of sarcophagic limestone lay on chairs beside the low bed.

Eagerly Areta painted. From behind I saw that the effort was to preserve the august likeness in death; and already I was able to predict failure: no truth could an eye so wild interpret to a hand so unstable. I sat near her in the numbness of awe, and hours of the night rolled over us.

Later, I crept from the room. As I passed through one of the outer halls, a stupendous stalking figure moved diagonally across a far corner of it. The light was dim, but his step slow, and my eyes searched him fully. I knew the Elder, Theodore. A simple garment of blood-red silk, with amice of orphreyed black, tuned on the marble an intermittent musing to his strides. A mist of hair, crowned with the fanon, floated in wide white vagueness over his back. A great veil of yellow cloth covered his face, as a veil covered the face of the Prophet of Khorassan. I cannot at this moment picture forth all that passed within me at this sight: the intense impressions of first youth stamped themselves once more deep upon me. Once more it was Theodore, the omnipotent, that I saw. And though his head was immobile aversion as he passed through, I knew that he knew my presence.

I inquired of the old serving-man who attended me in my room at supper an hour later as to the arrangements for the burial of Sergius. He answered, "At the next rise of dawn he was to have been interred in the vaults of the rock-chapel."

"*Was* to have been?"

"But since your arrival — within the hour, in fact — time Elder Theodore has come in person from the Tower, and suggested to the lady Areta that the body be embalmed."

I started, understanding enmity — a deadly thrust at my own heart.

"And she?"

"Eagerly consented. The constant presence of the body will be her unhoped consolation. The Elder, skilled, sir, in all designs, has himself undertaken the work, and the coffined frame has even now been conveyed by boat across the water to the Tower."

I retired weary to my bed. But though morning was near, sleep was an ambition merely. I lay and swept clean the house of memory, building in the deep the old life up again. Of Sergius I thought, and his singular likeness to the boy, Christ; his questionings, answers, parables; his sibylline intensity of interest in sounds, and strata, and the shapes of things, and the hues of birds; how eagerly he accepted anything out of the ordinary course as a doubly-direct revelation of Omnipotence to himself. After a time, every appearance was to him a rune: like old augurs and æonoscopi, he followed within musing eye the course of all winged creatures. The fragments of a rainbow had pythmic meanings for him. He contrasted the notes from the vocal organs of many living things; showed how this sound or odor was really identical with that appearance, and how the difference of their mode of occurrence was not intrinsic, but due merely to the differentiation of our own sense-organs. His little museum was full of strangely sorted specimens of this and that: seeds, zoolites, spotted eggs, fuci, spawn, spongiadæ, chips of chert, bars of bast. Once, having spent the night in the forest, he came at dawn to where I, enfolding Areta, sat on the sea-terrace. His white brow was radiant. He told how all the night he had listened in a thicket to the song of a nightingale: a song which, he said, *was not her native.* I long remembered the impression which the quaint high things he thereupon uttered made upon us. And I thought of his smooth-mindedness, as of that Jesus whom he aped. If by chance he encountered rudeness, dullness, it was good to see within how lightlike a power he appeased it. I would often cavil at the obscure and loosely-metered *extravaganzas* which he sometimes sang to us; and always would he graciously pause to show how under the appearance of ease lay a strenuously-reached fitness; how beyond the cloud was light. "To what meter," he asked one day, "do earth-sent angels tune the dithyrambs of their exultation?" "To a meter," I answered. "which 'ear hath not heard,' nor can hear." But he: "Oh yes! heard indeed, but with scentless and purblind ears." He then took jewels of different sizes and colors; laid them in a line. All the syllables of each foot of the meter he marked by stones of the same hue; the *length* of the syllables he indicated by the varying sizes of the stones. No sooner had he done this, than Areta, perceiving a vision of some beauty in the combination, clapped hands; while I, observing indeed a picturesqueness, ended. "You here see," said Sergius, "that the first foot is a trochee (long followed by short syllable), while the last is an iambus (short followed by long): a symbolism, you will at once say, of the fall and rising again of Man; and, if you compare nearly all the Shemitic dialect-versions of the hymn I have in my mind, you will find the same general alternation: a beginning of long-and-short, and an ending of short-and-long, or long-and-long." And then, with exquisite clearness of rhythm, he proceeded to chaunt in Hebrew an improvisation of the angel-song of the Gospel, beginning, "Fear not," and ending, "shall be called the Son of God." Night-dews gathered in the eyes of Areta as the melody rose from him; myself not all unmoved. Nor did Sergius ever leave the reason restive. He pointed out now, for example, the coincidence that in the Greek version, too, of the words their alpha is a trochee, and their omega an iambus, and so even in later versions, as the Latin, French, English, and many others. It was at moments such as this that Areta would rescue her hand from mine with a rashness almost angry, and sidling towards her brother, lean a passionate face to peace on his bosom; and many hours, many longing days, might pass, before her dear favor returned to me. In such constant rivalry for her lived Sergius and I. I have won her from him by a hairataghan of agates, a cameo of onyx, or a bird from the sunset, spoil of my skill with the bow; and he back again by the solution of some problem in ciphers or lines, by a psalm, on earnest chansonnette. A very slight divergence, I remember, once occurred in the march of their thought. It was the custom at the time for one or other to read aloud by a deep-shadowed brook in the Wood, the "Giornale di un Viaggio di Constantinopoli in Pohonia," by the idealist mathematician Ruggiero Boscovich: a book of books for my cousins. During one such *séance*, Areta set up claim to Boscovich as supporting the cosmothetic view of the impressions of the senses, her own strongly marked leaning being toward that subjective idealism of Fichte which attributes the orderly succession of sensible changes to the nature of the individual mind in which they are perceived. To Sergius, on the contrary all was directly God — every event, sight, sound, God's quite special act: and hence it was, perhaps, that in *his* eyes the Bishop of Cloyne loomed immense, as the greatest who ever breathed. The divergence, I say, was slight, for to neither mind, as a thing of course, did any such idea as the absolute existence or agency of matter ever occur: yet Sergius frowned at the interruption — a sign in him of strong displeasure. Boscovich, he said, austerely, was *"other than she thought."* Morning redness overswept Areta: a vice caught her nether lip. For a week she abandoned herself wholly to me. Deep in the glens and bowers we wandered, hiding through the night in the darkness of caves, folded together. Sergius was a mateless bittern by the pool. One other singularity I may mention as often noticed in my love: her birdlike flightiness of motion, giving sometimes the impression of translation through space. Walking with her along the path of the wood, I have lifted my head to a squirrel's perch, or stooped to a fallen catkin, and turning again, lo, have seen her rapt well beyond me, beckoning airily perhaps from the summit of a rising ground. Her computations, too, of the dial's variations were not always in strict harmony with common notions; when, after my long absence, I returned as related to Phorfor, she said, "You are come, then," and the murmur had precisely that intonation with which one speaks of an interval of hours.

I lay in the darkness, and I swept clean the house of memory. Of the Elder Theodore I thought. We children called his name in pious, lower voices. Vast powers over nature, vast mystery of lore, we gave to him. Our imagination crossed itself at him. Only at night, on every seventh day, in the reluctant gloom of the rock-chapel, did we come at sight of the hem of his garment; for our awful lids would not lift to his veiled face. Here, kneeling, we took from his hands the elements of the Holy Supper; whereupon he made haste to disappear into the black *adyla* of the sanctuary. He was, Sergius hinted, of Aramæan, or Syro-Chaldean race; or else he derived from among the priests of the Cophti. The veiling of the face might be due to some disease of the blood which rendered him all too chill a horror for the glance of a fellow-mortal. The Tower was his solitary abode: a tall structure rising from the sea of our land-locked bay, about two stone-throws from the beach; it tapered upward pyramid-wise in seven brick terraces, each lacquered in a glaring color. By day it cast on the vaporing purple water the reflection of a gaudy basking lizard. Above all was the observatory. There the sun sometimes fired through narrow openings a tangled refulgence of sextants, armillary spheres, gimbals, the cannon of a telescope, azimuth compasses, pictured charts. In the deepest night we opened the eyes and thrillingly knew that the Elder pored into the ever-written red-letter scroll of the past and the to-come. Neither I nor the orphans ever understood what had been his precise relation to their parents; that they had revered him above mortal we understood; also that the guardianship of our lives was in some sort bequeathed to his hands. But was it by childish sure instinct, or a series of trivial and now forgotten incidents, that I came to know that *I* was by no means included in the scheme of Theodore's providence? that I, the waif, the Hagarson, might become, perhaps was, an obstacle to the unfolding of that elaborate forethought? This consciousness at any rate grew gradually mine. When at last I fled from Phorfor, I was a missile from the suggestion, tense, compelling, secret, of the Elder of the Tower.

Thus I built in the deep. But with the morning I dispatched a note to Areta, asking if I might hope that day for the sight of her face, but for a word from her. She apparently did not receive, or read, the paper; for I waited without reply. The galleries, park, gardens, fed my memory with here an ancestral effigy, there a grove or stream. Another day passed, and another. But at the fourth dusk, a boat lay moored at the water-steps of the terrace. Its benches sustained in a glazed coffin of light pagodite the body of Sergius already cured to perpetuity by a miracle of asphmaltum, natron, bitumens; a dwarf rower of dark skin held the skulls of the bow; fastened to the stern by a twine floated a little shallop of mother-of pearl. I, standing near, waited. Areta in purity of white came slowly from the portico of the mall, walking down an aisle of the double xystum of Corinthian columns which lined the terrace; palms on either hand overshaded her; and she came the full and sudden moon through the palms, walking in shining. My hand touched my mouth; I was at once abashed and excited at her developed splendor. As she passed, she extended laterally her left hand, without seeming to see me. I burned it within a kiss. She descended the stairway, looked upon the steadfast face of Sergius, and stepped into the shallop. I following, the dwarf began to paddle.

Here the sands and the low cliffs all along the two folded claws of the bay are of a very pale pink coloring; the sea being an extremely vivid purple resembling the hue of the dye called Phœnician, and remarkably shallow throughout. Here and there the cliffs project bluffly quite into the bay, thus blocking the continuity of the sand. The water is but very slightly brackish. A bright-hued seaweed, scallops, and star-fish visibly carpet the bottom; while moon leaved water-growths cluster into groups of silvery greenness over the surface. From the terrace our rower slowly conveyed us a hundred yards to the left, and there turned into a opening in the coast-rock about four feet wide through all its length; up this the sea, far-winding, slumbers in breathless gloom, covered thick with the drowsy grace of Egyptian lotus-lily. Three wide steps near the end of the inlet lead into a low square chapel excised from the mountain-rock, its roof being supported by the ebony columns of twin stylobats.

Areta had not spoken. Her face was the uttermost expression of a rigid woe. Arrived at the chapel entrance, she looked up, and stepped readily from the shallop. The dwarf and I bore the now lightened body in its shell to trestles near a purple catafalque before the altar-rail. On the craped altar itself a taper on either side of the pyx nimbused itself with a little sphere of little rays, giving all of light we had. The black hangings of gold-fringed velvet made the distant places of the excavation a vastness of darkness.

Areta, seating herself on the altar-step near the body, motioned to us to leave her. I, seeming to obey, retired; ordered the dwarf back to the Tower; and took my place in the obscurity of a recess. Hence I could watch her tearless pain. She leaned her head on the rail sideways, and watched obliquely the steadfast dead. She did not move. As the spaces of the night marched by, the taper-flames began to leap duskily, and one of them puffed suddenly out. She rose then; and opening a cista behind the altar, obtained two others; and was about to light them, when I, buying up the opportunity, stepped boldly forth. I took the tapers and lit them, and adjusted them to the candlesticks. She showed no surprise at my bodily presence near her. We sat together on the altar-step by the coffin; together we gazed. The face before us was unchanged and Sergius's own; a mournful richness of gold involved him. Her hand did not refuse the ring of warmth in which till morning I fostered it.

When the deeper shadows had thinned to a twilight in the chapel, she rose and walked to the doorway. I, entering with her paddled in the shahlop down the winding way, and so out to the sea. The sun was now bright above the circling blue mountains of Phorfor; nature looked wide-eyed in pricked alertness; the water a flushed and many-gifted soul under the blaze of light and the roughening reel of routs of zephyrs, morning home-returners. White, long-necked birds, scarlet-legged, flew hither and thither, uttering a swan-call akin to the viola-note. I watched anxiously to read the countenance of Areta. For a moment the throes of vacillation had her; for a moment she struggled to maintain the grey face of grief — but a single sobbing gasp of laughter burst suddenly forth from her bosom, and instantly the hilarity of the sky, and the frolic of the world was in her look. She hurriedly buried a crimson face in the draperies of her arm.

To this I had looked forward with the precision of certainty — if she remained at all the same Areta that I knew. Never was Areta other than the unfailing exactest mirror of environment; a condition which no doubt arose from her belief — so deep as to be part of herself — that environment was, in fact, the exact mirror of herself; and this again from her disbelief in the existence of matter. Now, it is no doubt true that most cultivated people of the outer world accept such non-existence as an intellectual thesis, whether tentatively in the form presented by Malebranche, Geulinx, and the so-called Cartesian school; or in the form of the absolute phenomenalism of Hume, Browne, and the middle German teaching; but in most minds, as I imagine, a lingering half-faith in Lockes "thing in its real essence" (Kant's 'thing in itself') must persist to the end, for the very reason that the fancy, by long habit of youth, has already grown to hold the earth-rock genuine solid, and the sun very "substance." To my cousins, however, even from the first dawn of thought, all was pure spirit; the one "substance" the consciousness of their own inner souls; the world a thin picture on the senses, resolvable as mirage. And this knowledge, so far from being an affair of the mere reasoning understanding, was their very life itself. To them no other possibility suggested itself. The slightest change in the environment of Areta would indicate to her a preceding change in her own mental being. Sergius, looking up, would question the causing Mind; she, looking inward, asked, How has the alteration been produced in *me?* I remember them thus affected by the disappearance of many things around them. In the bursting Spring I have known Areta a wild ass's colt on the hills with twinkling feet and bacchant stare; in the chiller season puritan and wise. That her consciousness should now evolve a gay picture of nature, she, feeling the discord within her sorrow for Sergius, doubtless marked as a strangeness in herself.

Having arrived at the terrace-steps, she raised her face, and leapt to the land. I proceeded to make fast the shahlop, but on reaching the top of the handing-stage, saw her already beneath the pediment of the portico, on the point of disappearing within the castle. There I heard that she had retired to a distant part, and would be seen no more until sunset.

It was dark when she reappeared at the waterside. We then proceeded as before to the chapel, and renewed our silent vigil. Her face had lost nothing of its hard misery. She seemed not to know me, though I clasped her hand. Within the intrusion of the morning, I suggested that we should return to the castle. She slowly turned her head, and within the raised eyebrows of surprise, looked at me fully; then, frowning, said, "Leave me! leave me!"

I could not but obey. Later I heard that on the preceding day a side-apartment of the chapel, of which there were many, had been fitted up as a chamber for her. This then was to be her constant abode of gloom.

In the evening I returned. She frowned, but did not deny me place by her side. There watching through the slow circle of the night, I was near happiness, for I was near her. Yet she was far from me. So months, many months, passed over us. Every sun divided us, but with the drawings of the moon we flowed together again. Upon the steadfast face of Sergius our gazes fell.

*R*arely at midnight would the Elder Theodore step from a boat at the entrance, and walking toward the sacrarium, reappear huge at the altar within chrism and plaque and chalice, bearing the Host and Wine of the Eucharist. Blessed then it was, as we knelt, to see the face of Areta, adoring spirit's more than woman's. We sang no hymn; a few muffled Greek words rumbled like the echo of a reverberation from Theodore; whereupon his feet resought the way they had come. Areta might then melt somewhat; speak a word to me; her kindled pity for the Redeemer's trouble seeming to suage into twilight the starlessness of her own crude night. She might produce from her chamber hooks, and I at her bidding would read, perhaps von Hardenberg's Hymn to the Night commencing: "Once when I was shedding bitter tears; standing by the grave which hid the Form of my Life; chased by unutterable woes; forward could not go nor backward; lo, from the azure distance fell chill breaths of Twilight; and the band of Birth, the fetter of Life, was rent asunder; thou, Night's inspiration, Slumber of Heaven, overcamest me; to a cloud of dust that grave expanded; through the cloud I beheld the transfigured features of my Beloved"; or the mystical aphorisms of *Siris* would fit her mood; or Arthur Collier's ideality in *Clavis Universalis*. And sometimes within the passing months I would tremble to see her wan face dimple fleetingly into the very smile of Areta; and noticing one night her spinning-wheel of electrum — quick-gleaming alloy of gold and silver — stand by contrivance of my artifice with violet-dark wool on distaff near the coffin, she did at length stretch out doubting fingers, and commence a woven undertaking. And the droning incessant circle bred a stirring in the roots of speech. At last — I shot a glance of triumph at Sergius — she yielded to the impulse of words. "He had long, you know, been ailing: phthisis was his worm. And the intense contemplation of sleepless weeks was its fattening aliment. For the last few months of life the spirit might be said to sway half-disembodied; but eschewing his bed, he still studied and roamed. I never left him. You know the unspeakable sympathies which from our dual birth united us; but now for the first time our two souls lost definiteness, and hovered into one. I was lifted at times into awful heights to share his apocalypse of the world. Nothing seemed any longer secret to him. The illusion of Time, for instance, ceased to cloud him: he knew the past and the future. He re-arranged his little museum, changing the relative position of this and that, into a quite wonderful beauty; then locked the door, and threw the key into a hot sulfur-spring in the forest. Once, as he lay in languid sleep at noonday, I heard him twice call your name, 'Numa! Numa!' When he woke he said, 'Numa, I know, is moved toward us again; but I could wish he were now here; I could then commit you, with confidence, to him.' Speech was now a gasping difficulty with him, and I wondered especially that he should speak so of you and me. He seemed to forecast — I know not what. Soon subsequent, absolute powerlessness confined him to an easy chair in the chamber where you first saw his body. I read to him through the day from the Hebrew scriptures, from his beloved Bishop Berkeley, and the hymns of Pindar. At every sunset he swooned to sleep; and slept happily to the next noon. Once, surprising from a mid-day trance, he dictated to me runningly in Hebrew three of those his imponderable metrical *capriccios,* and then fell back wearily to instant sleep again. I had followed him far, but as to these last words, the meaning was of subtler element than my spirit, and out-soared me. They may have been simple prophecy of quite simple events; they may have been parable or rhapsody, or prayer. His dear hand could no longer lift the pencil's weight; his eyes were two twice-illumined moons. A little yellow bird called Beatrix, which it had been his whim to overpaint to a somber grey hue, fluttered constantly in his breast, shrilling his name. He had so trained it from its motherless birth. I have everywhere sought it since his death, but in vain. At the beginning of the last week he again sighed your name; and henceforth every noon hoped aloud for you. On the third day he minutely directed me to draw a Key on paper, which, when it was finished, I immediately recognized as the 'key' figured in Wilhelm Meister's *Wanderjahre;* beneath this he told me to write the opening words of the angels' song in the Gospel of Luke beginning 'Fear not.' These two, the former above the latter, were to be inlaid in gold on the headpiece of his inner coffin; and this, as you see, has been properly accomplished by the Elder. On the next day he called me close; I kneeling before him, his hand rested upon my head. 'I do not doubt,' he said in the whisper of the dying wind, 'that he for whom I wait will come speedily. The hoofs of the rider's horse are urgent on the mills. I bless you then, Areta, and say good-bye. Yield yourself utterly to God, little one. Give to every passion its wine, to every pulse its throb, to every song its dance. *He,* in truth, is pulse and blood, song and singer. Yield freely to him. If you would be perfect in divinity, let the Wind, passing, win from the whole intense gamut of your chords a wafture of richest perfected humanity. Ah, little sister, quick — my harp! my harp!' Quickly I reached him his kithara; held it before him; handed him the quill plectrum. He faintly delved from it a distant air — ah me, an air known even in the highest cycle of heaven — which since childhood I had not heard from him. He then had measured it to the Gospel words: 'Fear not . . . he shall be great . . . and shall be called the Son of God.' Ardently did I pray that while the harmony still clung in the web of my consciousness I might have opportunity to transcribe it into musical signs; but at that moment a hot messenger entered with your note of announcement. Even while I glanced through it, Sergius knew its meaning; and having uttered a sigh of rest, the visual body slid from him."

"But the melody?"

"Passed utterly from me. In vain have I mined into myself for it. If I could hear it again — ah me, but once again — I think that the love and the hope of life, which seem dead within me, might yet — again —"

Sudden tears shined from her uplifted eyes. Her hands clasped rigidly.

So she spoke with me through the show circle of the nights, spinning. The chiller season passed, and the spring, and the leafiest weeks of summer. She had settled into an unvarying morne mood; words she uttered, only livid in hue, and pregnant always with the odor of the grave from which they winged. But to sit always and watch her loveliness, so sad, so lunar, was already the dizziness of frenzy. She had dressed herself in the mourning of loose purple draperies, made of a very flimsy diaphanous cloth. A fillet of gold circled her head. My blood railed at its channels; with torrent fury I leapt the barriers, and spoke to Areta — of our old loves among the caves and crannies — of the wild hopes which had led me back to Phorfor. I think she did not at all comprehend my meaning; quite simply, with mournful gaze upon the dead, she said: "Our whole love is hid in him now — yours and mine; conscript to the memory of what he was, and to this little all that remains to us of him." It was then that I knew that Sergius, living, was strong; dead, was invincible; and it was then that I called down upon that Argus cunning which, on my coming, had impregnated his body with eternity, the bale of every imprecation.

Yet, I too, won my small triumph. For on an afternoon of beginning autumn, when the sun had sunk not yet below the west-looking harbor-hills, I — induced her with me to the terrace! It was my tingling Marathon. "Bright! bright!" she cried, hiding her face. Blood surged to her lewd limbs; visible to me was the raveling of the cerements from the risen, pulsing flesh. We sat on a couch of alabaster on the lowest stratum of the terrace, quite near to the marble balcony-rail overlooking the bay.

In the circling pink arms of the sands the purple basin of sea looked a dew-splashed violet cozy in the heart of a rose. Areta lived again. Sweet-linked waftings from the parterres set out staggering-adventurous to reach her, and reached her fainting. The sun, all glory-clouds and shekinahs, like the God of some mad universe belalalah'd *en route*, with cymbals and with dances, flamed down afloat in the *gluth* of a passion which he never assumes but when he would enkindle to mutual ardors the light-thoughted mother-hills of Phorfor.

Areta was simple childhood itself. Looking abroad on the rich vision, she laughed a laugh of perfect *bonne camaraderie;* nested herself snakily at the end of the seat; I reclining at length, watching close the spiritual play of her face. And we really spoke at last of things other than Sergius and his mummy.

"See," I said, "how the sun's rim demarks into seven contrasts of fire the colors of the tower. The glazed bricks have the appearance of red and blue and yellow heat."

Looking, she laughed.

"Mens agitat molem."

"The Elder's mind —"

"No, the sun-god's: kindled by us; and kindling by means of us."

"And in another sense the Elder's, too, — from within."

"In literal truth, yes: man, as Novalis without metaphor said, being a sun, of which his senses are the planets. In the case of such as Theodore above all."

"Singular man!"

"He walks his uplifted way alone: dead to sorrow, hope, desire; in a strict sense king of the world."

"But listen, Areta: you miss the mark here: Theodore, I know, is not dead to desire."

"Not? Then to what desire not dead?"

"The conservation in his hands —"

"Of the meanings of the stars."

"Of the opulent territories of Phorfor."

"Fie! of the revelations of God."

"The keeping of *you* safe —"

"From what?"

"From me."

An oval "O!" of lower comedy answered nine.

"And I tell you truth, Areta, the day may come when you will confront the necessity of choosing between me, your cousin, and the Elder Theodore, whose face you never beheld."

"Really so? and whom think you I would choose — my father's

prophet, the guiding forefinger of my brothers thought, grey hunter in old alchmymics and astrologies — or you, a worldly wanderer, lithe hopper in every grass?"

"I know well whom you would *once* have chosen; but as to now, of course"

Sweetly she smiled.

"And am I then so greatly changed in — how many years? — six, I think? You are, as of old, 'Numa'; a light-footed boy, I remember, somewhat empty of thought, lengthened now only by a six-fold growth of the leopard's beard — which also could be sheared."

"Call the beard 'fantasy of your dream,' and me still rubious Numa, capricious with you in the long grasses of the valley."

"What other than 'fantasy of my dream'? and yet to *me* very hyacinthine real."

"Card it with carding fingers: I promise you no dream but substance enough."

"If my finger's would but assume the office of the carder's comb! But is feeling then less fantasy than sight? You do not mean this that you say of 'substance.'"

"So men speak and think in the world, Areta."

"You mean among savage tribes?"

"No, but among races considered civilized."

"The gravers of their great men must scratch a shallow tracery on this 'world' of yours!"

"Oh, very shallow indeed! There are many conflicting voices, you know; the writings cross and re-cross on the basalt; and as they rather lack the genius of sharp distinction between the really great and the only seeming, so confusion comes, and continual movement in a circle in place of locomotion."

"But you do not mean that they have a genuine conception of a material universe?"

"Extremely genuine and material, in the case of the great majority at least."

"They are not Christian?"

"Oh yes!"

Areta's laugh had a resemblance to the chirping of the cicada: so shining, and lalling, and dry.

"Not Christian: for what account can they possibly render themselves of the many feats of magic performed by Jesus?"

"The feeding of the multitude, and so on? I hardly know. Some disbelieve them; some nebulous-shruggingly neither believe nor disbelieve; some, in a fury of faith, charge them to the conniving *legerdemain* of Omnipotence."

"The con —! but these last are either hypocrites or self-deluders. They cannot conceive the inconceivable. If nature be phenomenon and nothing else, it *is* conceivable how one mind may, by its forceful action upon other *minds*, effect in them a sense of variation from the usual succession of phenomena. With such a hypothesis, magic becomes natural and easy. But like only can conceivably act upon like; you cannot, for instance, feed mind with broths, or blood with thoughts. Where therefore you introduce a conception of packed matter, the conceivability of magic — or indeed of any action whatever of spirit, divine or not, upon the phenomena perceived by other spirits — utterly collapses. And in the case of those who only half believe in the eyewitnessed performances of Jesus, there is, of course, no pretension to belief —"

"But there is: many of these last indeed cling on with quite riotous vigor to the *rest* of the torn Book."

The sun had set, Areta's profile looked duhhwan, a misty crescent in the sudden dusk. Her drooped lash was as a trait of seaweed dark on the spume of breakers under the Cyprian moon. Her voice tuned every moment to a lower sadness.

"Yet Jesus was the most ideal of the idealists. 'Matter' to him was less than the dream of a dream. What, for instance, do these persons make of his saying: he that hath his spirit in such and such a way shall announce to the mountain: Be thou plucked-up! and it shall obey him? They must either think that he had a meaning, or hold him for a rhetorician — or, lower still, an orator."

"But the world, Areta," I said, "does not, you understand, call itself a thinking world, but an acting. Very slowly indeed, in its preoccupation, do the thoughts of its deep ones filter through the whole: and the reason is that pointed out by Des Cartes in *Principia*, and I think also by Malebranche, that the faculties we have are few, and designed for support and pleasure, rather than to penetrate the essence of things."

"But — I like your distinction between thinking and action. If there be nothing but spirit, upon what can action act, and by means of what? There is in truth no action but thought; to aspire is to be an adventurer; to dream is to be practical; to feel is to be a man of affairs; and when your world calls itself an acting one, it may simply use a euphemism for vague or wrong thinking. As for the Cartesian view which you mention, compare with it Berkeley's saner one: that 'some truths there are so *near* and *obvious* that a man need only open his eyes to see them; and such I take this one to be, that all the choir of the heavens and the furniture of the earth, have not any substance without a mind; that their being consists in being perceived.' And now, having proved that, say, *fire* is nothing more than a particular combination of color and form, and that color and form can no more exist without a seeing spirit than a sound without an ear, Berkeley, you know, disdains to proceed to prove that this purely notional appearance cannot, for example, *burn:* merely remarking that that at least is *obvious;* and this is certainly the conclusion of Hume, Comte, and the rest. So that the faculties would seem to require no very 'penetrative' acumen for the perception of truths so superficial."

"And yet," said I, baiting my hook, glad at the drone and harping of her voice, "I venture to say that these truths are in fact so far from 'obvious' to the untrained mind, that they may even seem rather ridiculous to it."

"And why? Does the untrained mind then suppose that fire or rock is anything *more* than color and form? and if so, what? what invisible, inconceivable thing does the color and form hide from us? They would, at least, make the same impressions upon us, if this singular thing of which we are never cognizant were not there: and we cannot, therefore but assume it to be absent; since, too, we cannot imagine the unimaginable, to *speak* of it is to use words without meaning. If, moreover, a thing perceived be really nothing more than color and form, the 'untrained mind may readily arrive at the certainty that it can neither burn, nor do anything whatever; and hence that no power, as no substance, can be other than spiritual. As to how, in such case, phenomena have the 'power' of producing impressions upon our consciousness, one opinion may differ from another. Singular Jonathan Edwards in his *Original Sin* is, you know, actually driven to assume the constant re-creation of all existing objects for the purpose of reimpressing us at every moment; but to me there seems no necessity for the creation or recreation of anything; it is only necessary that *we* should he, and should dream. Only in the mysterious loom of the spirit can the woof of the world be spun; for if phenomena were in truth external, how could they, not being spirit, make impressions upon spirit, unlike upon unlike, especially as, being passive, they can do 'nothing whatever'? There may indeed be a law of our mind that every the we are conscious of proximity between a form and color called 'hand' and a form and color called 'fire,' we shall also be conscious of pain: as to which, Sergius, you know, declared that every such consciousness of pain was the special act of the Divinity, — thus bringing Him in very deed 'closer than breathing,' 'in our hearts and in our mouths.' But at any rate, we can have no certainty that such law is universal, or that such special acts are inevitable: for is it not too probable that there are fingers in the universe which, plunged into flame, would feel torture indeed, but the torture of Arctic cold? the flame then must be without property, substance: and only substantial the nervous, visionary *ich*. And even for us, the law, if it exists, may not be always strict; the dream of yesterday was well-ordered; but as sometimes happens in the less lucid visions of the night, the phantasmagory of tomorrow may melt and writhe into strange distortions. Nay, on a night, I actually *had* the trance that he, my splendid dead king, held to the furnace a barchment which, like the bush of Moses, burned unconsumed. Ah, but let us return — to him!"

She stood upright, tall and grey. The moon was abroad in the heavens. I, conquering her hand in the trouble of love, kissed it.

"Areta! Areta! this one night grant me, I implore! Do not return. For one night only leave Sergius to his death. Sleep, for me, in the castle!"

She smiled at my zeal with a shaken "No!"

"Only this one night, for me?"

"Shall we not go and sit *together* by him?"

"My first prayer since I have come back to you: ah, Areta!"

"Really your first?"

"You know."

"You make it late."

"Then grant it early!"

"Always willful of bead, little Numa! and a lubricant for persuasiveness!

It was really night. I, twining round her arm, led her pouting recalcitrant, to the portico. Far within the halls she must needs part from me; mounted on wings the marble stairway, torch in hand; waved me a swift spirit's good-night; calling, 'the *second* may be harder i' the winning!'

I had no hope, no wish for sleep. Plying the paddle of the shallop, I circled many times the basin of the bay, now halting in the shadow of a bill, now basking in the moon's utmost noon. A red light, steadfast to the changing hours, burned through a slit of the ripple on the shelly sands F peace, low-sobbed, of an night tense in an agony of stars, distraught of eye as the patient stricken ox, and dumb with the pains of its passion, as I with the pains of Areta. Her words, the odor of her, her sweet yielding, had purged my blood to the ultimate element of flame; her name was nightmare in my aching gorge. I came to the inlet; passed upward. It was midnight. Here no gloating ardor of the heavens trenched upon the supremacy of Shadow in which the reach of fan-shaped lotus, close-clustering, slept a perfect nepenthe. I stepped from the shallop; entered the chapel. The darkness was complete. Long on the altar-step, on the spot, where she sat, I sat. Aloud now I found utterance to call her name. Then falling to my knees, I overcast the coffin with my arms, my head fallen above his head, beseeching him as a god. "Sergius! if death have ears, solicitudes! if ghosts be veined with the ichor of human pitifulness! open your lean and lungless bosom – stretch your adamant arms of Polar ice: grant me, still quick, lustful, craft to wrest her from your mortality! give her back to me!" A sudden glimmer like a taper-light seemed to glance behind me. I sprang panting to my feet: but all was dark as before. I returned to the shallop, and so out upon the bay. The steeply-slanting constellations, stepping foot and foot with the night, were evidence of its revolving. Having surfeit of the water, I came to land; and finding beneath the portico a hung heptachord, took it, and made a circuit of the spread castle. I was faint with the long sickness of desire; my lips lay dead for lack of the carnal life-flame of her kiss. To the East I stood beneath a square turret in a garden of spices. In a chamber on the second stage I knew that Areta slept. It was beginning morning: night, throeing with dissolution, spread out, like old misers on lamp-lit deathbeds of velvet, a gluttony of bulging jewels; a languid, low-looming moon wrapped in elfin satins the crimson of pomegranate, and the grey-green of the tower, and the sardius of asphodel-berries, and the purple of myrtle-fruit. Here in galaxies fireflies poise uncertain, sun-birds and droning coccinellæ dart. Turtles and nightingales hang their harps upon its willows. Inconsequent hints of zephyrs, both with the fragrance of clove and jasmine, came with healing in their wings to my parched lips and forehead. I sent up from the lyre a lullaby, tuned to the splash of a fountain which gushed from a basin of cipolin – a cold white spirit in the midst of the garden; muttering; wreathing with aureoles of the lunar rainbow her far-tossed hair of dew. I sent up the melody, and with it my soul, hoping for her face at the window: when a sudden consciousness of danger, a sense of some luminous descending mass, appalled me. My eyes being turned upward, I clearly saw whence it came – from a window of the third stage, that immediately above Areta. I had but the to rush backward before it fell to the earth. It appeared in the moonlight to be a great quantity of grey powder; and almost immediately on contact with the ground, it uttered a tremor of froth, and burst vividly forth into a carmine flame, mingled with writhing tongues of cobalt.

I hurried to the terrace. The red light burned steadfastly in the topmost Tower. Till morning I watched in vain to see a huge expected form emerge from the castle. Expected, I say, and yet with endless doubts; for Theodore's boat was a visible spot of blackness floating by the Towerwall. I was confounded. Was his arm, I asked myself, indeed longer than the arm of man? Soon after the full dawn, the dwarf set out from the Tower, broom by side, towards the chapel. I beckoned him to me.

"Is the Elder Theodore," I asked, "now in the Tower?"

He nodded.

"And has been throughout the night?"

"Ha, master! that I do not know."

"You know with what knot you last moored the boat; has she been since removed?"

"Not, for certain."

I loitered for some hour or two among the parterres. It was a dank, secretive morning. The mountains donned grey veils of pudicity, low-lashed matin nuns after the glut and riot of a night. Areta came to the portico, looked abroad, her face sedate. My heart leapt to see the purple mourning gone, and a peplos of saffron in its stead. A broader regency of gold chapleted her head. The mists seemed to rarify at the yellow sun of her. I went and took her hand.

"I heard your sleepless moonings."

"And did not show a face?"

"Being sleepier than you! and their end, moreover, was so abrupt."

I said nothing of my narrow escape.

We walked to the parapet. Just then the dwarf, paddling near the shore, was returning from the chapel.

"Call him that he may take us back," she said.

"Already, Areta — already!"

"It is fitting now. Let us look with quiet joy —"

"Give me till noon."

"Till noon, persistent Numa? Well, till noon. You shall read to me in the castle. Call him that he may fetch the book."

"I will myself bring it. What book?"

"John Norris."

I set off rapidly in the shallop, passing on the way the dwarf, who was making for the terrace. In the chapel I lingered a very long time, and when I returned, returned without the book. I had forgotten it. Strong agitation, half joy, half fear, throbbed within me.

Areta, looking, saw my pale face, and caught its pallor, fore-knowing. As I sprang to the stage, the dwarf, coming with a weighted basket from the castle, descended the steps to the boat.

"You were even now in the chapel?" I said to him. "Yes, master."

"Did you miss sight of nothing?"

"Of nothing, sir."

"And all you found as usual?"

"Yes, master."

"What is it? What is it?" cried Areta. I sprang to her side.

"Areta — love — I know not how — I swear to you — but the coffin and the body of your Sergius have vanished from the chapel."

Never could I have expected such result. With the sudden curvature of a cankered lily, her head drooped forward. Heavy she lay on me as a white column of Corinth aslant in arms of a bower of bindweeds. I bore her to a couch in the castle, and there till the gathering of darkness watched the wanness of her apathy.

She rose, a straining, a luminous strange questioning in her deep eyes; dashed back her hair; Niobe bereft; and instantly fled from the room. Swiftly as I followed, she was already far in the shallop when I reached the landing-stage. Having no boat, I sprang to the sands, and ran along them till stopped by a projecting cliff; thence made my way to the inlet through the sea, which at no point reached me above the middle. On the altar of the chapel a light glowed. Areta, sitting on the altar-step, pored upon chasms, a pity to see. Sergius had left not a rack. It was a second death of the beloved to her; a twice-whetted knife piercing home from breast to back; acuter than at first, suddenness lending point. She was such that her heart was as a quicksand, deep-secretive of every cherished object. Excision implied always the drawing of blood, and, it might be, the tapping of life. And the vitality of her ideal view of the world was oil to these flames; the loved thing, held the creation of her own soul, grew into the substance of its god, pant of her pulse, beat of her blood. And the embalmed body was all she had possessed of her Sergius; for the unfinished stained head of her attempt had been thrown aside as worthless. Thinking so, I stood near, moved with pity. She lifted her eyes and saw me; flashed a ray of mistrust at me.

"How of the body, Numa?"

I started.

"Were it not well to question as to that the Elder Theodore?"

"The Elder? No! The Elder was in the Tower: I, standing by the parapet, saw no one pass on the water: the dwarf had the boat: left all as usual in the chapel! *his* strength could not have sufficed to move the weight: then *you* went to the chapel —"

Her head followed her wringing hands downwards. I was appalled at the close welding of this chain of inference.

"You suspect me? Areta! With what motive —"

"Alas! it is hard to tell: with no motive but one unworthy our race! Except indeed my fantasy be all awry — my love to him unknowingly estranged — or his to me — some punishment for I know not what —"

She stopped suddenly short, and together we darted wild eyes around the chapel in the infinity of new surprise. A voice in the air, in liquidest falsetto, in breathless impatience, called: 'Sergius! Sergius! Sergius!' And instantly from the depths of the black recess behind the reredos of the altar there slid like slanting light-rays through the air a little creature, a tenuous grey bird, an embodied breeze, a flash of life. It settled, still minstreling its luted shibboleth, to a fluttering rest in the panting bosom of Areta.

"Beatrix! Beatrix!" she called, in a note lucid-high as that of the tiny thing she fondled, "Beatrix! little herald! whisperer of his secret! fledged dove of my comfort! Thou art come then?" Close she hugged it, trouling, laughing, trilling, light-wheeling to the hint of a dance, a maiden-canephorus tripudiary in the comus of the Dionysia. The transit from despair to frolic was perfect. No question she asked as to whence the bird of Sergius had come after so long an interval. It was a heavenly benison — a dear revelation — unaccountable but real: she made no scrutiny. The slim-sloping little bird, nothing but a winged voice, unappeasably garrulous of its Becket vocabulary, throated and throated again its shrill *euion* of Sergius! Sergius! — and every twittered sesame availed to open wide the heart of Areta to ever a fresh flood of Libyan buoyancies. Breast fluttering to breast, she flitted and whirled with the new love to the door of the chapel; and, heedless quite of the old, floated rapidly in the shallop down the inlet. Following, I dimly saw her disappear behind a winding of the rock; heard yet a last echo of the ceaseless pipe. Then walked drearily backward, as before, through the sea.

After this very many weeks passed away before I again looked upon the face of my love.

I won from the mysterious tongue of an old stepdame almost daily whisperings of her; how she spent herself upon the bird; fed it at every hour from her own hand; slept only tranquilly when it lay warm in the happy valley of her breasts; laughed with it, danced with it, was a wanton in the abandonment of her kisses; never wearied of the hypocrite zeal of its monotone. How sometimes, she would descend by a narrow stair to a side-garden of the castle, high-walled between two buttresses; daily there an hour or two; but how, as the suave winter of Phorfor drew on, her chamber had her always. This I learned. Several letters I wrote to her, protesting my innocence in the matter of the mummy; my constant longing for her; and once received a verbal reply that she would see me shortly. Hope burst at once into flower within me; but after many days of straining outlook, I dropped limp from my watchtower, and fell to wide listless roamings over the domain. During all this time I was wary as to my life, knowing it in danger; kept circumspicent eyes; barred my doors; never slept twice following in the same bed.

When the mourning-doves had once more resumed the practice of their elegies in the copses, I stood often near the small side-garden; and when spring had blown into still freshest summer, I quickened every day more ears at the gate than Typhon guardian-eyes before the garden of the daughters of Hesperus. Areta came at last one noon; I heard her step on the shells of the walk; the call of the bird. Outside I bent listening to her stirrings; listened till, after an hour, she walked back into the castle. At the same hour of the next day she returned. I, procinct with the sword of adventure, tapped at the wicket. She instantly lifted the latch, opened, and was before me, laughing cascades and carillons.

"Little Numa! *you?* say 'little Numa! little Numa!'"

"Sergius! Sergius!" shrilled Beatrix, picking a crush of grapes and rose-buds from her lips, upturned.

She was dressed only in a thin llama Greek robe of umber brown, and through the shaken folds her limbs glanced, bluish to aspiration's eye, as limbs of new-sprung Aphrodite mirrored fluctuant among brown seaweed in the Paphian shallows. Her head thrown far back gave me view of the full convex of her throat, white as brandished legs of hamadryads in Apidamian glens by moonlight. Blue-blooded Areta! long-legged! — she was younger than the summer; she was the hopeless Ideal to the spring of the *folie* of perfect loveliness.

We sat beneath an almond tree in blossom, obstinate snow beneath the universal sweat and glister of the sun. Before us a monarch-peacock, Argus-tailed, stormed its little hour on the path. The air of the garden was full of roses.

"And Numa has not been to see us!" she cried, billing to Beatrix, larks prattling to the sunlight in her voice.

"Sergius! Sergius!"

"Areta! — you are light with me."

"Not at all: I have been here: you might have come."

"But could I know —"

"You have been brooding upon the death of Sergius! He has been giving way to melancholy broodings upon the death of our sw-e-et, sw-e-et Sergius!"

"Sergius? Sergius?"

"I! — you certainly mistake me as to that. Sergius is dead, Areta — dead as flint — as carrion —"

"He vibrantly lives!"

"Dead, Areta! and so long ago —"

"Fie! you let the delude you so? It was yesterday as much as a year ago, a thousand æons ago. Time is the counter by which plowmen — and little sw-e-et Beatrixes — reckon the number of their successive ideas; we surely should feel in subtler algebras."

"That is so, Areta: that I know to be so: yet, as you must see this same Time is the fated element in which we breathe. And Sergius, as men reckon, actually did die —"

"Did I tell you that he dictated three far-meaning fantasias to me just before death? One of them had clear reference to this subject of Time, though of none have I been able to follow more than a footprint or two. Would you hear them?"

"Them — or anything you say to me."

She repeated the compositions, slinging a knee between catapult arms, looking up, wondering at distance. Two of these, on later familiarity with them, I tried to translate into common English verse from the rhythmic Hebrew in which they were dictated; but I found their metrical parallelism packed with those archaisms and Chaldee-Aramæan enrichments (often obscure) in which the prophets delighted; so that owing to this, as well as to the extreme tenuity of their meaning at all points, I failed in the attempt. In the case of the opener third, however, I may have come somewhat better out of the thicket:

"Shapes in the Fire come and go: an orb from Scorpio swoons — (empurpled woe!) and horns hath she, and eyes, and lethal trance, and voice that, as she hies, the swan's death-nocturne tunes.

"I see a headlong Messenger: her robe a crocus flame — (confide in her!); thrills shake her plumes amain: her passion's load, the burden of her pain, is the burden of A NAME.

"There smiles a lady, veiled, in death; bright angels round her chaunt — (mellifluous breath!); she, from the VIIth sphere, regards the VIth where gleams her lovely bier, and sighs her ancient haunt.

"List to the Organ's roaring throat! Hymen's loud *euois* swell — (triumphal note!): this day two souls entwine: their purple orgies drenched in aphrian wine, and Priap loves, a-dell!

"I doze below four lax-zoned moons: nude wails of woman rave — (lugubrious tunes!); nude, by a beach of bones, their pallid pomp in torchlit dolor moans, seeking a new-oped grave.

"Lo! — one I see — a child of man! his outlines laved in light — (complete in plan!); eternal smiles he wears: no clothing on his chiseled luster bears, and yet is clothed in White."

So for a long time I sat by Areta; she lithe as phosphorescence, and full of aery, moth-winged words; yet words infect always with the lues of Sergius and his mortality. And the next day she again admitted me to the garden; and so at every noon we sat beneath the almond tree; amid saw the long-trained peacock, proud as a lady, step; and talked together in the interludes of the Corybant *orgia* of Beatrix. Once she came with me beyond the garden-gate. It was a morning magnificently broad and bright. Deftly I snatched the bird from her finger, and before she knew my meaning, ran backwards with it to the castle; passed up a stone stairway, along three corridors, and so to her chamber; saw all windows closed; posited the bird up on her square low bed, of ivory, arabesqued in a fan-tracery of gold; reclosed the door; and flew back to regain her. She, coming to meet me, stood: rather scared to see at first: then, guessing my thought, with the shaken pendulum-shoulders of half-comic reluctance. Further and further that long day did I first, then she, beck like folly-fire into the glades of the forest; umbrageous valleys of Phorfor thick with dews and gloom; Calypso-antrums disheveled with maiden-hair, for all that diamond intergleams of stalactics pin the frivolous tresses; azure-brown steep-banked rills we knew of old; boskets dim and tremulous and secret as the soul of treasure-finders; and where, at midnight, dumb footfalls heat to syrinxal lutings not of men, and routs of freakish ægipeds chase eye-sidling Kupris under the tense-lipped leer of the witched, subconscious moon. Areta, finding herself in the very lap of summer, was impotent; resigned herself; fled before me, unattainable, calling; was a town-bred *grisette* rolling concupiscent in feathery beds of heather. Not till dusk did we return, languid; passed slowly by the terrace; saw the shallop bobbing in the quiet twilight by the landing-stage; and the large boat by the Tower-steps; round in the little garden fell wearily to the seat, she leaning a pale face against the tree-trunk; then, with closed eyes:

"Haste and fetch me my little Beatrix."

As I passed along the second of the three angled corridors, I seemed to hear a rustling train on the floor of the third; but when I reached it, found it lonely. Entering the chamber, I looked for the bird; looked long in the agony of interest. Fearing, doubting, I returned to Areta.

Glancing, she saw me come from the door without the bird; and sprang pallid to her feet.

"Areta! the bird —"

Again that under-look of mistrust, heart-piercing!

"Where is she, Numa?"

"It is very singular — she seems to have left — or been taken from — the chamber —"

She, suddenly tragic, cried: "Oh why — why are you here to plague me! If I but walk with you, talk with you — pain — bitter — falls to me —"

drooped then to the seat, face caught in hands, weeping.

Presently she rose, and with grave bent head, walked slowly without speech into the castle.

Diligent search was made for Beatrix, the servants all requisitioned. Areta pined in her chamber; "heart-broken," said her waiting-woman. Beatrix had swerved like a vision into the breaths of the wind, slipped quite back into the jaws of the abysm whence she came. On the fifth evening, however, a letter, as I heard, was handed to Areta from the Elder Theodore. Though it was then near midnight, she at once set out alone; passed over the bay to the chapel; and the next morning sent word by the dwarf that daily food should be taken her from the castle, as in the days of her first seclusion.

That night I, too, took boat to the chapel. Areta, I found, had retired to her side-chamber. In front of the altar, on the spot where the body of Sergius once lay, another coffin, a malachite shell, now shimmered dully under a taper-glow; stretched, open, on the old trestles. In the headpiece was gold-inlaid the Key and angel-song, as before. Supine within lay a figure — a marble statue. I wondered at the minute burin, so intimate with the genius of death, subtle to catch in stone the inmost thought of the Azrael. Here was flesh twice mortal; here was Sergius himself, stiff-fixed in a sleep doubly eternal. As the Greeks in the days of their hairiest niceties overpainted every part of their marbles, wreathing the lips in rosy smiles of supernal loveliness; so here, with opposite hope was the figure painted overall. Too clearly with opposite hope: for I knew not which to say prevailed in naked ghastliness, the stained face and slumbering lids, yellow as fennel; or the beard and lashes, matted black; or the leaden lips, or greenish ears, or livid fingertips, or winding-sheet of gold.

As I stood regarding this effigy, lo, black velvet hangings parted before a doorway, and Areta, licked below the haunches by curling purplish tongues, loomed cold in a splendid unbroken gown of soft silk, all whiteness, like taper snowbergs, sun-smeared, clear against the black of Polar precipices.

"You see, Numa," she said, coolly splenetic in voice, "I am not all alone. The Elder, knowing my loss —"

"Stay, Areta!" I cried, "can it be that you still suspect me of that wanton act?"

"In the *first* case, I seemed to wrong you; in the second I knew not how to imagine — the inference looked so clear —"

"But you cannot believe this! I had no wish to rob you of your Beatrix! Were we not happy together? Can you not see that in all this there is a design deeper than our probing — a force stronger than we? That your suspicion is quite ill-aimed? and your trust?"

"Forgive me then if that really so." Her voice mellowed. "The objects of our apprehension come and go, melt and harden before us in endless flux, and we are apt to seek for explanation in the activities of other minds, when perhaps it is we that vary in the temper of our loves and hates, passions and wills. At any rate, with the sight we now see before us I am well content; it has been graciously fashioned for me by the Elder's own cunning and will more than replace —"

"But, Areta! you will not look upon this hideousness from day to day — promise me —"

"Numa! it is the very placidity of Sergius in death; full of a mournful greatness. If to your eyes hideous, to mine far from that. But I will sleep now. In the day-time you will come and sit by me."

She turned and went.

As I passed over the water to the castle, a sudden thought took me, as when deserted ships are smitten fervently aback into new lays on a gusty day. It had reference to the Key and Angel-motto ordered by Sergius to be inlaid on his coffin, and it was the fresh sight of these that night which must have pricked me to the thought. A troubled instinct seemed to rise in me that the significance of the device — too well I knew Sergius to doubt that it had significance — might not be deeper than earnest study. I knew that he had *sung* the words to an air of his finding; that he had measured them out in metrical feet. For many days after this I kept close, profoundly engaged upon the task. Long years before, on reading the *Wanderjahre* of Goethe, I had wondered at the introduction of this figure into the work; wondered that so meaningful a writer, with no apparent reason, should plump this seemingly absurd drawing, without intimacy with the context into the thick of his seriously-intended book. The 'key' had then seemed to me not only very frivolous, but even rather stupid. But later on I came to the certainty that in Goethe's mind at least (with its strong bias towards the mystical) the figure was alive with some secret meaning; and now assurance was doubled in me; for I knew that this must have been the thought of Sergius also, to the flame-jet of whose genius the hardness of the riddle had doubtless soon solved to fluid clearness.

I reproduce the figure; and it may perhaps be well if I barely indicate the very slow and steep road by which I toiled to some sort of apprehension of the significance given by Sergius (and I presume by Goethe) to this singular key. And first I was led by the extreme non-resemblance of the figure itself to my own ordinary notions of the *genus* key, to ask myself for what reason the author could have chosen to call the drawing a "key" at all; and hence was confronted, in the first place, with the necessity of defining the word "key." What then, I asked myself, is a "key?"

"That which opens," I at once answered; and that this is the commonest conception I was convinced by the occurrence in most languages of such metaphors as the "key of the situation," etc.: so Bosphorus was called the "key" of Pontus. But reflection showed me how far is this from a satisfactory definition; for crowbars open, hands, winds, many things; nor do all keys open, as in those cases where the casket or safe, once locked by one key, can only be reopened by pressure upon a secret spring — a spring which is, in fact, *another* key. And what I needed was a definition inclusive of all keys, and exclusive of all other than keys.

I was therefore compelled to step deeper, and then arrive at the certainty that a key is that rather which *locks* — which alone locks; nor are any exceptions to this truth other than apparent, as when automatic locks fasten keylessly, in all which cases the key-principle is, of course, concealed in the mechanism; and this fact is expressed in the German Schlussel (key), *i.e. locker,* and so with clef, clavis χλειζ (all related to English cleave, close, include, etc.). The key, then, I said, locks, welds together; and I thus got the idea of binding force. But looking at the figure, I could not but observe how the four small circles at the corners of the handle are bound to the large central circle by the two lines running at right angles within the handle; and how the fifth, further away, at the top of the key, is also (less directly) connected with the same large circle by the shaft, or body, itself. Whereupon there arose within me the conception of a sun *binding* to itself five surrounding planets; and instantly I remembered Areta's repetition of von Hardenberg's apothegm that "man is a sun of which his senses are the planets" — *four* senses (of sight, smell, hearing, and taste) closely connected with the cerebral center of light and thought; and a *fifth* (of feeling) more distantly related to it by its diffusion over the body; there thus took shape in me the double notions of flame and human life: notions, indeed, so closely allied as to be almost one — as is proved not only by their interweaving in all the theosophies that have been, but by the common use in language of such expressions as "glow," "fire" of life; and etymologically by the identity between such words as breath, spirit, etc., and *p*urify, *p*urge, *f*ire, etc., all connected with Greek *pur* (fire). With the notion, too, of flame is allied (indirectly through the notion of breath) the notion of *music*; especially of such music as is sung, or won from wind instruments. But, says Goethe, in reference to the key: "Does it not remind you of arrows with barbs? God help us!" Arrows with barbs — the unvarying symbol of flight with wings! and having reached this point, a glimmer of the connection between the key and the coffin-motto, "Fear not . . . he shall be great . . ." "lit me — the motto *sung* by the *flaming* and *winged* and *human-shaped* messenger to the maiden of Nazareth; and since this motto had yielded to the scrutiny of Sergius a meter, and been hymned by him to a melody, I no longer doubted that in the key would in very deed be found the key to this melody.

Remembering, then, my twin notions of flame and the human being, I set myself to seek in the key itself more definite expression of them; nor was it long before I observed that the whole figure is little more than a reproduction over and over again of the figure ϙ . *This figure, it will be* seen, is formed by the "binding" lines in the handle with each of the small circles at the corners; and formed again by each of them with the large central circle; and formed again by the shaft with the circles at its top and bottom; above all the whole key, if inverted, is, in its *ensemble* (omitting the barbs or *wings),* a general reproduction of it. But the figure ϙ *is the antique and* most elementary conceivable representation of the *wingless* human form, regarded as consisting of head and body; it also represents a burning and haloed candle or torch; a globed lamp; a tailed and flaming comet.

The figure ϙ , then, I assumed to be the *rationale* and *motif* of the whole key; and having determined this, I could not fail to remember that this very figure is also the obsolete Greek letter *koppa*. Now, *koppa* occurring between *pi* and *rho* would, had it been retained in the alphabet, have occupied the very place which the central *u* now occupies in the word *pur* (fire); it accordingly corresponds with our Latin *q,* and its line extended upward through its circle in fact makes a kind of double-*q*: φ But as the whole Key, inverted, is koppa, so *q,* inverted, is none other than *b;* and the elements of this letter *b* (a semicircle and a straight line) are actually formed no less than eight times in the key by means of the "binding" lines and the central circle. If, then, the Key indeed represented the key of the melody sung by Sergius, I had at last (remembering the flat delineation of the figure) the tangible result of B flat. And in this conclusion I was confirmed, when I considered that by means of the "binding" lines within the handle, in conjunction with part of the central circle, and part of the curves bounding the whole handle, the elements of the "flat" sign in music are produced no less than eight times over: thus ♭; and now I was able to see for what reason these boundary curves had not been made to bulge *outward* (a conformation which would have made the key a perfect *koppa*) instead of inward: for the inward curve was absolutely necessary in order that they might touch the central circle at four points, and so help to produce the eight repetitions of the character ♭.

It now only remained for me to take the Hebrew version of the words "Fear not," etc., and write down all the successive letters corresponding to the first seven (*a* to *g*) of the Latin alphabet: I thus obtained my *notes*. *Time* I determined by dividing two such letters, if they occurred consecutively by the semi-quaver, using quaver, minim, or crochet as one or more of the letters subsequent to *g* intervened. (In this convention I counted the Hebrew vowel-points as real letters.) Turning now to the organ, and trying my result in the key of B flat on the treble notes, I won — as anyone may henceforth win — an air so Orphic-wild, and — to *my* seeming — so mournful, that it bore me captive as it floated upward; an air, too, at which the ears of memory pricked: I gradually coming to realize that this was no other than the very tune which in early childhood I had heard from Sergius.

All this time I sat often with Areta beside the statue. Autumn and winter supervened. Her quick fictile spirit likened more and more to the marble shape of gloom upon which she looked. "Deathes dreeriment" prevented and pervaded her. She sat and read and wove and gazed. Her mood deepened to resemblance within that of the more hyper-spiritualistic of the Herrnhüters, and the Moravian and Bohemian brethren — the complex religiosity of the Brahmin *yati* basing itself upon the simple Christian faith. Her only books now were Spinoza's *Ethics,* and the three treatises of Jacob Böhme: The high and deep searching of the three-fold Life of Man according to the Three Principles; the Introduction to the real Knowledge of the Great Mystery; and the Supersensual Life. She reverted to her habit of watching through the night, and sleeping by day; she clothed herself in the black habit of a recluse; the wanness of long fastings made her in the grey darkness of the chapel stranger than water-ladies hair-wringing beneath unnatural gloatings of the moon; her diet was cream thickened with raw crushed Persian apples. I wondered that two environments could so of one make two: such varieties were infinite in Areta! Not now was she the same but lately mænad-irrational with the lechery of spring. One link only seemed to bind her anymore to me: her eagerness that I should convert to sympathy with her feeling. It was a quiet settled mania with her. She besieged me with meek persistence at every point.

"Little Numa," she said, taking my hand in her two, "were you not ever my unrelenting shadow, hot-hunting me whither I fled from you? So now must you follow me where I go — as I *him.*"

She kissed me, once and again, motherly-familiar, on the forehead, I maneuvering flagrant lips to the tingling transport of her cheek.

"And where that is you know. Is it not" — summoning the *Uebersinnliches Leben* of Böhme — "there where no creature dwelleth? where, having ceased from all thinking and willing, we hear what God unspeakably speaketh? To be real sovereigns of nature and ourselves, must we not be silent and quiet, and then are we as God was before nature and creature. We must learn to distinguish between the thing and that which is only the image of it; that which is properly angelical, and that which is no more than bestial. For" — what says the writing? — "if thou rulest over the creature externally only, and not from the right inward ground of thy renewed nature, then is thy ruling verily in a bestial kind, and a sort of imaginary government; but if thou hast put off the bestial or ferine nature, then thou art come into the Super-imaginariness, which is a state of being above figures and shadows: and so rulest over all, being reunited to thy original in that very source out of which they came; and henceforth nothing on earth can hurt thee, for thou art all things, and nothing is *unlike* thee."

She held my hand: she kissed me — lingeringly — again and yet again, on the brow.

But I: "Yet here you seem wayward, Areta. As for me, I fly from my mast the flag of Sergius. Sergius and Jacob Böhme, it seems clear, looked through eyes of different-colored irises. For, so far from bidding you cease from all willing, did he not say" — was it not his last word to you — "give to every passion its rein —"

"Sh-h-h!" She extinguished my mouth with swift smothering hand, "you cannot suppose that the maxim will fit *you* — rudderless little Argonaut that you are! Nor yet me. Sergius it fitted: for in him every 'passion' was spiritual, and winged colt born of that instinctive mother-purity of his, which everywhere saw God: to give to such its rein was to be snatched into heaven. But *you* — thick, all clay —"

She swooped like a fishing-bird upon a sighted kiss in my hair.

But I again: "And is clay then, Areta, less divine than spirit? Not so, I am certain, did Sergius think. 'Give,' he said, 'to every song its dance' — and to you he said this, specially to you. Ah, Areta! is not body sweet as soul? Does not God beat and burn in both? To feast then must be divine as to fast: to kiss sublime as to pray. For is He not kiss, and kissed, and kisser; prayer and shrine, and pilgrim? So said Sergius."

A disdainful sidling look, pouting resentment, kept her from answer.

One night — it was then beginning spring — she, looking upon the statue-face, said, frowning:

"I somehow seem conscious of some sort of change. Look, Numa, see if the same effect is not wrought upon you, too."

I looked, but shook my head. Yet the change, very gradually growing from day to day, had long been far from unknown to rue.

"And with this consciousness of change, Areta, does not your fondness for the marble lessen?"

She seemed astonished.

"How could that come? You appear to cling most persistently to the notion of some inherent reality in the things we see. If I see a thing, which I *know* can be nothing more than the image of my own mind, must I not also know that any seeming change in it is an exact reflection of some real change in me, by some means produced? so that, supposing I love the thing, my relative position to it must be at all times unaltered; and love, so long as it can realize the identity of the thing, follows it through all its modifications, as Boötes hunts Harmaxa, or as the suns in the tail of the Bear follow it through all its circhings round the Polar star."

"But suppose," I said, "you know the *means* by which the change is wrought in you — the definite will of another mind working upon yours; suppose, for instance, the Elder, willing that you should be conscious of change in this statue, effected his purpose, in the fashion taught by experience to be possible and easy, by applying to it a burin, while you slept —"

"In that case, indeed, some loves might spread wings from their object; but as for me, even in that case, I feel sure — and your supposition is as wild as little Numa hunting hares of old on the mountains!"

She caught my head between antipodean hands, and dipped at it a steep kiss, motherly-playful.

Little by little Spring slackened her girdle, swelling nymphic-gravid. Change in the statue now grew amain.

For this, not Theodore, but I, was responsible. Despair at its ghastliness and the deepening gloom of Areta had spurred me at last to come to the chapel during her sleeping-hours, and with furtive tremulous chisel to soften the face into a semblance somewhat more lifelike; the chipped part I would then resmear with a hue less lethal, yet not too discrepant. And the effect upon her was very quickly evident.

One noon a mountebank, from a townlet beyond the mountains, arrived laggard at Phorfor. I hurried to the chapel.

Down a side-aisle I ran to her chamber. She slept. I intruded my head between the velvet hangings of the door-way, and called:

"Areta! Areta!"

She was as when the first presentiment of morning stirs in the plumage of the eider-duck; strained the ivory coronal of a bare arm lazily round her head; jerked suddenly stark, as in the last throe before death; and lay outlined sidewards, hills and a central mountain in Lihhiput under the thin green coverlet, eyeing me through imbecile eyes.

"Areta! a punchinello!"

"A punchinello! O joy . . . ."

Fleeter than the ether wings of instinct, more oilily than interfluent mercury, she leapt instantly before me, standing hot and rosy, clean-cut through the smoke-puff of a night-veil of gauze. Then quickly scarlet with remembrance —

"Numa! go. . . ."

I waited in the chapel, dubious, yet buoyed on the memory of all the craze and fervors which the appearance of a mountebank had meant to Areta, a girl.

She came presently, dressed in black. And mournfully negative, said:

"I cannot go with you."

"How! you will not let the man return —"

"Let him be fed and paid."

"I certainly shall not stir without you, Areta." She stood looking at the changing statue.

Then rushing furiously downward at its eyebrow a skew and still-born kiss, throttled my wrist. "Come then!" Dragged me toward the door.

We sat beneath the almond tree of the little garden, and the punchinello set his stage and puppets before us; fussy puppets with breath to grin, and caper, and perorate. Areta looked — mostly pale, averted, — with nostrils panting thorough-bred; now and then flushing into crimson; now and then rippling into sheer oblivion of laughter. The new sunlight seemed to wind her with ecstasy. That night I was able to force her to sleep once more in the castle. The greater part of it I spent in chiseling at the statue.

In the morning I returned within her to the chapel, she guilty and silent. We stood by the altar rail — for a long the stood dumb, gazing on the emptiness where the statue had lain. The spirit of its pallid granite had passed into Areta; only, she just moved her head measurely from side to side, woe-ridden. Two hours before I had left the coffin safe by the rail.

All at once paroxysmal in queenhiness, horizontal from shoulder-blade to rosy-armed forefingertip, she cried to me —

"Oh go! go! — far from Phorfor — whence you came —"

I bowed. The suddenness of high blood had ever been a trait of our race, nor was I all undowered with its quiet-quick arrogance. I bowed — and walked instantly from the chapel, through the sea, to the castle.

So then Areta had dismissed me as a hireling from the ancient home of my family. I passed to my chamber, crammed a few pieces of clothes into a traveling-bag, and descended to the stables at the back. I saddled my horse, and was about to mount, when the dwarf, appearing from behind an angle, shambled briskly toward me, and handed me a parchment.

"From whom?"

"The Elder Theodore, master."

I broke the seal, and read:

> "The Lady Areta has now commanded you from Phorfor. I, her protector, suggest that this injunction meet instant obedience.
> "THEODORE"

On the document I made haste to scribble in pencil the words:

"I shall *not* go: and I defy you, Theodore"; handed then the parchment to the dwarf; unsaddled the horse: and returned to my chamber.

The thought which shadowed me all the day was the wonder that Theodore should know of Areta's "go! go!" He had heard it, then: but how? We two stood alone in the chapel; his boat was by the Tower. Had he asses' ears? My faith in magic, to Areta possible as nature, was small. I sought deeply for explanation. I remembered how, praying one night by the coffined Sergius, a taper-flash seemed to glance behind me in the chapel: yet Theodore's boat was by the Tower. And I thought of the fall of luminous powder as I harped beneath the turret-window: yet the boat was by the Tower. And from what hand had Beatrix flown to us out of the chapel-recesses? How had she disappeared? The boat was then by the Tower.

At midnight I dressed in white, and crawling flat-faced along the marble terrace, reached the landing-stage; thence dropped to the sands; and so, still crouching, entered the sea, four-square; with hands bloody from the barbed star-fish of the bottom, I came to the inlet, fairly sure that I had thus cheated the eyes of Theodore. Having reached the reredos-end of the chapel, I struck light to a taper, and passed straight onward through a draped doorway. Never beyond this point had I dared before, nor, as I knew, had Areta, nor Sergius. A long and steep corridor, with branches veining out every-way stretched before me. After hours of search, I found that the alcoves, vaults, chambers of every shape, both along the main corridor and its ramifications, were past numbering. Many of these were doorless; many had doors, but open, admitting me to examination; one only, near the end of a long and very precipitate corridor which was the branch of a branch, hid from me behind a locked door. The position of this I marked, and judging that the time had now come when the night shudders into a deeper gloominess at the instinct of the near darts of morning, I returned with like secrecy to the castle.

At the next midnight I crawled back with the same furtiveness to the chapel, and made for the marked door. I carried a bunch of old keys, one of which chance at length fitted to the lock: there was no creaking, and I guessed a well-used mechanism. Within I found a large chamber, black every-way with its own bare rock, and empty. I walked round it, once and again, and met everywhere — nothing. Surprised, I again set out, holding the taper high; but happening now to come nearer one of the corners than before, I stepped upon air; plunged downward into the throat of an abyss; and bumping in my descent upon steep stone gradients, arrived at the bottom all shock and amaze. But I held the taper: in five minutes I was conscious of this. And light was in my pocket. I rekindled the flame, and found myself at the angle of two subterranean galleries. And now truth dawned upon me. For it was clear from their general directions that of these, one led beneath the sea to the Tower, and one beneath the inlet and the land to the vaults of the castle.

Here, too, having passed cautiously along the Tower-gallery, I found a honeycomb — clefts and crannies everyway, veins, chambers. The chief artery itself was full of windings, angles. For about two hours old Erebuses blinked in every nook at the innovating flicker (if my taper. I went so far sea-ward as to see the steps leading down from the lower: their length showed me the great depth of the excavation beneath the water. Then back again into the side-catacombs, eyes stepping in my careful feet, a thief in the might, all leers and tremors. Once, far in the labyrinth, I stumbled over some rock-debris. Instantly there was an answering sound: a faint stirring as of shaken plumage, and this barely-whispered, sleepily-voiced interrogatory: "Sergius? Sergius?"

It came from behind a bolted door opposite where I stumbled. I drew the staple; entered; roused grey Beatrix in her hung cage of reeds to a sage lateral interest of round eyes in roe; saw the mummy of Sergius in its shell; and near it the statue in its coffin; then, knowing morning near, rebolted the door; returned to the chapel-level; locked the door of the stair-chamber; and with elaborate secrecies made my way to the castle.

Before midnight of the same day I had toilsomely lifted the statue-weight from its coffin, and round its neck fastened a provided rope: with this, having slung the Beatrix-cage upon my back, I dragged draft-cattle-wise, barked at by Cerberus echoes. Progress was slow. The taper, carried in an alternate resting hand, showed me now, what I had previously noticed indeed, but not in such numbers — large cloth bags, stuffed with some soft substance, laid here and there on the ground of many parts of the labyrinth. Resting, I happened to see a little of the powder which as (I concluded) filled the bags, spilt by chance at my feet; it was grey, and I remembered the descending mass beneath the turret-window. I stooping to examine it, a flake of hot grease fell near. The powder instantly volleyed me such a hoot, that space seemed to split fragmentary round me, and I woke to sense prostrate against the wall, deaf but to the booming buzz of my own waltzing brain, and blind but to the two bluish round ghosts that hovered before me in the darkness. When I had relighted the taper, Beatrix was still fluttering and screaming with fright. I had now passed through the length of the vein, and was near the main artery. I dragged the statue after me up a step, and proceeded slowly on this final stage toward the stair. I had not consumed many yards, however, before there sounded upon my palsied consciousness from behind an angle of the corridor the stalk of an approaching step — and, O Heaven, the rustle of silk. I spun motionless, fled riveted, was fixed in sick gyrations, like the statue of a whirlwind, was everything in a moment and nothing, a circle in flesh, symbol of infinity, sign of zero. But only for one eternal instant: in the next I had extinguished my light, had lifted the statue in my arms, and, shuddering under the incubus, had plunged into the dark orifice of a cranny near me; just as Theodore, holding a candlestick, loomed into view. He came close, tremendous, heavy, veiled, himself a phalanx, a marching pyramid — passed close to my breath, unsuspecting — went yet a few strides beyond: when Beatrix, tempted, called, as if uncertain, "Sergius? Sergius?" Theodore stopped statuesque, angled his head sideward; his ears a pair of scales, zealous to weigh the very dust of sound; and so for a full minute stood. Hearing nothing, he again strode two steps forward; and again the new sound stirred the bird to call, briskly now and loud. Theodore turned, hesitating, came towards me, glanced at the black mouth in which I hid, and passed somewhat beyond. Once more the bird uttered a note, and once more he halted short, the stone monument of an ear, grandly patient, his back towards me broadly immobile. Not now did I hesitate a moment: my shoes were already done off. Creeping from my retreat, I drew on tiptoe near him, all bloodless, collected, a concentrated corpse, and stretching a sudden head above his shoulder, puffed utterly out the flame of his candle. An "Ah — h — . . ." broke from him like the menace of thunder. I flew back to my cranny, expecting him now to return to the Tower for new light; instead of which he immediately came in my direction, and walked away towards the chapel, blocking my exit! In the chapel, I knew, he would procure a light, and return armed. I, clasping desperation to my bosom, grasped the statue-rope, and tugged towards the Tower; and finding progress all too slow, summoned the cracking thews of Atlas, and lifted the burden, running, laying it down, running again, until I stood at the foot of the Tower stairway. All this time, Beatrix, wildly swinging in her cage, was two ecstatic winnowing-fans in a granary of chaff. From the step-foot I half hoisted, half dragged, the burden up the stairway, and had overcome more than three-quarters of its steep length, when I beheld Theodore heaving rapidly towards me along the corridor a mountain in travail, steel glinting in his right hand, as when a regiment winks moving on the hillside. Upon the strength of Atlas I piled the fury of Samson — the statue grew light at my maniac tendons. Before the Elder of the Tower had halved the stairs, my head was prising up the trapdoor of iron above: it gave sluggishly — I urged and hunted the statue through the aperture — pelted myself madly after it — and slapped down the ponderous metal upon the snapped point of Theodore's blade.

Having spindled the hasp on the top of the trapdoor, I found myself in a dark room; but quickly discovering the locked door, the key of which projected inwardly, I opened it, and easily towed the statue over the glazed bricks of the flooring to the boat by the Tower-steps. The wakeful dwarf, dumb at my apparition, gazed upon me with fish-mouth vacant as his eyes. I was soon by the landing-stage, and so with my burden reached the castle. Looking in the darkest morning from a casement, I dimly discerned Theodore wading to the Tower through the sea — vast as a reef when it awfully forges through the fog athwart the drifting mariner.

I cull some few sentences from a journal which I kept at this time:
Elaphebolion, 3rd *(hist.)*. Areta, then, will not see me. Will let me go without one last look or word. My note of today was the third in which I have declared my power to prove the quite natural means by which

her mementoes of Sergius have disappeared. She sends no answer. Her old waiting-woman has been with me again by stealth: is all in my favor, and full of sibilant talk, breathless news. Theodore, it seems, plies Areta with missives: warns her presumably against seeing my face. I work all the night, and nearly all the day, upon the statue and the bird. The thought that I have thereby made the spirit of Areta somewhat brighter will be to my exile like fruit in winter: she will see my hand, my care for her, and remember how I loved.

Elaph. 4. This day I have received the first message from Theodore since the incidents in the galleries. My minute outlook seems to have filched him of the hope of assassinating me by cryptic drugs and dirks. And so open murder is to sit arbiter upon us. His parchment was a conjugation of the verb dare: you dare, you have dared! "We cannot *both* abide at Phorfor." Foolish old man! he does not know how soon Phorfor will heave a rid bosom at me. I wrote on the parchment: "*I* will not go. Swords punctually at midnight of the 9th in the chief underground gallery of the chapel." An hour after the answer came:

"It is well."

Elaph. 5. I am toiling as before at the statue and the bird.

Elaph. 6. By the 9th all will, I conclude, be ready. I shall leave a note for Areta, and set out by dawn of the 10th, provided only that Theodore's sword do not prove longer than my life.

Elaph. 7. Areta's room is constantly warm with her: so the old dame reports. The Mahlström of the spring, it is clear, has not caught her in its now widening whorls. The three last troparions of Sergius she has written out afresh, and studies them long. These, and a few books marked with his name, are all she has of him.

Elaph 8. This day I have been pondering upon my appointed meeting with Theodore. An unwillingness has arisen and grown almost compulsory within me. He is an old man; many reasons come to me. Yet he must not think me dreadful of his power. Time must decide for me.

On the 9th no entry appears. During the evening of that day I sat and wrote my letter of farewell to Areta. The room was the one in which I had chiefly lived of late; vastly domed; tapestried in Utrecht velvet of red, but blood-black under the orbed moon of pink light pendent from the center. It jutted from the castle on the second stage, somewhat basilica-shaped, the roof being low and flat over the semi-circle at the far end. On one side it looked east towards the mountains, and west over the bay on the other. A palisade of taper stained-windows, Gothicmullioned, surrounded it. Half the length of the west side was filled by a ponderous organ, the most important of the three in the castle. I sat and wrote my letter, and had not finished, when, hearing an opened door, I looked, and saw, to my confusion, Areta herself stand; simple in silver-white linen *chiton*, zoned with gold-cloth; an azure and rosy diamond in her forehead flirting lissome at hide-and-seek with the various spirit of light.

A thick sadness veiled her face.

"I have come, Numa, in friendship, to bid you farewell — having just heard of your resolve to go from us tomorrow."

"Ah, that is kind. And you do not fear the Elder's malison, I hope?"

"I fear nothing, Numa. But you speak lightly, sir, of the great Theodore."

We sat together on a couch within a small recess. The hangings before us half hid us from the room.

"It is a pity," she said, "that you have so acted as to rouse his gentle mind to displeasure. You and he cannot, it is certain, now live upon the same atmospheres. One must disappear — you are a boy — he hoar with the snows of reverence — ah me!"

"Yet not for the displeasure of Theodore do I go: be sure of that, Areta: but because you, with your own lips, have bid me."

"That was the mere wind of the blow which struck me; the flash of the sword which pierced me. I was deeply wounded, you must know. Forget that, Numa. But now a far stronger reason urges. Theodore is mortally angry with you, sir."

"And because I have committed the sin of loving you."

"Of — ? No! of *not* loving me, you mean."

"Areta! why, the pebbles on the beech moan with the torment of their thirst when you pass on them — the callous heart of ocean flares into scarlet flames at you! And how have I shown this impossible lack of love? By removing, of course —"

"Yes, Numa."

"But in that case my only motive must have been jealousy, which is but the yellow mustard flower of love."

"And some such half-notion it was which has helped me towards softer thoughts of you. Yet it was a base jealousy — of one far nobler than you — and so venomous bitter in its effects —"

"And now, if after all it be not true that I did remove your treasures, Areta?"

"In each case the Elder saw you in the act: in his wisdom, though absent in space, not merely saw, but foreknew: and warned me beforehand that if I laughed with you, went abroad with you, you would be led to do so and so, with such and such motive. All which unheeding, I rushed on, and was punished."

"Have you slept today, Areta?"

"Yes."

"Then stay with me tonight — the last — till midnight, at least. It will be a memory to me."

"And why midnight?"

"I may leave you then for a while. Before, I should without advantage pain you by turning all you hold light into the blackness of darkness; your childhood's *eidolon* of truth into the very Isis of lies. But after midnight, if fortune steer my steel, I may to good purpose hold to your eyes lenses rather less distorting."

She did not understand. We sat together silent. The spaces of the night marched by us. She was the grey symbol of apathy beside me, a grey pen in the gloom of the recess, still wearing on her pensive forehead the jewel without name of her lost celestial home. Did she not care that I should leave her lonely in the morning? Was Sergius still the just dead bridegroom of her widowhood? She took from the *sinus* of her dress a small roll, the three new-written fantasias of his deathbed. Pored over them in the dim light, bent, forgetting me. Then suddenly vocal:

"What, think you, did he mean by 'suns whose rays are *living* lutes'?"

"I cannot tell, Areta. Read the whole."

The cooing doves of her voice were like a bath of lukewarm luxury to my wallowing. She read the poem.

"Sergius best knew his own winged meanings, Areta: they may, as you once said, have been prophecy, or rhapsody, or prayer.

"The *second* was the prayer of a Moses dying at sunset on Pisgah."

She read it, bent grey in the gloom.

"The third seems mere poetry."

"Do not think so! — he never conceived *mere* poetry." This too she commenced slowly to read:

"Shapes in the Fire come and go:
an orb from Scorpio swoons —
(empurpled woe!)
and horns hath she, and eyes,
and lethal trance, and voice, that as she hies,
the swan's death-nocturne tunes.

I see a headlong Messenger:
her robe a crocus flame —
(confide in *her!*)

thrills shake her plumes amain:
her passion's load, the burden of her pain,
is the burden of A Name."

"Areta!" I cried, breaking in, ecstatic. A sudden flash seemed to enkindle a whole landscape of truth to me. "Areta, love!" I sprang to my feet. "A crocus flame! — thrills shake her plumes — my God! the burden of a *name!* You shall see!" Heedfulness died in me, moderation, remembrance, and hurrying to an opposite recess, I dashed aside the draperies, mounted on moveable steps, and threw wide the doors of a high-hung cage. There was a stirring, a meditation, a poising, and instantly a little saffron bird, yellow-bright as orpiment, took flight, clipping within twinkling tongue and wing a ruled and fluid pathway through the air — alighting upon the high white bosom Areta spread to it.

Her face changed to the beaming sunlight of joy. She knew Beatrix, though changed by my earnest lavings from the grave grey of Sergius to her native gold of Canary.

"And thou hast come back to thy Areta's soul" — whispering low — "ah wild, wild aeronaut" — hugging it to her throat — "come back in gaudier robes — and yet I love, I love, I love thee just so, too — no other than just so, little prodigal! But say your master's name — lisp, lisp it to my secret ear — sw-e-et — Sergius!"

"Numa! Numa! Numa!" shrilled Beatrix, recovered in breath, eloquent of the briefer euphony of my own arduously inculcated name.

Areta slid into waltzing with the bird, her head tossed back, laughing.

"O changeling Beatrix! O wanton breeze! O whirling whisp! What, another name, then? No longer deserted Sergius? And does the new-launched burden loll move lightly, then, on the ebb and flow of its little, little, liquid throat? Ah, it is well! it is well!"

We sat again within the recess, the bird swiftly fickle from her to me, an incessant slim bobbin zealous for the net, a frantic plowshare in the sands, stitching us together with a million airy threads. Numa was her constant burden.

"Confide in *her,* Areta! ha, love! can you not now believe that the mighty soul of your brother lovingly foreknew me?"

She looked upon me and smiled.

A huge clock of greenish-black augite under the rosy central lamp tolled midnight.

"It is midnight. Whither was it you spoke of going?"

"Nowhither, Areta. I will not leave you tonight."

The indecision had frozen together into sudden resolve within me.

No blood, I decreed, of me or by me, should spill at that final parting-time. Theodore, if he dared, might think one of my race a coward. In the morning he would know me gone forever.

But I rose, and bearing the steps to one of the high western windows, mounted upon them, and slightly opening a stained half on one side of the mullion, peeped through. Theodore would probably go to the meeting place by the underground way, but if he took boat, I was there to wave him signal of my changed purpose. He would not wait to see me leave the terrace in the shallop, knowing that I now knew the subterranean way from the vaults of the castle.

Several minutes passed; then concluding that he had by that time reached the *rendezvous* I commenced to descend; but was arrested — seeing a shadow, the shadow surely of Theodore, pass by a blind of the Tower. Awe and confusion filled me, dread of his dreadful subtlety. What woof did he weave? He was not in the Tower having *returned* from the meeting place: for this the time since midnight was utterly insufficient. He had not therefore gone at all. But for what reason? As I stood debating, a horrible bursting and cracking, uproars of wrack and shock, earth-heavings, throbbed and thundered at my ear, loosened my knees. Enceladus, compact with tremors, crawled beneath us. The castle, flicked but by the tail of the explosion, shivered as with the coldness of horror. Looking in the direction of the chapel, I saw the wide winging of smoke, flying rocks, a dull lurid flare. Then I knew in my hurrying heart how precipitous was the ruin I had shunned; how stern, majestic the wrath of Theodore. There came a moment of lull — a sickening treachery of peace — and in the next instant the Tower in the sea sent up to heaven a wild shrieking bellow, and from the center of its summit an infinite clean spear of crimson and blue and greenish flame laddered yells of horrid menace to the stars. The earth-shock, immeasurably fiercer in its effects than its author's thought, had communicated the fury of its fires along the underground gallery to the witches' cauldron of volatile chemicals in which Theodore brewed the sorceries of his dark will. The Tower throed, and frittered, and spat red bricks as a grounded pugilist his bloody teeth. For a moment, on the topmost parapet of all, a hunted monumental form appeared — a veilless face — with a similitude of excrescent horns on the forehead — a face which was but a dead and thick and featureless lump of lavender-leprous flesh, lit and lashed by scorpion whips of flame from his silken robes and wide-burning fleece of hair; but the gallery cracked from under him; he lurched ponderously, and lancing a far-circling shrill, empurpled, to my fancy, with a strange chaunted hint and cadence of a death-melody, fell — like holocausts slung flaring from the battlements of heaven — old Lucifer hurtling rotary in somersaults of steep combustion through -the interspaces. And immediately thereupon the whole fabric burst, and rumbled down upon him, building him a funeral mound of hissing bricks broad above the surface of the water.

Of all this Areta had seen nothing. She stood in the middle of the room, three-eared, with lifted auditory hand.

"O Numa, tell me — what is it?" she cried, wan in voice and face.

I led her by the hand to the recess.

"Listen, Areta, and believe serenely that all is of God — the Elder Theodore is dead."

She doubled, hiding her face in her lap.

"Dead. . . ."

To her it was the dissilience of whole Scorpio from the zodiac.

I, in solemn peace, spoke low, unveiling all. Her face was buried from me; she made no sign; only, when I told how that Theodore had lied to her, she shook her head, quick-sobbing:

"Oh no, no, no. . . ."

For a long the then we sat speechless. Her face I could not see, but I knew it veiled with the crape of tragedy. The spaces of the night marched by us. The clock chimed three.

"What can *he* have thought, seeing all?"

"Sergius?"

"Yes."

"Sergius, I incline to think, probably mastered long before death, to a far greater degree than you or I, Areta, the alphabeta of that dark Sanskrit in which Theodore's soul languaged itself. But he, like Theodore, is dead now; and it can be of little moment to us what he thinks."

There was silence between us for a while, till she, as if reasoning with her own thoughts, said, "But strange! strange!" and began again to read slowly the vision of Sergius:

Shapes in the Fire come and go:
an orb from Scorpio swoons —
(empurpled woe!)
and horns hath she, and eyes,
and lethal trance, and voice that, as she hies,
the swan's death-nocturne tunes.

I see a headlong Messenger:
her robe a crocus flame —
(confide in *her!*)
thrills shake her plumes amain:

her passion's load, the burden of her pain,
in the burden of A NAME.

There smiles a lady, veiled, in death;
bright angels round her chaunt —
(mellifluous breath!);
she, from the VIIth sphere,
regards the VIth where gleams her lovely bier,
and sighs her ancient haunt.

List to the Organ's roaring throat!
Hymen's loud *euois* swell —
(triumphal note!):
this day two souls entwine:
their purple orgies drenched in aphrian wine,
and Priap loves, a-dell.

"But," I cried aloud, suffused, and, as it were, electrically shocked, by a revelation, "this — this was no voice of man, but of a glowing spirit from heaven!" and rushing to the organ, I furiously filled its mighty frame with wind; sat before the notes, and in victorious euphony, in pealing acclamation, I sent boasting and gaudent through the timid silence of the morning the angel-song of Sergius. The air was his intact; but instead of the sad minor-key, transposition to a major; instead of the solemn serenity, the light step and golden pomp of wedding marches. The bass was my own. Never so shall I play again. Areta was behind me, her hand on my shoulder, trembling; her face pressed hot to mine. Beatrix, long since flown to her sleepy perch, but pricked to sympathy by the practice of her own native art, warbled a continuous drowsy serenade of my name. All this has self-maturing memory brought me back. But for the time I was lost to sense. Music was a well of living water within me; the broad bosom of the organ shivered at me as when a Pegasus finds its unappeasable rider. I leaned faint upon it when my tyranny was accomplished.

"O Numa" — her two hands on my shoulders, her face a rosy lake-ripple looking up at dawn — "O Numa, you have —"

She stopped.

"And whence, of whence, have you drawn this power over me? You seemed to me a little Numa-god as you played!"

"The piece, you see, is changed in movement and key from the melody as sung by Sergius."

"Changed — and glorified."

A pain went lightning through me.

"You like it better so?"

"Yes — that even *must* be."

"The written music, if I go in the morning, you shall have."

"*If* you go. But not the pippling of every popinjay is a prophecy, nor the whisper of every wind a warning!"

She laughed, mocking my impotence.

"And do you not see it surely true, Areta, that the great soul of your Sergius lovingly foreknew me?"

Her look rested upon my face: her hand fell to mine.

We sat again within the recess. I opened to her the pit whence I had digged the lost jewel of the melody. Grey spaces of the morning now shivered past like home-turning ghosts. After long intimacy with her, I bent the trickle of our talk to our child's friendships, delights and abandonments together in the deep places of Phorfor. She turned herself from me.

"Children," she said, "are —"

"Yes?"

"Are —"

"Tell me!"

"Sensual."

The word rived her with a shudder; but if of luxury, or if of self-retention, I could not say.

"And men too, Areta, and women. Is it not the barm of the Holy Spirit lovingly uneasy in our bodies? So said Sergius."

She made no answer. Stealthy mists of seriousness had again crept gradually large around her. Contact was no longer possible. She became burrs to me and a battery, memorable to pilgrim fingers. The shadow of some thought in her stretched between us.

Morning threw wide casement after casement: the cock was as a herald with clarion vacillant between hand and lip, tiptoe-parturient with the yet unvoiced evangel: Behold the Bride-groom.

An aged man-servant for whom I had drawn back the lever of a bell, appeared, bearing comfitures on a salver, and a mama of wine. I, pouring a glassful, presented it to her. "No! the day now begun is marked as a fast-day with me."

"See, Areta, how the night hops away with bedraggled wing, like a faint, wounded raven:

'And now does the cock,
  Half anxious its crow
Of tribrach and long,

Shrill: doesn't it GROW . . .'

my hour them is near: will you not drink me a parting *salve* in this glass?"

This I said craftily, with hope in her answer. Her eyes leapt upon me in eager query.

"Oh . . . you do not mean —"

"Have you not *bid* me go? and you have not yet unbid me."

Her lashes fell in long curvature upon a perfectly pallid cheek. I could see that she debated keenly within herself. After a time she spoke, arguing to her lap:

"Well, if you will go, you will go. I here will give myself utterly to those vigils and tears and prayers which made *her* saintly; prayers, Numa, in which *you* shall not be forgotten."

My heart sank horribly.

In saying "her," she pointed to a picture in oils of a long-dead lady of our race hung on the opposite wall: a middle-aged lady, with meekness in her look, and a radiance of unearthly sunlights in her smile, far known of old beyond the bounds of Phorfor as St. Anna, the blessed.

I, pale as she, held the wind before her.

"Drink for me, Areta!"

"No! why urge me so? I have told you no — no."

The flash of her anger singed me of enterprise. I sat again mouse-quiet by her side.

"To what a point," she said, looking up at the beatitude of St. Anna, "must she not have adventured on the greased mast of spiritual attainment! Her life was a long upward gaze: an eye turned white to heaven. Before death she is said to have been familiar with the facial expressions of many of the winged things of the cycles of the skies. But — how singular — that we should speak of her — tonight!" and she repeated:

"There smiles a lady, veiled, in death:
bright angels round her chaunt —
(mellifluous breath!);
she, from the VIIth sphere,
regards the VIth where gleams her lovely bier,
and sighs her ancient haunt.

List to the Organ's roaring throat!
Hymen's loud *euois* swell —
(triumphal note!):
this day two souls entwine:

their purple orgies drenched in aphrian wine
and Priap loves, a-dell!

I doze below four lax-zoned moons:
nude wails of women rave —
(lugubrious tunes!)
nude, by a beach of bones, their pallid pomp in torchlit dolor
moans,
Seeking a new-oped grave.

Lo! — one I see — a child of man!
his outlines laved in light —
(complete in plan!);
eternal smiles he wears:
no clothing on his chiseled luster bears —
and yet is clothed in White."

"Then, Areta — then —" I cried, frantically stamping to my feet, *"then* was the Sergius we knew indeed true prophet, and sibyl, and seer!" — and flying towards the far semi-circular end of the chamber, I sent hissing apart along a brazen bar the two halves of a silken curtain, and revealed between the divided drapery, standing poseful on an *estrade* in the alcove, a statue of marble. Areta at the sight flew wide-winged towards me, rhythmic-swaying to the throb of timbrel and cymbal, eating up with inconceivable swiftness the vast length of the room. And we looked together, she leaning heavy upon me. Soft glamours of blue and crimson light, leveled by the now high-prospering day-spring through the stained windows, lotioned the head in a dream of colors. Only by the thick-matted black hair could she know it the very block of the Sergius-statue: in all else death had been wonderfully burined into life — the painted cerements all chipped from it, and in their place the white clothing only of its own immaculate marmor.

"But, Numa — it is you! it is you!"

She compressed from my sight a face all inflamed in her two tight hands. Twin-sisters, lake-women, rowed competitive to rhymes in the milky hollows of her breasts!

"It is you, Numa! It is you!"

It was indeed I; I smiling rosy patronage; I nude; express; accomplished Man.

Areta blushed. She was a vomiting Ætna of blushes.

But I violently tore her hands from her face, and I held them in mine, both in both, swinging them. And she, with prudish under-glance, looked up into me, I deep into her.

O broken heart of Love! in her eyes were films, and meanings, and the everlasting and impetuous YEA.

*T*hat morning a thievish sprite in my feet led me a-hunt through all the nooks and byways of the castle. By a studied plea I had escaped from Areta. Yet Sergius, either with design or without, had left little of himself behind: some sandals I found, a few gowns woven without seam, three books of Bishop Berkeley marked with his name. These I took, and kissing them one by one, worshipping, praising him as a god, I locked them in a cabinet, and flung the key far. An hour thence, I, rejoined to Areta, was with her in the woods, gathering flowers: she dancing raillery at every rein. Her lips and pure white dress were stained with the dribble of the syrupy magenta wine of the grapes of Phorfor, her eyes all glairy with its tipsy yeast. We had, indeed, tippled freely of its whispering nectar; and as the garland of ivy and violets with which I had crowned her had toppled aslant on her head, my riotous love had somewhat the look of an awry Bacchante rather drunken among the forest-glades. For many generations no marriage at Phorfor had been dehymenized by any such thing as benefit of clergy, and the laying on of frog-chill agastric hands: nor, as I knew, would Areta have tolerated any such. But from a slight gash in my fingertip she stained her tongue with my sucked blood; I mine with hers. Then repairing to her chamber with the gathered flowers, we bent to build the Altar of our Covenant: and, truly, it was upper Aiden and the very hair-curling tortion of delight to watch Areta, with what sighing pains, wifely collusions as of Bertha the Good, she took part in the making. It was low and broad by the side of her bed, and directly faced the rising sun. Plushy we made it, and furry, with riches and thicknesses of velvets; overshading it with canopy of silk; and over and around the velvets we heaped a strew of ivy and violets (the blend worn in chaplets by the *phallophoroi* in the Great Dionysia); and over this we sprinkled poppy-flowers; and over this parsley mixed with barley-groats; and over this tufts of wool; and over all — on the front, and on the back, and on the sides, and on the top — we traced out in characters of the immortal flowers of amaranth this word:

APHRODITE PEITHO